THE NEXT
WHATEVER

Rebecca Phillips

The Next Whatever
Copyright © 2021 Rebecca Phillips
All rights reserved.

www.rebeccawritesya.com

ISBN: 978-0-9920753-6-1
Cover Design: c8design.ca

Chapter One

The town of Granesville has three pizza joints, two gas stations, and one set of traffic lights. I'm sure there's more to the place, like a post office and library and all the other usual town amenities, but these are the things I notice as my mother and I cruise down Center Street, the aptly named road that runs through the middle of town.

Mom brakes at the intersection and glances over at me. Dark sunglasses hide her eyes, but I can tell by the way her mouth twitches that she's nervous about this latest move. I'm not sure why. We've relocated enough times over the years to make Moving Day feel as normal and expected as Thanksgiving.

"The way your dad described this place, I thought it would be smaller. But this isn't bad at all." She says all this in her calm yoga instructor voice, which she uses almost constantly, even when she's not teaching a class. "I know it's a big change from the city, but we'll just have to make the best of things while we're here," she adds as the light finally turns green and the car lurches forward. "We always do, right?"

I say nothing and turn up the radio. We've lived in much smaller places—like Vance, population 869, where I spent the entire seventh grade—but Granesville still feels like a major downgrade from Weldon, a city of almost one million, where we'd lived for the past two years. Where I thought I'd get to stay longer.

I prefer big cities. Cities have plenty of room to get lost in. But it's not like I get any say in the matter, anyway. As my dad always says, we have to go where the work is. And for the next year or so, the work is here in Granesville, population 6043.

"Avery?"

I jump a little and look over at my mom. The tinge of exasperation in her voice tells me she's probably said my name at least twice. "Sorry. I'm just tired," I say. I don't want to tell her I was thinking about Weldon, and the little park I used to go to after school sometimes with my friend Mia, who I've been texting with nonstop during the long, two-day drive here. If I mentioned Mia, or any of the other friends I'd managed to make during our last move, Mom would want to talk about it. Then I'd have to explain how awful it feels to constantly leave people behind. Then she'd probably suggest meditation to clear my head or cleanse my soul or whatever. Like it's that simple. I don't have the energy for it today.

Mom doesn't seem bothered by my daydreaming. She's totally focused on our surroundings now, both hands gripping the wheel. We've left the commercial area of town and are currently zooming down a narrow, pothole-ridden road. On our left, a large lake shimmers under the midday August sun. It's a familiar sight. My dad is a structural engineer and designs bridges for a living, so every town or city we settle in has a body of water of some sort nearby. Lakes, rivers, channels, bays…we're well acquainted with them all.

"I need you to tell me what street that hotel is on again," Mom says, swerving to miss a pothole. We hit it anyway, causing Hazel, our Pomeranian, to let out a surprised *yip* from the backseat.

I check the map on my phone. "*This* street. Waterview." Granesville's street names are nothing if not literal. "It's just ahead. And it's a motel, not a hotel."

One of her toned, tanned shoulders lifts in a shrug. "Oh well, we're only staying there a couple of weeks. And they were the only place that allowed pets."

On cue, Hazel catapults herself between the seats and settles on my lap. "It's closer to three weeks, actually," I correct as I stroke the dog's soft, cream-colored fur. Dad found a house for us to rent last week, but we can't move in until the end of the month. So it'll be nineteen days of living in a motel room with just our bare essentials while everything else we own waits in storage.

We veer around another bend in the road and the motel suddenly appears on our right. I squint up at the blue-lettered sign. *Waterview Motel.* Of course. The property is huge, with a sprawling manicured lawn and flower gardens and clusters of trees. The motel itself is less impressive, small with dingy white siding, but I've seen worse. Clearly, the top selling feature of this place is the view of the lake. Hence the name.

"How cute!" Mom chirps as we pull into the long driveway.

I hug Hazel to my chest and wonder how my mother can be so unfailingly positive after being stuck in a small Toyota for sixteen hours with a bored dog and sullen teenage daughter. Why can't she be hungry and cranky like a normal person?

As we're turning into the parking lot, we spot Dad standing in front of the motel, beneath a sign that says *Office*. He waves, and Mom's face breaks into a giant smile. We haven't seen him in two weeks; he'd moved early to get organized and meet the crew of his newest bridge job, while Mom dealt with the sale of our house in the city. But for my parents, a two-week separation may as well be two years.

Mom parks and jumps out of the car while I'm still clipping Hazel's leash to her collar. The dog and I exit the car just in time to see my parents' reunion, which reminds me of those videos of couples reuniting after one of them returns from a long stint in the military. A lot of hugging and nuzzling and—if I cared to watch, which I definitely do not—probably kissing too, and not just a friendly *hello* peck.

Hazel runs ahead of me, thrilled to be outside, and I follow her to where my parents are standing, still locked in an embrace. They break apart when Hazel crashes into their legs.

"There you are," Dad says, hugging me and then reaching down to pet the dog. "How was the drive?"

"Long," I say. I did not inherit my mom's optimism.

"Well, I'm so happy you're here. I missed my girls." He hooks his arm around Mom's waist and they both beam at me. Together they look like an infomercial for gym equipment, my father tall and trim and my mother tanned and muscled, neither of them carrying an inch of extra fat. Something else I didn't inherit. "Come on, I'll show you the room."

As Dad leads us to where we'll be living until the end of the month, I silently count doors. I do this almost unconsciously, like breathing. I'm not obsessive about it...I just like knowing the sum total of things, and people, and anything else that can be tallied. There's something about the consistency and permanency of numbers that makes me feel safe.

Sixteen. This motel has sixteen units altogether.

We're in room 112, by the ice machine. Dad opens the door to a surprisingly modern room, with dark laminate floors instead of the standard industrial carpet and light blue accents instead of gaudy floral. The temperature is deliciously cool after the heat of outside. I'm about to plop down on the bed when something hits me.

"There's only one bed."

My parents look at me, then at the king-sized bed, neatly made up with an ocean-blue bedspread and white throw pillows. I haven't slept in my parents' bed since I was three and I'm not about to start again now. Am I supposed to sleep on the scratchy-looking loveseat? The floor?

"Oh!" Dad smiles and crosses the room to a closed door. I assume it's the bathroom until he pushes it open, revealing a room identical to the one I'm in, only backwards. "I thought you'd like your own room, Avery."

5

Mom beams at him like he's a genius, and I try to smile and appear grateful for the extra space and privacy. And I am grateful, kind of. My parents want to be alone, I get it, and I'd rather not be around to witness them reconnecting. But just this once, I wish they'd make room for me inside the invisible bubble that surrounds them, at least until I start to adjust to the newness of this place.

"Awesome," I say. I step into the adjoining room, Hazel trailing behind me and sniffing everything within her reach. It's even colder in here. *Too* cold. I go over to the window, open the heavy drapes, and stand in a patch of warm sun.

After we're settled in, we go out for dinner to celebrate our first night in Granesville as a family.

Dining options are limited, so we quickly agree on First Choice Grill, a steakhouse/sports bar type place that serves a million varieties of beer on tap and features a wall of TVs, all tuned into golf. A colorful sign near our booth says *Finish Our Sizzlin' 72oz Steak in Under an Hour & It's Free! Plus Win a T-Shirt!*

"This place is great," my father says as we look over our menus. "I've been here a few times. I recommend the buffalo chicken wrap."

Mom orders what she always orders—salad—and I opt for a burger and fries. While we wait for our food, my parents discuss the new house, which we drove by on the way here. It's a medium sized bungalow style, with white siding and red shutters. Mom's excited about the flower beds in front, and Dad likes the two-car driveway.

All I care about is what my room looks like, but we can't go inside until the current residents clear out.

"And the high school is within walking distance," my mother says, turning to me. "Isn't that convenient?"

I almost tell her that my own car would be even more convenient, but I decide to save that conversation for when things settle down. Instead, I think about Granesville High, where I'll be starting my senior year in twenty-four days, four days after we move into our house rental. According to my internet findings, the school's total enrollment last year was 654 students. At Thompson High, where I spent sophomore and junior year, I was one of 2378 students. There, I blended into the crowd. Here, I'll be an outsider in a sea of tightknit cliques and kids who have known each other since preschool.

I definitely prefer big cities.

After dinner, Dad takes us to the area on the lake where construction on his latest bridge design is about to begin. Right now it's just a cleared section of woods, the ground muddy and pitted with tire tracks. I try to muster some interest, though this stupid bridge is the reason I'm not still in Weldon right now. When we moved there before my sophomore year, Dad assured me that it would likely be our last move as a family. I was thrilled, and eventually I grew confident enough to think of the city as home. I got comfortable there. I made friends. Found a boyfriend. But then this bridge project popped up unexpectedly, Dad's company won the bid, and after weighing the pros and cons, my parents chose to see the opportunity as "our next adventure" rather than another loss for me.

I look over at my parents as they stand at the edge of the water, arm in arm. It amazes me how adaptable they are to different places. I stopped trying to adapt a long time ago, when I realized it wasn't worth the time or effort. Now I'm just indifferent.

My father points across the expanse of water. "That's McMahon's Island. See that campground? The bridge will connect to the left of it." His eyes light up like they do whenever he talks about work. "It'll be beautiful. A through arch design, two lanes, seven hundred and eighteen meters in length."

Dad loves numbers and statistics almost as much as I do. I shield my eyes from the evening sun and peer across at the lake. From here, all I can really make out of McMahon's Island is the campground he pointed out, dotted with RVs, and a line of trees.

"How do people get back and forth now?" I ask.

My parents exchange a glance, then my father looks at me, his brown hair ruffling in the breeze. "A ferry. You can't really see it from here. It's a few miles down the road."

"A bridge crossing will be *much* more convenient," my mother adds.

That's my mom. Always pointing out the positive.

On the way back to the motel, we drive by our future house again, and then the high school, so I can see just how close it is. Granesville High is small and L-shaped. Both the parking lot and the building are starting to crumble, in need of a renovation. But Mom assures me that it's supposed to be a good school. A fine place to graduate.

That's good enough for me. Since I started school, we've moved seven times. Seven different schools. Seven different sets of kids. By the time I was thirteen, I stopped seeing our moves as adventures and started thinking of them as pit stops to college, where I can finally settle for longer than two years. Granesville is the last pit stop, the end to seventeen years of feeling restless and unmoored. My goal for the next year is to keep my head down and work my ass off in school, so that for once in my life, *I* get to choose where I end up next.

Chapter Two

Waterview Motel has an outdoor pool, but I've only gone in it once. The day after we got here, a horde of people descended upon the motel, families in town for a wedding or reunion or some sort of big gathering, and filled up the rest of the rooms. The pool has been teeming with squealing children ever since.

As a rule, I prefer to swim in water that's not diluted with pee. So for the past three days, I've either been hanging out with Hazel in my room, binging *Supernatural* on my tablet and raiding the mini fridge, or sunbathing with my mom by the pool and trying to avoid getting trampled by little toddler feet.

This afternoon we're at the pool, and the giant family clan must have left for the day, because it's actually quiet for once. Just us and a couple of senior women in bathing caps, bobbing around in the water. My mother, who claims their room is too small to stretch properly, has unfurled her yoga mat right on the poolside concrete and is currently in boat pose, her body bent into a perfect V shape. I'm a few feet away in one of the lounge chairs, reading a Stephen King novel and pretending not to know her.

"Hey, Avery," Mom calls, blowing my cover. "Want to join me?"

She's moved on to bridge pose, her torso thrust into the air. It's about ninety degrees out here and she's not even sweating. You'd never know she's close to fifty, only a couple of decades younger than the wading bathing cap ladies in the pool.

"No, thanks," I say, and return to *Carrie*. Her mother just locked her in the closet, so I guess I should be grateful that mine is only asking me to do yoga asanas. She always asks, even though she knows I'm not flexible or athletic like her and Dad. She teaches yoga for a living and plays tennis for fun. He runs three miles every morning before work. The only exercise I do is walking, and only when I have to. If I didn't have my mother's thick dark hair and my father's brown eyes, I'd wonder if I was somehow switched at the hospital as a baby.

"Avery, why don't you find something constructive to do?" Mom is flat on her back now, feet spread and palms facing upward. When she reaches corpse pose, I know she's finished.

"I'm good here," I say, turning a page in my book. Sweat drips down my back and I think about going inside to bask in the air conditioning, but then Mom would just bug me to go back outside again. After the two-day drive here and being cooped up with her for four days at the motel, even the sound of her voice is starting to annoy me. She's got her resume in at every yoga studio within a twenty-mile radius of here, but she hasn't heard back from anyone yet. Which means I could have several more weeks of public yoga and parental nagging ahead of me.

Maybe I *should* do something constructive.

"Actually," I say, putting *Carrie* aside, "I think I'll go into town and see if any places are hiring. Can I take the car?"

Mom sits up in one fluid movement and smiles at me. I knew she'd approve of the job hunting—she and Dad expect me to work and contribute, and I've held part-time jobs since I was fourteen.

"That's an excellent idea." She stands and rolls up her mat. "Yes, you can take the car. But no more than an hour, okay? I need to get to the bank later."

I promise her I'll be quick, then head back to the motel room to change. Hazel greets me with a bark, then sits at the foot of my bed while I exchange my shorts and sweaty tank for a light, striped sundress. There's nothing to be done for my needs-a-trim hair, so I scrape it back into a ponytail. Once I'm presentable, I transfer my resume from my laptop onto a memory key. Our printer is in storage somewhere, but there must be a place in town—the library, maybe—where I can print a few copies.

"Wish me luck," I tell Hazel as I grab my purse. She snorts and rolls around on the bed, a one-dog cheering section.

My stomach flutters with anticipation as I slide behind the wheel of my mom's Corolla. I've had my full license for sixteen days, and since then, I've driven alone a total of three times. Not having a lot of friends means I don't go out much, so my excursions so far have been limited to trips to the store and picking up my parents from a restaurant after they'd both had a few drinks. And now this. Puttering around Granesville isn't exactly the height of excitement, but after being cooped up for several days, it feels like freedom.

Once I'm on the road, Waterview Motel shrinking behind me, I roll down my window and jack up the stereo. The tightness in my chest that's been there since we left Weldon finally loosens, and I hum along with the music all the way into town.

Center Street, home of most of the businesses, seems like the best place to start. I roll along slowly, checking out the possibilities. First Choice Grill, where we ate the first night. An ice cream place called Cherries, with a round, red cherry dotting the *i*. Primo Pizza, Pizza Ladies, Matty's Pizza—all within a few yards of each other. The Snug Mug Café, where my dad gets his morning coffee because the motel restaurant coffee "tastes like ashtray" (his words). Sadler's Subs, a tiny eatery tucked between a convenience store and a dry cleaner. As I pass the sub place, I notice a girl standing outside, tapping on her cell phone. She's about my age, and she has long black hair and a look of intense irritation on her face.

A new song starts up on the stereo, its fast, thumping bass vibrating the entire car. The girl glances up from her phone, her annoyed expression deepening at the loud intrusion, and catches me looking at her. She raises her eyebrows like *Can I help you?* before turning and disappearing inside the sub shop. Yikes. I guess not all the town locals are the friendly sort.

Slightly rattled, I turn down the stereo and keep driving until I reach the library, a tiny brick building at the end of the street. Luckily, the place is almost deserted, so I have the single printer all to myself. A few minutes later, I step back out into the heat, clutching my ten, still-warm resume copies—at least double what I need, seeing as I haven't spotted a Help Wanted sign anywhere.

Now that I have my resumes, I'm not sure where to start. My last job was at a movie theater, making popcorn and working the cash. But there's no movie theater in Granesville, and going by my Google search, the closest one is a half hour drive away. I toss my phone in my purse and sigh. Why did we have to move to the sticks? I miss the city more with each passing minute.

Okay. I'll just have to make the best of things while we're here, as my mother is fond of saying. I pull out of the library and turn right. There's a tiny mall on the edge of town, with a Target. Considering I'm brand new to the area, I might have a better shot at getting a job there than at one of the little locally owned shops on Center Street. I have a feeling they'd rather hire their own.

Finally armed with a plan, I relax a bit and crank the music again. I'm singing along by the time I roll up to the intersection. The light is red, so I take the opportunity to check my reflection in the mirror. I smooth a strand of wayward hair and then turn my gaze back to the road just as the light turns green. And just in time to see an old blue car, careening through the intersection. Straight toward me.

At first, I can't believe what I'm seeing. Time stops, followed closely by my heart, and then survival instinct takes over. Without even thinking about it, I pull forward and veer sharply to the right to avoid impact. The blue car skims past me, inches from my door, taking out the rear view mirror as it goes. I'm so focused on that car, so consumed with my desire to move out of its way, that I don't even notice the cyclist on the other side of me until he or she collides with my passenger side door.

I slam on my brakes. Oh my God. *Oh my God*. I just hit a person. A car hit me, and then I hit a *person*.

For a moment, I'm numb, unable to move. Or breathe. My head swims with dizziness until my body, deprived of oxygen for too long, suddenly forces me to open my mouth and suck in some air. As my mind clears, I reach over and shut off the stereo as if on autopilot. In the abrupt silence, I start vaguely registering the noises outside my car—doors slamming, voices, gasps of surprise and alarm.

The cyclist. With shaking hands, I turn off the car and get out. People are starting to circle, their faces either curious or horrified. I'm scared to see what's waiting for me on the other side of the car, but I go anyway, my legs like water beneath me. Relief blazes through me when I realize the person I hit isn't dead. He's splayed out flat on the road, his bicycle half on top of his leg, but he's alive and breathing.

"I called 911," I hear one of the onlookers say as I kneel next to the cyclist, my bare knees pressing into the asphalt. He looks young, about my age or slightly older, and he's staring up at the sky and blinking like he can't figure out why he's suddenly on his back.

Still partly numb, I glance around the intersection, looking for the blue car. It's gone. The asshole hit me, causing me to hit someone else, and then he just left. What the hell kind of town *is* this?

15

I refocus on the cyclist. "Are you okay?"

He lifts his head—which is thankfully encased in a bike helmet—and then immediately drops it to the pavement again, his face contorting. "No." He pats his chest like he's checking for broken bones. "I just slammed into the side of a—ahh."

I lean back, wincing. He's not dead, but he's clearly pissed off and in pain. Oh my God. This can't be happening. It feels like a dream, a nightmare, not quite real. I did this. I hit this guy. I could have killed him. My vision blurs, and I close my eyes and swallow, trying to hold down my lunch.

The same man who called 911 steps forward to lift the bicycle off the injured guy's leg. He groans again, his face turning pale.

"Is it your leg, dude?"

The guy lets out a jagged breath. "I think…I think something's broken."

"I'm so sorry," I tell him. My eyes burn with tears. I hit him *and* broke him.

His gaze flicks to me. "You're the one who swerved into my space?"

"I swear, I didn't even see you. There was this blue car and—"

"Old Man Jenkins," says someone from behind me. "I saw him. Probably didn't even notice what happened. That guy's license should've been revoked years ago."

There's a murmur of agreement from the bystanders. I have no idea who Old Man Jenkins is or if this is a regular thing for him, but now seems like the wrong time to ask. Especially since the police and ambulance have just arrived. Within what feels like

16

seconds, two paramedics appear and tell people to move aside. I'm not sure if that includes me, so I scramble backward toward the curb, giving them plenty of room.

"What's your name?" the paramedic with braided red hair asks the cyclist as she gently unbuckles his helmet and takes it off. Underneath, his hair is dark with sweat.

"Liam Kavanagh," he says through clenched teeth.

"Can you tell me what happened, Liam?"

He just groans again. His pain seems to be getting worse.

"I hit him," I blurt out, and my tears finally spill over. I swipe them away and point to my mom's silver Corolla, still sitting in the intersection, windshield glinting under the sun. The police have blocked off the intersection, and the mostly empty road makes me feel like I'm in some kind of dystopian movie, which adds to the surreal vibe. "I was driving and I…I hit him."

The paramedic looks at me for a moment, then catches the eye of her partner, who's busy examining the cyclist's—Liam's—ankle. Her partner nods, and the red-haired paramedic approaches, crouching in front of me as I sit on the curb.

"Are you injured? Do you need help?"

I shake my head. "I'm not hurt. I'm just…I think I should probably call my mom."

Someone—I'm not even sure who—hands me their cell phone, and I punch in my mother's number with trembling fingers.

"Hello?"

The sound of her voice does something to me, melts the icy shock in my blood and puts a lump so big in my throat that it takes me a few seconds to speak. "Mom? It's me."

"Avery? Whose phone are you using? Where are you?"

"I'm at the intersection just off Center Street. I…um, there was an accident." I swallow hard and look over at the cyclist, watch as the paramedics load him onto a stretcher. "I think I broke some guy's leg."

"*What?*"

She keeps talking, asking me questions, her voice sounding as panicked as I feel. But I don't have any answers for her, because I don't really know anything yet. The only thing I'm sure of, with one hundred percent certainty, is that my year in Granesville is off to the worst possible start.

Chapter Three

My mother arrives in a taxi while I'm sitting in the back of an ambulance, getting checked out for injuries and shock. Luckily, I'm okay. The only thing I'm truly suffering from is guilt for maiming some random dude.

"Avery!" Mom rushes over to me, still dressed in her yoga gear. Her face is chalky white under her tan. "Are you okay? What happened?"

Before I have time to answer, a police officer approaches and stops in front of us, his girth blocking the glare of the sun. "You're the young lady who was driving the Corolla?" he confirms.

Mom and I both stare at him for a moment. A calmer, less distressed part of my brain notes that he's tall and muscular and bears a vague resemblance to Idris Elba. I immediately scrap the thought. What is wrong with me? Who notices hot cops right after getting into a car accident?

"Yes," I say, shifting my attention to his shiny badge.

"I'm Officer Porter. Can you explain to me what happened, uh—" he glances at my license, which I'd given to a different cop before going with the paramedic—"Ms. Bishop?"

I look at Mom, who's watching me expectantly, waiting for the answers I wouldn't provide over the phone. "It was all such a blur. I was in the intersection and suddenly this car was heading straight for me. Someone said the driver's name was Jenkins?"

Officer Porter nods and scribbles in his note pad. "I'm aware. Three different witnesses have already named him. Go on."

I tell him about my panic, my instinct to swerve. My obliviousness to the cyclist, coming up on my right and unable to stop in time. "Do you know if he's okay?" I ask, my eyes burning again. "I didn't mean to hit him."

"Of course you didn't," Mom says, then frowns at the officer like she's expecting him to accuse me of something.

Officer Porter doesn't respond. He finishes writing whatever it is he's writing and hands me back my license. "Thank you for your cooperation. I'll be in touch." He strides away, leaving me to wonder what exactly he'll be in touch about, and if it's possible to go to jail for accidentally hitting someone, even if I did it to avoid a head-on collision. How much trouble am I actually in?

Fresh tears slide down my cheeks. I never should have left the stupid motel today. I should have stayed inside with Hazel and finished Season Eight of *Supernatural.* This is what happens when I try to put myself out there—something happens to remind me that

I'm better off staying inside, away from the general public.

"Come on, Avery," Mom says, touching my elbow. "Let's go see if we can leave."

We can, and we're even allowed to take the Corolla home, even though it's missing a rear view mirror and the passenger side is dinged up from the guy's bike. I'm no longer running on adrenaline, so my mind is now free to latch on to more practical matters, like how much it will cost to fix the car, and how my parents will react once they get past the immediate concern for my health and safety. I've never been the type of kid to cause trouble, even by accident. Now I've damaged a car *and* a person, all in the span of a few minutes.

"Did you call Dad?" I ask on the way back to the motel. My mother is driving much slower than usual, like she's afraid more pieces of the car are about to fly off.

"Yes." She glances at the empty space where the mirror used to be, her lips stretched into a thin line. Her *I'm slightly annoyed but I'm trying not to show it because I'm such a positive person* face. "I couldn't get a hold of him, so I left a message."

A dull ache begins in my left temple; the first sign of an impending migraine. Great. "I'm sorry about the car. I'll get a job and help pay for the damage."

Mom's expression softens and she reaches over to pat my knee. "We'll figure out a sensible solution. Let's discuss it when your dad gets home, okay?"

I nod, even though I don't want to discuss "sensible solutions." Just this once, I want her to treat me less like a mature adult who has it all together and more like the scared, insecure seventeen-year-old girl that I am.

***

My migraine is worse by dinnertime, so I give in and take one of my triptan pills. Sometimes I try to avoid taking medication for as long as possible, because the side effects are almost as bad as the pain itself. But I take it and brace myself for an evening of nausea flashes, exhaustion, and extreme foggy-headedness.

"Tell me again how it happened."

I swallow the food in my mouth and look at my father. The three of us are sitting at the small table in their room, eating the rotisserie chicken and premade salad Dad picked up at the supermarket on his way home from work. He heard the story from Mom the second he got in, so I'm not sure why he wants to hear it again now. I rub a hand over my face and, for the millionth time in the past few hours, explain about the intersection, the blue car, the panic, the cyclist. I've said it so many times now, it feels like I'm reciting a story from a book.

"Could've been worse, I guess." He spears a baby tomato with his fork and swipes it through the stream of vinaigrette on his plate. "I know it's an instinctual reaction," he adds after chewing and swallowing it, "but swerving to avoid an obstacle can be even more dangerous than meeting it head on. Sometimes it's better to just take the hit."

Mom nods. "It's so easy to lose control on the road."

I shove a large piece of lettuce into my mouth to dam the flood of words bubbling up in my throat. Words like *It wasn't obstacle, it was a car and it was coming straight at me* and *I've only had my license for sixteen days and I don't remember any "dangers of swerving" lessons from driver's ed* and *Yeah, it could've been worse, I could have killed the guy instead.* But talking back to my mother and father in any capacity usually earns me a furrowed-forehead, concern-mixed-with-disappointment look, which I can't handle while on strong meds.

My parents expect me to be mature. Even when I was three, they expected me to be mature. When I played with other kids, I had to be the one to acquiesce whatever toy everyone wanted, even if I got to it first. I had to be the one to rise above. The one to sit quietly and answer respectfully and be on her best behavior. Before me, my parents were nomads, going wherever Dad's job sent him, interesting places like Dubai and Rome. Then I came along, prompting them to at least limit the traveling to one continent. I was a "very unexpected surprise," which is just a nicer term for *accident.* I could always sense, from the way my parents related to me—almost like I was their peer rather than their child—that parenthood was never a part of their original plan.

They love me, of course, and they've always taken care of me, but it's easy to see that they generally prefer each other's company to mine. And they always, *always* take each other's side, even when the opposing side is me. Like our so-called vote on Granesville, for example. Months ago, when Dad found out about the job opportunity here, the three of us took a vote: stay where we were, or go. I chose stay, of course. But my father wanted this job, and my mother has wanderlust in her blood, so I was overruled. I'm almost always overruled, but I'm supposed to be mature enough to suck it up.

Screw it. The want me to act grown up and responsible? Then they should respect what I have to say next. I finish chewing and put down my fork. "I want to go see him."

Both my parents look up. "See who?" Dad asks.

"The guy I hit. The cyclist. I want to apologize and make sure he's okay."

Mom leans over to shoo away Hazel, who's been inching progressively closer to the table since we sat down. "I'm sure we could ask that officer you spoke with today," she says when she straightens back up. "He'll probably know."

I push away my half-full plate. The meds kill my appetite too. "I asked him, remember? He didn't answer. I just want to see for myself."

"Avery," Dad says, frowning. "We don't know what's going to happen yet. This guy might be planning to press charges against you. He might—"

"I don't care."

My words surprise all of us. I rarely talk back. Hardly ever disagree or interrupt. But I won't be overruled this time. This is different, a special case. Important enough to speak up and stand firm. If I don't see this guy— Liam—with my own eyes, then I'll always wonder about him. I'll always have this unshakable guilt, eating away at me, forcing me to replay the sound of him smashing into the side of the car, the sight of him lying in the road, in horrible pain. Because of something I did.

"There's only one hospital nearby," I say in a calmer voice. My parents aren't giving me the concerned, furrowed-forehead look like usual. Instead, they're starting at me wide-eyed, like I'm a doll that's suddenly come to life. "I'm sure he's there. I know his name, so I'll be able to find him if he's been admitted." If the swelling around his ankle when the paramedics loaded him onto the stretcher is any indication, he'll likely be there for a day at least.

"Well," Mom says. She meets Dad's eyes, and they have one of those silent conversations that only people who've known each other forever can pull off. "If you really feel like you need to see him, then I guess you should. But not tonight, okay? It's getting late, and visiting hours are probably over soon anyway. You can go tomorrow morning. Your dad's leaving his car here with me until mine is fixed. I'll drop you off at the hospital on the way to the bank."

Relieved, I let out a breath. Tomorrow is better than nothing. Maybe I should start asserting myself more often. "Deal," I say, and reach for my dinner again.

Chapter Four

"Shouldn't you bring something?" Mom asks the next morning.

I yawn and rub my eye. It's only nine a.m., too early for questions and conversation. "Like what?"

"I don't know. Usually you bring something when you visit someone in the hospital. Flowers, maybe?"

"Flowers," I repeat as she brakes at a stop sign and we both lurch forward. She's not used to Dad's big work truck, so she keeps braking too hard and accelerating too fast.

"Or a card?" she says, making a wide left turn.

I yawn again, picturing the card I'd give this guy I injured. *Sorry I hit you with my car. Get well soon!* "I don't think I need to bring anything," I tell my mother.

She shrugs and stays quiet for the rest of the short drive to the hospital. My parents still don't approve of me going to see the guy who might potentially sue us, but they seem to understand my motives, at least. Knowing I'm doing the right thing doesn't help the quaky feeling in my stomach, though. I lay awake for most of last night, my mind spinning images of broken bones and big shiny cars, zooming straight toward me. I thought about today too, what I'd say to this stranger who was unlucky enough to be in the wrong place at the wrong time, and how he might react to my words. How would *I* react if the situation were reversed? I like to think I'd go easy on him, accept his apology and tell him it wasn't really his fault. Or maybe I'd be angry because it *was* his fault, because he swerved and hit me instead of staying put and taking the hit himself.

As my mother pulls into the hospital parking lot, a surge of doubt washes over me. In the daylight, after a restless night, showing up here unannounced suddenly feels like the dumbest idea I've ever had.

"Text me when you're ready," Mom says.

My stomach constricts around the Pop Tart I managed to get down for breakfast. "Okay," I say. Then I take a steadying breath, swallow back the raspberry-flavored acid in my throat, and get out of the truck.

The hospital, like the town, is small, quiet, and easy to navigate. I head straight for the reception desk, silently repeating the name I'd heard the guy give to the paramedic yesterday, his voice weak and strained. "Liam Kavanagh," I tell the woman behind the desk when she asks who I'm visiting.

I hold my breath while she types it into the computer, then let it out again when she says, "Room 347." She writes it down for me on a little piece of paper. "Third floor, turn left when you get off the elevator."

Relief trickles through me as I walk across the lobby, even though I know it's probably not a good thing that he's still here. If it wasn't bad, he probably would have gotten a cast and been sent home. What if he's hurt even worse?

Again, I'm overwhelmed with doubt, but I force myself into the elevator and up to the third floor. I step out into a sea of white and pastel green. The walls are decorated with painted cartoon dogs and cats and rabbits, all smiling big goofy smiles. I haven't spent much time in hospitals, but I know a children's ward when I see one. Which means Liam Kavanagh is under eighteen. It was hard to gauge his age yesterday, with his features contorted with pain.

I automatically count doors as I snake through the corridors to room 347. When I reach it, I stop short just before the open door. Voices drift out into the hallway, a low, deep tone followed by a higher, louder one. A woman. I hesitate in the hallway, wondering if I should come back later.

"Don't you worry, I'll think of something," the woman says in a confident, slightly accented voice. Scottish? British? It's hard to tell.

The other voice—Liam?—responds to her, but I can't make out what he's saying. I start to edge closer, then jump back again when I hear footsteps approaching the door. For some reason, I move a few feet down the wall and pretend to study a poster about a fundraiser as the woman emerges from the room. I peer at her out of the corner of my eye. She's about my mom's age, plump, wispy blond hair, fair skin. I watch as she waves at the person in the room and then walks away in the other direction, not even noticing me.

My feet feel rooted to the scrubbed white tile. Now what? Should I…walk in there? Knock first and wait?

I end up doing a combination of the two—knock and then walk in before he even has a chance to look up. My eyes zero in on his left leg, an oversized lump under the thin hospital sheets. Oh God, it *is* broken. *I broke his bones.* Now that I'm looking at it, at him in this hospital bed, proof of my possible negligence, I suddenly feel like I need to either sit down or run away. Or vomit. I do none of these things. Instead, I just stare.

"Uh, hello?"

I look up, catching the eye of the boy in the bed next to Liam's. He's about twelve, and there's an IV sticking out of his hand. Otherwise he looks normal.

"I'm here for him," I say, pointing numbly at Liam. The boy nods and goes back to watching his TV, and for the first time since I walked in here, I raise my eyes to Liam's face.

He looks different than he did yesterday. Not quite as pale. His hair is lighter now that the sweat and road dirt has been rinsed away, golden brown instead of dark. His features are smooth, the evidence of yesterday's pain erased, though the tense set of his mouth makes it clear that he's still uncomfortable. Or maybe it's me who's making him uncomfortable.

"You're here for me?" he asks, glancing at IV Boy and then back at me.

Damn. He doesn't recognize me. Suddenly it hits me that he only looked at me once yesterday, and I was hanging over him at the time. Plus he was in acute agony. Of course he doesn't recognize me.

I inch closer, coming to a stop at the end of his bed. A huge bouquet of Get Well balloons sits on his table, swaying slightly in the air conditioning. He's been here less than twenty-four hours and he already has gifts?

"I'm Avery Bishop," I say in a shaky voice. "I'm…I'm the one who was driving the car that, um, hit you."

He stares at me for a moment while my words sink in, then his gray eyes widen in understanding. Silence stretches between us, so long and heavy that my mouth goes dry and palms start to sweat. This is why I prefer to keep to myself and limit my social contact to my dog and the fictional Winchester brothers, none of whom will judge me like this real life guy sitting in front of me right now.

"Oh," he says, finally. He drops his gaze to his hands, resting on his covered lap.

Oh? That's it? "So I just wanted to apologize and to, uh, see how you were feeling," I stammer.

"How I'm feeling," he repeats slowly, like he doesn't understand the words. For a panicked moment, I wonder if I damaged his brain along with his leg, but then he blinks at me and lets out a joyless laugh. "Well, since you asked," he says, his tone and demeanor suddenly changing, turning dark. "My tibia is broken, and I've been waiting for hours for the doctor to decide if I need surgery to fix it. But even if I don't need surgery, I'll be in a cast or walking boot for at least six weeks, maybe even longer, which means I can't work, which means I might end up losing my job. And I really count on that paycheck because I'm saving up for the senior trip, which probably won't happen now because I won't have enough time to save up the money I need. On top of all that, my ankle hurts like hell, and now the person who hit me with her car is standing in my hospital room asking me how I feel, when it's pretty damn obvious that I feel like shit." He pauses to take a breath and lifts his gaze to mine again. "So, yeah. That's how I'm feeling. Thank you for asking."

All I can do is stare back at him, mute. One of the scenarios I pictured was similar to this, but even so, experiencing his anger first hand is way worse than my imagination. I swallow the lump rising in my throat and look down, blinking fast. I can sense him watching me, along with IV Boy, who clearly finds us more entertaining than TV. My dad was right—coming here was a bad idea. I've only made everything worse.

I force myself to look up, meet the hostile eyes of the guy whose next six weeks I ruined. "I'm sorry," I tell him. "I really am."

He looks away and shifts position in bed, wincing at the movement. Silence falls between us again. I don't know what else to say, what else I can do to make things right. All I know is that I have to get out of here now unless I want to cry in front of him, which I definitely do not. Luckily, a nurse arrives at that moment, saving me from further embarrassment. I use her presence as my cue to leave.

Liam doesn't even look up as I slip out of the room.

I manage to hold in my tears until I make it to the elevator, which is fortunately empty. Shame prickles in my chest. I've always hated confrontation and can't stand to have people—even strangers—mad at me. My mother calls it emotional sensitivity. I call it frustrating. I wish I could be tough, like her. I wish I could have told that boy that I'm not a careless driver, and he didn't have to treat me like I broke his ankle on purpose just to ruin his life.

The elevator doors slide open and I step out into the lobby again. I dig out my phone to text Mom. All I want to do is go back to the motel, hole up in my room, and process what just happened.

Mom texts back that she's still in line at the bank and will be at least another fifteen minutes. To kill time, I go into the hospital gift shop to get a bottle of water for my dry throat. On my way to the checkout, I pass a shelf filled with Get Well gifts. Fake flowers. Balloons. Cards. Stuffed animals. A display of little brown teddy bears, each with a set of tiny crutches and a cast on its leg. I pause to look at them and think about how, if I were in the hospital with a broken bone, having something like this in my room might cheer me up a little. And if anyone needs cheering up, it's that guy upstairs.

I can't just leave without trying.

After a moment of hesitation, I grab one of the teddies and buy it along with the water. Then I go back to the elevator and press the button for *up*.

Liam is dozing when I walk back into room 347. IV Boy, still awake and watching TV, eyes me curiously as I cross the room to Liam's bed. Liam looks up expectantly as I approach, probably hoping for the doctor, here to give him the verdict on surgery. When he sees it's me, his eyebrows shoot up. At least he doesn't look mad anymore.

"Forget something?"

"Sort of," I say, and place the injured bear on his table next to the balloon bouquet. "I forgot to give you this."

His head tilts to the side and he blinks slowly at the bear, like he doesn't quite understand what he's looking at. Again, I wonder if he has a head injury, but then I realize the nurse from before probably gave him a shot of something for his pain.

"Thanks," he says, then lets out a short laugh. "Did you run him down with your car too?"

My cheeks burn. Instead of answering him, I dig in my purse for a pen and a piece of paper. All I have is the receipt for the bear, but that will do. I write my name and cell number on the back and place it next to the bear. "If there's anything I can do to help you, just call me, okay? I owe you."

He looks at me, eyelids drooping. "I can't think of any way you could help," he says, the words slurring together. "I mean, unless you have a thousand dollars lying around. That's how much I need in the next three months if I'm going to pay for the trip."

Taking advantage of his mellowed state, I ask, "Where is it? The senior trip?"

"Europe," he says in a dreamy voice. "A ten-day tour of Scotland and Ireland…But I'm mostly interested in Ireland, since that's where my parents grew up. My father…This trip is probably my only chance to see it." His eyes slide shut, and his next words are barely a murmur. "*Was* my only chance."

I feel another stab of guilt. The woman from before, the blonde with the accent, must have been his mother. But what about his father? He isn't making much sense.

The only thing that's clear is how important this trip is to him, and how what happened yesterday might have messed everything up. How *I* might have messed everything up, because of one moment of instinctual reaction. Because the only way I could save myself from getting hit was to hit him instead.

"I'm sorry," I say again, even though it's pointless. He's fast asleep and doesn't hear me anyway.

Chapter Five

My mother is smiling when I shuffle into my parents' room the next morning. "Guess what?" she asks.

I grab a yogurt out of the mini fridge, only half paying attention. I miss my mom's scrambled eggs in the morning. Six days of motel living and I'm officially sick of it. "What?"

"That nice Officer Porter called a few minutes ago."

My heartrate accelerates. The Idris-Elba-lookalike cop from the accident scene. He said he'd be in touch. "And?"

She picks a dirty shirt off the floor, tosses it in the laundry bag by the dresser. "*And*...he had some news for us. After talking to several witnesses, the police determined that the accident was *not* your fault. People saw the man in the blue car run the light, and they saw you turn to avoid him. You weren't being reckless or breaking any laws, so you're not going to be charged at all. That's a relief, huh?"

"Yeah," I say quietly. It *is* a relief to hear that I wasn't legally at fault, but after feeling the sting of Liam's bitterness in the hospital room yesterday, I'm not so sure I deserve the reprieve.

"So that's that," she says, slipping her bare feet into a pair of flats. For the first time, I notice she's dressed kind of fancy, in a blouse and black skirt. "My car will be good as new in a few days, and it'll be like nothing ever happened."

I grit my teeth around a mouthful of yogurt. Liam's ankle won't be good as new in a few days. He won't be able to pretend like nothing ever happened.

"My insurance will probably go up because of this, though," Mom adds with a frown. She opens the drapes, exposing a rain-smeared window. "And the repairs on the car are going to cost a damn fortune. I know the accident wasn't your fault, but you *were* the one driving at the time, so I think it's only fair that you contribute to the costs."

"Well, I need to find a job first," I say, trying to keep the irritation from my voice. I finish my breakfast and dump the container in the trash can. "Are you going somewhere?"

Her smile widens. "I got my first job interview! It's at a yoga studio about a twenty minute drive from here." She glances at the digital clock on the nightstand. "Whoa, nine-thirty, I'd better go. Maybe I'll pick up some smoothies for us on the way home, how does that sound? Okay, bye!"

She waves at me and bounces out the door. I flop down on the unmade bed, exhausted already.

***

To celebrate Mom's interview—and my exoneration, too, I guess—Dad arrives home from work with a bottle of red wine. He cracks it open in the motel room and pours some into three plastic cups.

"Here's to good news," he says, holding up his cup. "And to Monica, my brilliant and sexy wife."

"Derrick." She laughs a little, her face flushed. "It was just an interview. I haven't gotten the job."

"Yet." He winks at me, like we know the truth even if Mom doesn't, and takes a drink of wine. I smile thinly and do the same, even though I think wine tastes like crap. My parents are really into it and have been offering me small tastes on holidays and special occasions since I was about twelve. I only ever have a sip, just enough to feel included in the festivities.

Hazel, unimpressed with our celebration, plants herself by the door and starts whining.

"I'll take her out," I say, grateful for the excuse. My parents are sitting together on the edge of their bed now, drinking and laughing like they're in some cozy tavern. At a table for two.

"Thanks," Mom says, shooting me a smile as Dad refills her cup.

I attach Hazel's lead to her collar and the two of us step out into the damp evening air. The rain from earlier has slowed to a heavy, humid mist, and my skin immediately turns sticky.

"Come on, Haze," I say, and steer her toward the trees and grass at back of the building. It's darker back here, and foggy. In the sunlight, Waterview Motel seems almost cheery. Now, it looks like a place where Sam and Dean might hunt for ghosts or monsters in *Supernatural*.

A shiver runs down my neck. To distract myself from the eerie atmosphere, I take out my phone to see if I have any texts. Nothing. I've pretty much convinced myself by now that Liam isn't going to contact me. Why would he? He's clearly feels bitter toward me. Or maybe he doesn't even remember me being there the second time, even with the bear on crutches as evidence. He probably thinks I was some kind of weird hallucination he conjured up during his morphine high.

Before putting my phone away, I scroll through my short contact list, which consists of my parents, my cousin Katie who lives in Boston, and the few friends I'd made during our last stint in the city. Only Mia, who I actually hung out with outside of school hours, has texted me since I left. Our contact has become more sporadic in the past few days—probably because she got a new boyfriend shortly before I left—but I'm used to the feeling of growing apart from people. I realized a long time ago that long-distance friendships have less of a chance of surviving when the friendship hardly has time to really develop in the first place.

The dog strains against her leash and I take a step forward, almost dropping my phone. I stick it back in my pocket and tighten my grip on the leash handle. Hazel is running around the grass at top speed, a light-colored blur in the mist. After a few minutes of this, she stops suddenly and looks toward the woods. A low growl erupts from her throat, making all my arms hair stand on end. I clean up her business as quickly as possible, then hightail it back to the front of the motel, heart racing. *A rabbit or something*, I reason with myself once we're safe in the well-lit area. *Ghosts are not real.*

My parents' voices and laughter filter through the closed connecting door as Hazel and I enter my cool room. They sound like they want to be alone, which suits me fine because I do too. I leave Hazel to her food bowl and head for the shower. Being outside has left me sweaty and disgusting.

My phone rings just as I finish rinsing conditioner out of my hair. I turn off the water, fling open the shower curtain, and grab my cell from the counter, assuming it's Mia. But it's a number I don't recognize. I press answer with a dripping finger.

"Hey," responds a voice to my *hello*. "This is Liam. From the bike? Is this Avery?"

I catch a glimpse of myself in the mirror, remember I'm naked, and quickly reach for a towel. "Um, yeah," I say, too loudly. My voice echoes off the shower walls. "Hi, Liam. From the bike." I wince at my words—why can't I speak like a normal person?—and step out of the tub, wrapping the towel around me.

"I hope it's okay that I called you."

His voice sounds deeper and stronger than yesterday, and he seems lucid, so I assume he's not calling me in a pain killer haze. "No, it's fine. That's why I left my number." I sit down on the edge of the tub. "Are you…did you get released from the hospital?"

"No," he says. "I had surgery on my ankle this morning, so I'm here until tomorrow."

"Oh." The guilt returns, coiling in my stomach. "How did it go?"

"The doctor said it went fine." He clears his throat. "Anyway, I called you because I wanted to apologize for yesterday. You were nice enough to visit me and I acted like a total jackass to you."

"Oh," I say again, slightly surprised. I was half expecting him to yell at me or something. "It's okay. You don't have to apologize."

"No, really. I know now that it wasn't your fault. The accident, I mean. Someone from the police station called my mom this morning and filled her in on the details. I had no idea Old Man Jenkins was involved. Makes more sense now."

I reach over to open the bathroom door, letting out some steam. "I just moved here a few days ago," I tell him. "Is Old Man Jenkins the town drunk or something?"

He snickers. "Not exactly. He's a bit senile, that's all. Okay, a lot senile. He's kind of known for walking out of stores without paying and wandering around Center Street in only his undershirt and boxers. He definitely shouldn't be behind the wheel of a car."

"I can vouch for that."

"So can my ankle."

I laugh, even though it isn't really funny. A long, awkward pause follows, and I search my brain for something non-idiotic to say. "Well…"

"Well…" he says at the same moment. Now we both laugh.

"Anyway, um, thanks for calling."

"Thanks for coming to visit yesterday. I'm sorry again for biting your head off. I was just really upset about losing six weeks of work and not having enough money for the senior trip. I've wanted to see Ireland since I was about six." He sighs. "My mom keeps telling me it'll work out, but I don't see how. The final payment's due at the end of November."

God, now I feel even guiltier. "Maybe you can go next year? If you don't get to go on the senior trip, I mean?"

"No. The school gets a discount with group rates or something, plus we can do a lot of fundraising to help with the cost. I wouldn't be able to afford it on my own." There's a rustling sound, like he's shifting in bed, followed by a soft grunt of pain. "Besides," he continues, letting out a breath. "I'm planning to join the military after high school, so who knows when I'll get another chance to take a trip like this."

My stomach sinks. One wrong swerve and I've destroyed his lifelong dream. There has to be some way I can fix this. Make it right. "I'm sorry. If there's anything I can do, like give you a drive somewhere, help you get around, whatever…Just let me know, okay?"

"I'll keep that in mind. Though my doctor claims I'll be zipping around on my crutches before I know it, so there's probably not much you can do." He pauses before adding, "Unless you want to stand in for me at my job or something."

He laughs after he says it, clearly not serious. Still, his words spark something in my brain, an idea, and a plan starts to form. A crazy plan, possibly, but one that might actually work.

"What's your job?" I ask him.

"I make subs at Sadler's Subs. I've been there for over two years."

Sadler's Subs. The tiny place I passed the other day, mere minutes before the accident. The place the black-haired girl went into after I annoyed her with my loud music. Okay. Perfect. I was worried he had some kind of complicated job, something that requires a lot of training I don't have. This, however, I can work with.

"But I can't make subs with a busted ankle," he goes on. "Have you ever been in the place? It's like a closet. There's no way I'd be able to get around in there with a boot and crutches. I'm probably going to be let go."

I stand up and adjust my towel. My hair, still soaked, drips cold water down my back, but I ignore it and leave the bathroom. Hazel's on my bed now, a poof of white fur blending in with the pillows. She watches me as I pace the room. "Maybe there's a way for you to keep your job," I tell Liam.

"Huh?"

"Okay, this might sound weird, but hear me out." My body suddenly feels damp with sweat, even though it's cold in here and I'm wearing a wet towel. "What if I *did* stand in for you, like you said? Act as your replacement? I mean, if your boss is okay with it. I have experience with food prep and cash. I'll work there until your ankle is better, and I'll give you every cent I make. That way, you'll have enough for your trip. You can still see Ireland."

He doesn't respond for what feels like minutes. Then, just as I'm wondering if we've been disconnected, he says, "Why would you do that for me? You don't even know me."

I stop pacing and sit down on the desk chair. Clearly, he thinks I'm out of my mind. And he's right—I don't know him, and I probably wouldn't have even thought of this yesterday, when he was lashing out at me in the hospital room. But now that's he called me, all nice and vulnerable and apologetic, I feel like I owe him the help.

Maybe I *am* out of my mind, but this is the only way I can think of to make up for my role in his current predicament. The only way I can redeem myself for the horrible first impression I've made in this town.

"I feel bad about your ankle," I say, because that's basically what's driving me. That, and my innate need to solve problems, especially when the problem was caused by me. I know it was more Old Man Jenkins' fault than mine, but I don't want to be part of the reason he loses his job and has to alter his plans. "Just think about it. Okay?"

After another long silence, he says, "The nurse is here, I gotta go."

We hang up, and I go back to the bathroom to finish drying off. By the time I'm in my pajamas, the second thoughts have started creeping in. My idea *is* kind of out there. I mean, who does things like that? Who makes an offer to a perfect stranger—someone they *hit with a car*—to temporarily fill in for them at their job? For free? Especially when the offer-maker in question needs an actual, permanent job, with wages, to help pay off the repairs on the car she managed to wreck?

I'm definitely out of my mind.

Vowing to forget about it for the rest of the night, I snuggle in bed with Hazel and my tablet and fire up Netflix. I'm only five minutes into a *Supernatural* episode when my phone chimes with a text.

I'll have to ask Doug and Linh.

It's Liam. What is he talking about? Did the nurse give him another shot? I pause the episode and text back *Who?*

The Sadlers. My bosses. I'll let you know.

I smile. Maybe my offer wasn't so out there, after all. He must really want to make it to Europe. Years of moving has turned me off traveling, but I can understand how living in a town like this could make someone want to see the rest of the world.

My phone doesn't ding again until eleven-thirty. Half asleep, I squint at Liam's words on the screen.

It's all set. Sadler's Monday at two. Bring your resume. Then, a few seconds later, he texts the words *Good luck,* followed by an ominous skull and crossbones emoji.

It takes me at least another hour to fall asleep.

Chapter Six

On Monday afternoon, my mother drops me off downtown on her way to the supermarket. "Good luck," she calls as I get out of the truck.

"Thanks." I told my parents over the weekend that I had a job interview, which isn't technically a lie. I decided to leave it at that for now, partly because I'm not ready to see their reactions when I tell them my plan, and partly because there's no point in going into it until the plan is actually in motion.

I glance down at my dress to make sure my bra straps aren't showing, then take a deep, steadying breath before opening the door to Sadler's Subs.

Liam was right—the place is like a closet. A long, narrow, walk-in closet that smells like fresh bread and onions. There's no seating aside from one padded bench against the window. A small counter divides the ordering area from the prep kitchen, which is fully visible from where I'm standing. The limited wall space is crowded with framed newspaper articles, advertisements, and large, laminated menu cards. I move closer to peer at them.

"Can I help you?"

I spin around to see a pretty Asian girl standing behind the counter. It's her—the annoyed girl from a few days ago. Only she's not frowning this time. She's looking at me expectantly, like she's waiting for me to order. I didn't even hear her approaching.

"Oh, hi," I say, walking up to the counter, resume clutched in my hand. Her forehead creases as she studies my face. "I'm—"

"Ariana Grande," she exclaims, her voice triumphant.

"Excuse me?"

She smooths her long, black hair off her neck, exposing multiple ear piercings. "You're the girl who drove past me the other day. The one in the silver car who was blasting Ariana Grande."

"Oh. Yeah." Warmth creeps up my face. "Sorry about that."

"It's a free country," she says, shrugging her thin shoulders. "So what can I get you?"

I hold up my resume. "I'm here to see Doug and Linh? I'm the, uh…" How do I phrase this? *I'm the one who broke Liam?* Finally, I settle on "I'm Avery Bishop. Liam sent me?"

The girl's expression immediately switches from distantly polite to openly hostile. "Right. You're ten minutes early." She crosses her arms and gives me a look so cold, it makes me want to shrivel up and run away. "I'll get my dad."

After another extra-long glare, she turns around and disappears into a back room. My stomach clenches uneasily. Clearly, someone's filled her in on who I am and why I'm here, and she already hates me. Great.

A minute later, a tall, smiling man in a white apron emerges from the back. The girl's dad? They look nothing alike. For one, he's white. Also, he's about three times her size and built like a linebacker.

"Avery?" He comes around the counter to shake my hand. "Doug Sadler. Come on back, I'll show you around."

I follow him into the kitchen area, almost bumping into the girl as we pass each other in the narrow space. She scowls at me again and continues to the prep area, where she picks up a large knife and starts slicing tomatoes. I step closer to her dad, out of stabbing range.

"So Liam explained the, um…situation," Mr. Sadler says, stopping next to a huge rack of sub buns. They smell delicious, and my stomach responds in spite of its growing queasiness. "I have to admit, I was reluctant at first. Your offer to work his shifts for him is, well, kind of unusual. On the other hand, it's also convenient. Interviewing takes up a lot of time, and with Liam out, we're extremely shorthanded. Kath can only work so many shifts once school starts, and my son Isaac is…" He shakes his head. "Anyway."

"A lazy, unreliable bum?" the girl supplies for him, her eyes still on the tomatoes.

"Nose out, Katherine." When he frowns at her, I suddenly see the family resemblance between them. Turning back to me, he says, "You're new around here, right? What brings you to this neck of the woods? People typically move out of Granesville, not into it."

I tell him about my dad's job, the bridge he's helping to build. As I speak, his bushy eyebrows scrunch tighter and tighter.

"Right," he says. "I read all about the new bridge project in the paper a few months ago. Man, that ferry to McMahon's Island has been running for as long as I can remember. My uncle Frank operated it for a few years back in the eighties. It'll feel strange not to have it there anymore." He shakes his head quickly, his brow smoothing out again. "Anyway, back to the topic at hand. Liam mentioned you have customer service and food prep experience?"

I nod and hand him my resume. "I worked at Quiznos last summer, and then made popcorn and worked the cash at a movie theater for nine months. I had to quit because I was moving here."

"Quiznos," Mr. Sadler mutters, his blue eyes scanning my resume. Katherine lets out a short laugh, earning another pointed look from her dad. "Nothing against the big chain sub shops, but they can't compare to locally owned." He gestures toward the buns. "We get our bread fresh every day from the bakery. Vegetables are sliced fresh every day. We use only the best meats and cheeses. None of that cryovaced stuff. The key is consistency, attention to detail, and simple, quality ingredients."

"Dad, you sound like a commercial again," Katherine says, moving on to a giant Spanish onion. She expertly removes the core and then peels off the skin.

"So what?" he responds good-naturedly. "There's a reason why this place is still standing after thirty-eight years. I run it just like my father did before me."

Katherine places the onion in the rotary slicer. "*You* run it?"

Mr. Sadler grins at me and passes back my resume. "My wife plays a huge part in our success. You'll meet her next time. She's out running errands this afternoon."

I nod, unsure what to say. He's acting like I already have the job, but I don't want to assume. This place, him, Katherine…it's all a little intimidating. Maybe I should have offered Liam cold hard cash instead, though I only have $357.46 in my bank account and no potential windfalls on the horizon. So it's either do this or start selling my belongings on the internet.

Mr. Sadler opens the giant, stainless steel fridge and starts poking around the stacks of meats and cheeses. "What's your availability?"

"Totally open until school starts," I say.

"You going to Granesville High?" he asks, head still inside the fridge. "Katherine goes there. She's a senior this year. Liam too. Maybe they can show you around."

I glance at Katherine. She's ripping the skin off another onion, her shoulders stiff. The only thing she probably wants to show me is the bottom of her shoe as she kicks my ass. Why is she being so hostile toward me? Maybe she's Liam's girlfriend. I wonder if she thinks I maimed him on purpose so I could steal his job, or if she just dislikes me on principle. It's been known to happen. Mia once told me that I'm not an easy person to get to know.

"Liam works about twenty hours a week during the school year," Mr. Sadler says as he closes the fridge. "Usually five to nine on Wednesdays, five to nine on Fridays, and eleven to seven on Sundays. Sometimes more if we need him."

I run the numbers in my head. Sixteen or more hours a week for six to eight weeks, at minimum wage…by the time Liam's back on his feet, I'll have earned him at least a thousand dollars to put toward the senior trip. After that, we'll definitely be square.

"Sounds good," I say.

"Great." He turns toward the door as two middle aged men file in. Construction workers, going by their clothing.

"Hey, Dougie," one of them bellows. "Want to make us a couple roast beef subs with the works?"

Mr. Sadler waves a giant arm at the men. "You got it, Warren." He looks at me and gestures with his chin. "May as well show you how to work the board, since that's mostly what you'll be doing. Come on."

"The board" turns out to be the worn slab of wood directly in front of the stainless steel bins of toppings, and "working" it means assembling subs. I watch as he stuffs two fresh buns full of beef, cheese, sliced onions, shredded lettuce, tomatoes, mayo, and pickles. He tops off each sandwich with salt and pepper and a dash of oil. The result looks and smells amazing. He wraps each sub in wax paper and slides both in a brown paper bag. Then he hands the bag over to Warren, who gives him a couple of bills and tells him to keep the change.

"Easy peasy, right?" Mr. Sadler shuts the register drawer and then turns back to me, smiling. "So when can you start?"

I smile back. That *was* easy. "Immediately?"

"How about Wednesday at five? Kath will be here then, covering Liam's usual shift. She can show you the rest of the ropes." He meets his daughter's eyes, and they have a silent conversation not unlike the ones my parents have all the time. Only Mr. Sadler's gaze is sharp with warning, and Katherine looks unmistakably pissed. "You can fill out the paperwork on Thursday," he continues, eyes on me again. "Welcome aboard, Avery."

He turns and walks toward the back, disappearing through a door I can't see. The place is quiet now, *too* quiet, and I realize it's because I no longer hear Katherine chopping or the slicer slicing. I turn to find her leaning against the counter and staring at me, her face blank and stony.

"I appreciate what you're doing to help Liam," she says in a low voice. "But it doesn't erase the fact that you broke my best friend's ankle with your car. Probably because you were too distracted by your loud music to realize he was there." She stands up straight and looks me square in the eye. "Don't expect me to pretend like that didn't happen."

Not bothering to wait for my reaction, she turns away and goes back to slicing veggies like I'm not even here. The tense set of her shoulders and her overly forceful chopping tells me she probably won't be receptive to any excuses or explanations from me, so I don't say a word. Instead, I move quietly to the front of the shop, too stunned to do anything but leave.

Suddenly, I understand why Liam added a skull and cross bones to his *Good luck* text last night. This job might be the death of me.

Chapter Seven

The day after I get the job at Sadler's Subs, my mother gets the job at the yoga studio. To celebrate the fact that all three of us are now employed, we go out for a late dinner at First Choice Grill—which I've privately renamed the *Only* Choice Grill.

My parents are in a great mood, laughing and making house-decorating plans over their glasses of wine and beer. I sip my Diet Coke in silence, trying to figure out the best way to tell them the one detail I left out about my new job. The most important detail—that it's not only a job, but also my penance. A penance with no biweekly paycheck. Usually, I'm able to calculate my parents' reactions to things, but this time, I'm not sure what they'll think. Even *I* can't decide if I'm being selfless or stupid.

A waitress appears at my elbow. After we order, she collects our menus, smiles at us, and says, "I saw you three in here last week. I thought you were tourists, but tourists don't usually stick around so long. You guys new to town?"

One thing I've noticed about small towns—the people are usually nosier. And chattier. Dad smiles politely at the woman, who looks to be in her forties. Her nametag reads *Pauline*. "Yes, we moved here recently."

"How nice!" She winks at my father. "Let me guess—you work at that new IBM building over in Emerson."

Dad laughs, though I see why she thinks he might do that kind of job. He's definitely got the intellectual business man vibe going on with his button down shirts and expensive cell phone. "Not quite."

Annoyed with both her borderline flirting and the fact that she didn't ask Mom if *she* works at IBM, I cut in with, "He designed the new bridge."

My parents both shoot me the same, indecipherable look. I raise my eyebrows at them and turn back to the waitress. Her smile has gone plastic.

"Your food will be out shortly," she says in a clipped tone before walking away, menus tucked under her arm.

Confused, I meet my dad's eyes across the table. "What?"

He shakes his head and takes a sip of beer. Mom sighs—a rare sound coming from her—and places her hand over Dad's. "Not everyone in Granesville likes the idea of the new bridge," she tells me. "We don't like to…well, advertise the fact that your dad is involved in it."

"The ferry employs a lot of people in this town," my father adds, turning his hand over and twining his fingers with Mom's. "A few of them have been working on it in some capacity for over forty years. The bridge will put an end to that."

"Oh," I say, my gaze dropping to my straw. I've never really considered the negative side to this particular job. In most of the places we end up, the residents either welcome a new bridge or don't care about it, unless the construction interferes with traffic. I think about yesterday, the way Mr. Sadler's eyebrows drew together when I told him why we moved here. The flash of sadness in his eyes when he mentioned his uncle Frank operating the ferry so long ago. Is my new boss one of the anti-bridge people?

Thinking about Mr. Sadler reminds me of what I still have to tell my parents. I wait until our food is delivered by the considerably-less-chatty Pauline and then dive into my explanation.

"I admire your compassion for this boy and his situation," my mother says slowly when I'm finished. "But you're seriously going to volunteer at a sandwich shop?"

"No," I say, averting my gaze from their dual furrowed-forehead looks. "Not volunteer. I'll get a paycheck. I'll just be handing whatever I make over to Liam."

"Avery," Dad says with strained patience. "Your mother's car had thousands of dollars' worth of damage on it. Our understanding was that you'd pitch in on the cost."

"And I will. The sub job is only six weeks. Eight at the most. Then Liam will take his job back and I'll find something else." I pick a fatty piece of bacon off my clubhouse before taking a bite. "I have it all planned out."

They do their silent conversation thing for a moment, then Mom leans back and takes a big mouthful of wine. "It's *you* she takes after," she tells Dad.

Maybe she's right. Sometimes I'm too damn logical for my own good.

Mom reluctantly lets me take her car—now fixed up good as new—to my first shift at Sadler's the next evening. In my nervousness, I get there twenty minutes early, then wait in the car for ten minutes so I don't inadvertently annoy Katherine by showing up too early again.

I shouldn't have worried. When I walk inside, she's nowhere to be seen. A woman stands behind the counter, an older version of Katherine, except shorter and curvier. She's chatting with a customer and doesn't notice me at first, so I awkwardly wait by the door, wondering if my casual outfit of jeans and a V-neck t-shirt is okay. Mr. Sadler didn't mention any kind of dress code.

When the customer leaves, the woman smiles at me. "You must be Avery."

I step forward to shake her hand. "Mrs. Sadler?"

"Linh." She gestures behind her with her chin. "Come on back."

I follow her, breathing in the scent of bread and onions. We walk past the giant fridge and racks of buns to the office in the very back. The door is open, and as we approach I see Katherine sitting at the small desk, peering closely at the screen of a clunky old computer. She glances up as we enter the room, and her dark eyes flit toward me once before landing on her mom. "It's not fair, though," she says to her, like she's picking up a conversation in progress. For a moment I think she's talking about me, about my presence here, but then she adds, "Brooke leaves in eleven days, and all I'm asking for is a few nights off between now and then so I can spend some time with her before she goes."

"I understand that, Katherine," her mom says in a weary tone, like they've had this same discussion a million times and she's beyond sick of it. "But the schedule's not going to magically rearrange itself for you. I'm sorry…there's simply no one else to cover those shifts."

Katherine sighs and clicks the mouse a few times, squinting hard at the screen. "What about Sunday afternoon? You're honestly telling me that Isaac's not available then? What, is he too busy hanging out at the beach with his burnout friends?"

"Isaac's here on Saturday." Mrs. Sadler—Linh—shoots me an apologetic glance. "Anyway. We'll discuss this later. I need you out front while I round up some paperwork for Avery."

With another disgusted sigh, Katherine roughly pushes back her chair and gets up. She marches out of the office without looking at either of us. Linh smiles thinly at me and gestures for me to sit in the plastic chair on the other side of the desk.

"Okay," she says, taking her daughter's place in front of the computer. "Let's get you squared away."

Fifteen minutes later, after I've signed everything that needs to be signed, Linh presents me with an official Sadler's Subs apron and sends me back out front without her. Katherine must have gotten pre-emptive instructions to train me, because the first thing she does is look up from her tomato slicing and say, "A ponytail would be good. No one wants hair in their subs."

My face burning, I dig an elastic out of my pocket and smooth back my hair, cursing myself for forgetting to do it before leaving the motel room. As I secure the elastic, I'm hit with the realization that nothing about this job will be a seamless transition. I won't be easing into Liam's spot, into these people's lives, like nothing ever happened. I'm just a convenient replacement, useful in a pinch. Temporary.

But that's fine. After so many moves, I'm used to temporary. Still, even knowing this, I can't help but want them to like me. I always want people to like me. Side effect of constantly being the new girl.

"Um, Katherine?" I ask after watching her slice two more tomatoes, all the while acting like I'm not standing right behind her. "Can I…help you with that?"

She glances over her shoulder, knife still thumping against the cutting board. "Oh," she says, distracted. "No. I think we have enough of everything for now." She scoops the tomato slices into a stainless steel bin. "And it's Kath. Only my parents ever call me Katherine."

I nod and gaze at the door, hoping for a deluge of customers so I don't have to stand here like a lump. But we're still a few minutes away from the dinner rush, so the place remains empty.

Katherine—*Kath*—gets a cloth and starts wiping down the food prep areas in short, jerky movements. The fiery anger from before has faded somewhat; now, she looks more sad than mad. I long to ask her who

Brooke is, or find out what's up with her brother Isaac, but I'm afraid if I try, she'll turn that hateful glare from the other day on me again. I feel like I've already personally wronged her just by existing.

For lack of anything else to do, I head to the back, where I saw a broom leaning against the wall. Just as I'm about to start sweeping, the door opens and two little boys enter, followed by a woman wearing huge sunglasses.

"I want a turkey wrap with Ranch!" one of the boys shouts at the women, who I assume is the mom.

I look at Kath, awaiting direction, or encouragement, or *something*. She stares back at me, a slight smirk on her lips. "You're up, Ariana Grande."

Eventually—with no help from Kath—I figure out that there *is* no Ranch dressing, only mayo and salad oil, and that folding a fresh tortilla isn't as easy as it might seem. By the time I'm finished, their turkey wraps are being held together by wax paper alone, but luckily this is a takeout only place and I won't have to witness them discovering the mess I made. Kath rings them up while I peel off my plastic gloves and wipe my sweaty hands on my apron. This is way more intense than Quiznos, where I mostly bussed tables and worked the cash.

"Not bad," Kath says once they're gone. "Next time, though, you might want to fold in each end, *then* roll. That way, the filling stays put."

"Thanks for letting me know," I say with a touch more sarcasm than I meant. The stress of working the board on my own for the first time coupled with Kath's antagonism toward me has me a little on edge.

One of her eyebrows shoots up at my tone, but she says nothing. When another customer strolls in, I'm positive she's going to leave me here to destroy the business on my own. So I'm surprised when she stays by my side this time, overseeing as I bumble my way through a roast beef and ham with mayo and lettuce. The next few hours fly by with more of the same—me assembling sub after wrap after sub while she looks on and occasionally corrects my form. *Go a little easier on the mayo…Six slices of tomato, not four…Don't be shy with the pickles.* As my shift draws to a close, I feel like I have a better handle on things.

At quarter to nine, we start the closing ritual. Kath's mom left at seven, so we're on our own for cleaning up and cashing out. I'm exhausted, and my entire body reeks of onions and salami, but at least Kath's talking to me now. Sort of. If "You missed a spot near the corner" counts as talking.

When the door swings open at three minutes to nine, I almost start crying at the thought of making one more sub. I look up from scrubbing the sandwich board expecting to see a customer, but to my surprise, I see Liam. He's propping the door open with one shoulder, trying to maneuver his crutches so he can get himself—and his boot-encased left foot—inside.

"Liam!" Kath's face splits into a wide, honest-to-God smile—the first one I've ever seen on her—and she rushes over to hold the door for him. "How did you get here? Not your truck?"

Liam makes it inside and centers himself, hopping a little on his good foot. "My mom dropped me off on her way to pick up Brody from karate."

Kath switches the door sign to CLOSED and then carefully wraps her arms around his slim waist in a hug. "Look at you, up and around. Are you in pain?" After she says this, her eyes slide to me, vaguely accusing.

A fresh wave of guilt settles in my chest, and I reach around to untie my apron. *Liam's* apron, most likely. The one he'd be wearing right now if not for me.

"I'm good," Liam assures her, then looks over at me. "Just wanted to stop in to see how things went."

I wait for Kath to respond, but she says nothing as she untangles herself from Liam and takes off her apron, scrunching it up into a ball. In the silence, I retreat to the back to collect both my purse and myself. Seeing him in a hospital bed was one thing; watching him wobble around on those crutches with a cumbersome hunk of plastic on his foot just drives home how badly I disrupted his life.

When I emerge from the back, Liam and Kath are quietly talking, their heads bent together in that easy, familiar way of close friends, something I've seen a lot but haven't really experienced much firsthand. They both shut up when they see me, which confirms my suspicion that I was the star of their conversation. Kath was probably venting to him about how horrible it is to work with me and how much she wishes he were here instead. Not that I blame her.

"Glad you're feeling better," I say tersely to Liam, then slip around them to the door.

"Hey, Avery."

I turn around, half outside in the moist, late-summer heat, and meet Liam's eyes. In the bright light above us, they're a darkish silver. Like liquid metal. "Yeah?" I say as a prickly warmth swells in my stomach, surprising me. Has he always been this cute? How am I just noticing now? Maybe the onion reek is clouding my senses.

"Can I talk to you for a sec?" he asks, then glances at Kath and adds, "Outside?"

I nod and hold the door open as he crutches through. He moves down the sidewalk a bit, away from the window and Kath's eagle eye. I follow him, clutching my arms like I'm freezing, even though the air is damp and thick like a sauna.

He stops in front of the closed dry cleaner and pivots to face me, almost losing his balance. He catches himself from tumbling into the parking lot and straightens up, planting the tips of his crutches firmly on the pavement. "Still getting used to these things," he mutters, embarrassed.

I try to smile, but it comes out as more of a grimace. "I know I've said this already, but I'm really, really sorry."

He shrugs, drawing my attention to his shoulders, which are slim like the rest of him, but broad at the same time. *Jesus. It's like the hot Idris Elba cop all over again. Focus.*

"I hope today wasn't torture for you," he says, setting the heel of his boot on the ground. "Working with Kath, I mean. She can be a little…"

"It was fine," I say when he doesn't finish his sentence. "Aside from the damn onion smell."

He grins. "That never goes away. You'll be smelling it in your dreams."

"I believe it." Then, for no other reason than because I'm a huge dork, I lift my arm and sniff it. Liam just laughs.

"Anyway," he says, moving aside as two guys pass us, smoking. "I wanted to talk to you about the whole paycheck thing. I think we should make some amendments to our previous agreement."

I wave away a cloud of smoke, coughing. "What do you mean?"

"I don't think it's fair that I get every cent you make. I mean, you're the one doing all the work." He bounces again, adjusting his position. "I think it should be fifty-fifty."

I gape at him. He can't be serious. "No way. *I hit you with a car.* It's the least I can do."

"Sixty-forty."

"No."

He smiles again. "Sixty-five thirty-five."

"No," I repeat, my lips twitching with the effort to remain firm and not smile back.

"Seventy-thirty. Final offer."

I cross my arms and sigh. Clearly, he's not going to back down. And I *could* use the money, however nominal the amount may be. "Fine. Seventy-five twenty-five. That's *my* final offer."

"Deal."

He leans all his weight onto his left crutch and offers me his right hand to shake. When I take it, the warmth in my stomach spreads out into the rest of my body and I forget, for the first time since it happened, the moment of disaster that brought us both here.

Chapter Eight

I'm lying in bed the next night, reading the end of *Carrie* by the dull glow of my bedside lamp. It's after eleven and all is quiet from my parents' room next door, aside from the occasional snore from my dad. Hazel is passed out beside me, also snoring, a light, poufy ball blending in with the off-white motel sheets.

Earlier tonight I'd made the mistake of drinking an herbal tea from the complimentary hot beverage basket in my room, unaware that it contained caffeine. I was hoping reading would help lull me to sleep, but I'm wide awake as Carrie wreaks havoc on her town, flipping cars and setting fires with the power of her mind. I'm so engrossed in the carnage, I actually let out a tiny shriek when my phone dings beside me.

Heart racing, I dig it out of the folds of the bedspread and click on the screen. My heart speeds up even more when I realize it's a text from Liam.

Kath wants to know if you'll come in at four tomorrow instead of five. She's supposed to teach you how to use the slicer.

Kath wants to know. I guess using Liam as our intermediary is preferable than texting me herself. *Sure*, I text back. Assuming that's the end of it, I put my phone on the bedside table and reach for *Carrie* again. Just as I find my place, my phone dings a second time.

Don't worry…no one's ever lost a hand. There's a pause, then: *Only a finger or two.*

Thanks for the warning, I type back, adding a smiley face emoji before hitting send. Again, I figure we're done, and again, he surprises me with more.

Get rid of the onion smell yet? You know, I kind of miss it. Is that weird?

I reach behind me and punch my lumpy pillow into shape before texting back *I'm currently missing my bed, so I'm probably not the best person to ask.*

Why do you miss your bed?

I type out an abbreviated version of my situation— Dad's job, the moves, the motel, our new house, all our stuff waiting in storage, how much I long for my nice mattress and blankets.

Wow, Liam replies. *I've lived here since I was a baby. Boring, huh?*

It doesn't seem that bad.

Yeah, I guess it hasn't exactly been boring for me since YOU moved here.

He follows this text with a winky face and an ambulance emoji, and I feel my cheeks get warm with residual shame.

Kidding. It's nice to see a new face around here.

Now my cheeks are burning for a different reason. Is he…flirting with me? Or is he just being friendly? And what does it mean that I like it, whatever it is he's doing?

65

I stare at his words, hesitating, my mind replaying the promise I'd made to myself back in the spring.

Never again. That was what I'd told myself as I lay in bed one night, crying over Noah Burnett, my first and only boyfriend. We'd been together almost seven months when my parents sprang the news on me about our upcoming move to Granesville. At first, Noah and I were committed to dating long-distance, but then something changed between us. I'm not even sure what. With the countdown to my departure constantly looming over our heads, we began to gradually drift apart. By May, we'd mutually decided that a long-distance relationship probably wouldn't work, and maybe it would be better if we just ended things early and started fresh. But of course we'd always be friends.

I never spoke to him again. Not even through text. Two weeks before I left, he posted a picture on his Instagram of him and Makayla Cross, their cheeks pressed together in a couples selfie shot. I never heard from Makayla again either, though we'd been friends. Or so I thought. Seeing them together, so carefree, made me feel like I never mattered to either of them. Not really. I only lived in Weldon for two years, while they'd lived there their entire lives. As usual, I was just a visitor, passing through, forever an outsider. I was only temporary.

Never again. I've honored my promise to myself ever since, never crossing the line between friendliness and flirting. There have been temptations, of course, like whenever I worked a shift at the movie theater with Sai Khurana, who had long, dark eyelashes and a dimple in one cheek. But for the most part, I've kept my eyes on my work, on my phone, on my feet. I've learned that getting too close to people isn't worth the risk of having to leave them behind.

So yes, I *am* temporary, especially here in Granesville. A year from now I'll be gone, living somewhere *I* chose, creating something permanent on my own. So there's no point in trying to put down any roots here. I need to keep my head down and focus on my end game—graduation, then watching this town disappear forever in my rear view mirror. No ties. No attachments. No distractions.

I look down at my phone screen again. Liam is waiting for a response, for me to give him a sign that I'm open to conversation and possibly even more. But even though I've willingly immersed myself into his life, and even though I feel this strange little pull toward him, and even though these past couple of weeks have been the loneliest I can remember, all I can think is *Never again*.

I turn the volume off on my phone, place it face down on the table, and go back to *Carrie*.

When I walk into Sadler's the next day, I find Kath in the middle of an argument with some guy next to the prep area. He's holding a head of iceberg lettuce in the air, out of her reach, while she scowls up at him, hands on hips.

"Don't even *think* about it," she snaps at him, lifting one hand to point a finger in his face. "You're banned from the slicer, remember? Dad said."

The guy rolls his eyes, then turns and notices me hesitating by the door. He face brightens in a smile, and suddenly I realize who he is. Kath looks like her mom, but her brother is a younger version of their dad—tall and beefy and brown-haired, with a wide, easy grin that seems completely at home on his face. He looks about nineteen or twenty, but I might be overestimating because of his height.

"Jeez," he says to me, shaking his head. "You try to slice up a tennis ball *one time* and you get banned for life."

I give him a small smile back, unsure how to react. He lowers his arm and tosses the lettuce to Kath, who places it safely on the counter before turning to me. "Ignore him," she tells me.

I try to follow her advice as I scoot behind the counter, but it's impossible. He has a presence, the kind that makes you want to stare until you figure out what's so interesting about him. But I can't stare without seeming rude, so I study him in fragments—longish hair peeking out from under a backward baseball cap. Cargo shorts and flip flops. Three leather bands on his right wrist.

"So you're the new girl," he says when I join them by the slicer. "Avery, right?"

I nod, my gaze dropping to his white T-shirt. *I Finished the Sizzlin' 72oz Steak at First Choice Grill!* is emblazoned across the front, the words in a semicircle over a cartoon picture of an ironically cheerful-looking cow. I remember the sign I'd seen the first time I went to the restaurant: *Finish Our Sizzlin' 72oz Steak in Under an Hour & It's Free!* I don't know whether to be impressed or repulsed.

"This is my brother Isaac," Kath says in a weary voice, like she's introducing me to a spirited toddler. "He's just about to finish his shift and leave for the day."

"You'd swear she was trying to get rid of me," Isaac says, tilting his head toward Kath.

She motions for me to move closer to the slicer, which is big and shiny and intimidating. "I *am* trying to get rid of you."

Isaac removes his baseball cap, shakes out his hair, and then returns the cap to his head, grinning the entire time. "What kind of name is Avery, anyway?" he asks me.

"Isaac," Kath warns, then glances at me as if checking to see if I'm offended. I'm not; his smile and the jovial way he speaks makes everything he says seem innocent and pleasant.

I slip on my apron and tie it. "It's my grandmother's maiden name."

"Ah." He nods and nudges Kath with his elbow. "Our mother named us. She's obsessed with the Victorian era."

"She doesn't *care*, Isaac. Don't you have a street corner to loiter on or a beer to shotgun or something?"

"Rude," he says, smile unwavering. "Okay, I'm going." He catches my eye as he walks toward the front. "She's drunk with power, you know. Don't let her boss you around."

Kath snatches an onion core off the counter and throws it at him, but he bolts for the door before it can make contact. "Assclown," she mutters once he's gone.

I keep silent, half contemplating the mysteries of sibling dynamics and half wondering if I should go pick up that onion core before someone slips on it. Before I can decide either way, Kath hands me the head of lettuce Isaac had earlier and sidles up to the slicer. For the next hour, between customers, she teaches me how to put different veggies into it and use the lever to push them toward the blade, while at the same time turning a crank to make neat, thin slices. My right arm gets tired quickly, but by the time the tutorial is over, we have several stainless steel containers full of fresh toppings. And all our fingers.

Next, Kath shows me how to clean the machine, which is infinitely more complicated than using it. She tasks me with wiping down the outer surfaces and does the more dangerous, inner cleaning herself. We work together quietly, but the silence doesn't feel as tension-filled as before. Her attitude toward me during the slicer instruction was businesslike and formal, but maybe that's just her way. Maybe she's starting to see how horrible I feel about hurting her friend, and that I'm serious about doing his job well.

"Did your brother really put a tennis ball in here?" I ask as Kath reattaches the blade.

"Yes, unfortunately." She pushes a strand of hair off her forehead with the back of her hand. "Isaac doesn't make the smartest decisions."

Encouraged by her almost-friendly response, I press on. "Is he in college?"

She snorts. "No. He barely got through high school. He skipped class all the time and never did homework, so it took him five years to earn enough credits to graduate. He's not, like, dumb or anything. Just unmotivated." She wets another cloth and wipes around the base of the slicer. "It drives our parents crazy. It drives *me* crazy, because guess who has to pick up the slack for him around here? He's my brother and I love him, but sometimes I want to throat punch him."

This is the most I've ever heard her say at one time. And it was directed at *me*. "I'm an only child."

"You're lucky."

I shrug and fold my cloth, exposing a clean patch. "Maybe. It can get lonely, though, especially when you move around a lot."

She looks up, face alight with curiosity, but then her expression suddenly goes blank, like she just remembered who she's talking to. The girl who hurt her friend. The girl she's supposed to be mad at. She turns away and picks up one of the full bins.

"Anyway, so that's how you clean the slicer." She moves to the sub assembly area, all business again. "Got it?"

"Yeah," I say, watching as she sets the bin in its rightful spot. "Got it."

Chapter Nine

Two years ago, when we moved into our house in the city, the neighbors barely noticed or cared. But here, in Granesville, I count seven faces staring out nearby windows as movers carry furniture and boxes into the open door of 28 Parkhill Crescent.

Aware of this town's affinity for literal street names, I half expected our new home to be near either a park or a hill or both, but it's just a normal suburban street, two rows of similar-style houses on small, flat lots, yards separated only by the occasional chain link fence. It *is* crescent shaped, though, our midsized white bungalow situated near the beginning of the curve.

"Avery!" My mother sticks her head out the front door, her expression harried. "Can you come inside, please?"

I supress an eye-roll. Ten minutes ago she was telling me to "go outside, please" with Hazel, who spent the entire morning barking her fool head off at the movers. She's still barking now, as I walk her up and down the sidewalk, drawing even more attention from nosy neighbors.

Inside, I find Mom in the living room, stripping the plastic off our couch. We've gone through Moving Day several times, but it's still weird to see our familiar things in this unfamiliar space. It's a pretty space, though, all hardwood and tile and bright, airy rooms. Like the town itself, it isn't the biggest or nicest place we've ever lived in, but it's not without its charm.

"What?" I say, grouchy from the heat and the chaos and the warning twinge in my temple, because of course a migraine would choose today to debilitate me.

"Those are yours." She points to a stack of boxes in the dining room, each labeled *Avery's room*. Apparently the movers think I sleep next to the kitchen. "Take them to your room, please, and bring the dog with you because she's giving me a headache."

"Me too," I mutter, tucking the smallest box under one arm and Hazel under the other. She wiggles and yaps as we pass the kitchen, where Dad is poking around the appliances, making sure everything is in working order.

The house has three bedrooms. My parents, of course, took the main bedroom with the ensuite bathroom, leaving me to choose between the remaining two. I immediately claimed the room furthest away from theirs, even though it's the smaller of the two. After three weeks of sharing a thin wall with them, I'm ready for some distance. The other room will be a guest room-slash-office-slash-yoga area.

Once inside my room, I decide that the rest of the boxes can wait a few minutes. I close the door behind me and set my box and Hazel down on the floor. She immediately quiets down and hops up on my mattress, which the movers placed directly on the floor, next to my disassembled bed frame.

My bed. I flop down next to Hazel and sigh happily as the mattress conforms to my body, like it's missed me as much as I've missed it. I feel like I could sleep right now, but instead I take out my phone and snap a pic of myself, smiling, stacks of boxes and my old familiar dresser in the background. I caption the picture *New digs* and send it to Mia.

She doesn't respond right away, so I stretch out on my back with my phone face down on my chest and stare at the ceiling fan, slowly circling. Just as I'm starting to fall into a trance, my phone beeps. I tip it up and read Mia's text: *Cool! Miss you!*

I reply with a smiley face and let my phone drop again, knowing the conversation will probably end there. My contact with Mia lately has been brief and sparse, and I'm not sure who's at fault. The city seems so far away now, and the friends I made there—Mia included—feel like people I knew in an entirely different life. Maybe we're just too busy. Maybe our friendship isn't strong enough to maintain online. Some people move around and collect lifelong friends like souvenirs, a lasting tie to each place they've been. And other people, like me, have learned that nothing in life is permanent, and sometimes it's better to drift along without making any real ties at all.

"Nope." Kath dangles one of the rings of onion I just sliced in front of her face. "Still too thick."

I sigh and let go of the slicer crank. For my past three shifts, I've been trying—and failing—to get the onions to the paper-thin consistency that the Sadlers prefer. Each time I fail, the defective onions end up in the trash, and I hate to waste so much food. I also hate the are-you-an-idiot look Kath gives me every time I mess up. A little over a week has passed since she taught me how to use the slicer and briefly opened up to me about her brother. She seems used to me now, resigned to my presence, but there's been no more opening up or friendly conversation. She teaches me things and corrects me in her impersonal way, while I do my best not to screw up too much.

Every time I wonder if we'll ever get to be friends, I remember my no-ties vow and tell myself it's probably better if we remain work acquaintances only. I can handle a year's worth of loneliness. My dog and Netflix will see me through.

I turn the slicer crank again, determined to do better. And I do, I think. My next batch is a tiny bit thinner. I hold one up for Kath's inspection, but she's distracted, looking at her phone. In fact, she's been distracted all evening, completing tasks on autopilot, checking her cell for either a text or the time.

"It's been totally dead for the last half hour," she says, pocketing her phone and looking up at me. "Let's close early."

I glance at the old-school clock on the wall. Ten minutes to nine. We've never closed early before, but Kath's parents aren't here and the place really is dead. Probably because it started raining at around eight. Not even the drunks and stoners are dropping in for a late-night snack.

"Sure," I say, dropping my onion.

She yanks off her apron and darts into the back room, leaving me to switch the electric sign in the window to CLOSED and bolt the door. Just as I'm reaching for the lock, two figures appear on the other side of the glass, making me jump. It's Liam, who I haven't seen since the night he showed up after my very first shift here, and a tall girl with dark-framed glasses, who I've never seen before in my life. I open the door for them.

"Jesus," the girl says as she enters. "It's really coming down out there."

I hold the door open for Liam as he maneuvers himself and his crutches inside. He's completely drenched, water dripping from the tips of his hair and down his face, his blue T-shirt splattered with dark patches. The whole effect is very appealing, and I force my gaze to the girl instead, who's combing her fingers through her dark red pixie cut. Liam's girlfriend?

"Perfect timing."

I turn at the sound of Kath's voice and watch as she heads directly toward the girl and kisses her on the lips. Okay, not Liam's girlfriend. Kath's.

"Where did you come from?" she asks Liam once her lips are free.

"I found him wandering down Seton Avenue," the red-haired girl says.

Kath frowns. "In the rain?"

"It wasn't raining when I started walking," Liam says, wiping his wet face with his equally wet hand. "Or

76

this dark. I was going to the store for my mom, but forgot to factor in the extra time it takes to get anywhere in this damn boot.''

"He said he was going stir crazy sitting around his house," the girl tells Kath. "So instead of taking him home, I brought him here to see you." She looks at me and holds out a hand. "And you. Hi, I'm Brooke."

We shake. "I'm Avery."

"Oh, I know." She tilts her head toward Kath and rolls her eyes a little.

I like her already.

"I'll be ready in a few minutes." Kath takes out the register till and backs away, a spring in her step. I've never seen her like this before. She's *happy*. "Just gotta cash out."

"Okay, but hurry," Brooke says. "We have *plans*, and it's already nine o'clock."

I remember what Kath said to her mother when I found them in the back room before my first shift. *Brooke leaves in eleven days*...And that was ten days ago, which means Brooke is leaving for wherever she's going...tomorrow. No wonder Kath was so distracted today. No wonder she was so eager to close.

I glance over at Liam. He meets my eyes for a second before dropping his gaze to the floor. "I'll call my mom to pick me up," he says to Brooke.

"We can drop you off before our date, Liam."

"No, it's okay. Your night is already being cut short as it is."

Damn it. He looks really good wet *and* he's a thoughtful friend too? So not fair. *Never again*, my brain reminds me, but the words seem muted now that he's standing right in front of me. Dripping. Being nice. Making me want to be nice too, even though I'm afraid my niceness might be mistaken for something else.

"I'll drive you home," I tell Liam. *I'm doing this for Kath and Brooke*, I assure myself. It doesn't matter that I barely know them and Kath's never been very nice to *me*.

Brooke claps. "Perfect! Problem solved."

"You don't have to," Liam says to me in a low voice.

"It's no trouble. I have my mom's car."

Kath emerges from the back and hurries to join us, her cheeks flushed from what was undoubtedly the fastest cash out in history. "Ready."

Brooke swings an arm around her shoulders. "Avery offered to drive Liam home. Wasn't that nice of her?"

At the words "Avery" and "drive," Kath's expression turns flinty and she levels me with a look of deep mistrust, like she thinks I spend my time just waiting around for a chance to break more of Liam's bones.

"Text me later," she tells him as the four of us leave the shop. She shoots me another look, this one a subtle warning. I give her a tiny smile of reassurance.

The rain has let up somewhat. Kath and Brooke go one way and Liam and I go the other, across the parking lot to my mom's Corolla. I'm nervous now, partly because we're alone together and partly because I'm scared that if I so much as bump him accidentally, Kath will find out and rotary slice my arm off.

"Weird." Liam stops by the side of the car and runs his hand over the spot where he hit. "It's like nothing ever happened."

I gesture to his leg. "That'll remind us."

He nods and opens the door. "True."

It takes five minutes and a lot of creative angling to get Liam, his boot, and both of his crutches into the car. Once we're settled, Liam positioned way back in the passenger seat and his crutches splayed across the collapsed back seats and trunk, I finally start the engine.

"I actually didn't know you'd be here tonight," Liam says as I back up. "I mean, it's my shifts you're covering and I rarely worked Saturday nights."

I face forward again, aware of what he's really saying—that he didn't purposely come to Sadler's tonight to see me. Not that I ever imagined he would. "Mrs. Sadler—uh, Linh—gave me the day off yesterday because I was moving into my new house. She switched me to tonight instead."

"Which street is your house on?"

"Parkhill Crescent." I brake at the edge of the parking lot. "Um, what about yours?"

He shakes his head and laughs. "Oh, yeah. I'll direct you. Take a left."

Silence descends upon the car, broken only by Liam's brief directions and the occasional squeak of the wipers. I'm socially inept in general, but sitting in the close confines of a car on a dark, rainy night with the cute boy I injured has to be my most challenging social situation yet. So of course I say the first thing that pops into my head.

"Kath seems really protective of you."

Liam shifts on the seat, adjusting his leg. "Well, we've been best friends since we were five, so yeah. I'm protective of her too."

My chest twinges with something close to envy. I've never had a best friend, at least not one that lasted longer than a few months. "She's really pretty," I say, because that's the only thing I feel sure enough about her to comment on.

"Yeah. I used to have a crush on her years ago. Around third grade." He glances out the window. "Turn right at the end of this street, after the big white church."

"Really? You had a crush on her?" For some reason, I can't picture this. They seem so sibling-like.

"Really." He laughs. "Then one day we were at her house watching the Disney channel, and she told me she wanted to marry Selena Gomez. That's when I knew we were destined to be just friends."

I smile. "How long have she and Brooke been together?"

"Over a year." He runs a hand through his damp hair. "Brooke's leaving for college tomorrow. She got accepted into this super-competitive program at Bowen Institute of Music. No one was really surprised, though. You should hear her play the cello—she's amazing. But the school is like six hundred miles away, so she won't be coming home very often. Kath's been taking it pretty hard. She's worried they're going to drift apart."

I want to tell him she's probably right, that it's a valid concern, but I concentrate on turning right at the big white church and keep my thoughts to myself. Liam probably doesn't want to hear about my many fleeting friendships—and one short romance—most of them ruined by drifting and distance. He doesn't want to hear about how challenging it can be to stay together when you're not close by to nurture the connection.

Liam guides me into a neighborhood similar to my new one, only the houses are older, smaller, and not as well-kept. I stop the car in front of his house, a plain, light gray duplex with a neat front yard and two vehicles in the driveway—a small red car and an old, decaying truck. The large window in front is lit up, throwing a yellow glow onto a kids' pink bicycle, abandoned on the grass.

"I miss my truck," Liam says randomly, gazing out the window at it.

"I thought you rode a bike."

He turns his head toward me. "Only when my truck's broken, like now. I'm saving to get it fixed."

"Oh." Familiar guilt prickles though me again, making me rethink our seventy-five twenty-five payment agreement. Between his trip and that truck, he clearly needs the cash more than I do right now.

He gives me a long, appraising look, like he knows exactly what I'm thinking. But before I can put a voice to my thoughts, he says, "I might need some help with my crutches."

I swallow the words on my tongue and step out into the rain, which has picked up again. By the time we get Liam settled with his crutches, I'm almost as soaked as he is.

"I'd better get inside before my boot gets too wet," he says, steadying his crutch tips on the pavement. "Thanks for the ride."

"Anytime." I flick a stingy piece of hair off my face, aware that I probably resemble a drowned rat. "I meant what I said about helping you with drives and stuff."

He smiles, and suddenly I'm glad for the rain on my face, cool against my rapidly warming skin.

"I guess I'll see you at school on Tuesday?"

"Um, yep," I say, like the eloquent conversationalist that I am.

He turns and lumbers toward his house, while I get back in the car, my stomach tight at the mention of school. A new school means new people. It means getting stared at, whispered about, and sometimes ignored completely.

I peer through the rain-smeared window at Liam, struggling to get himself through the front door, and the knot inside me starts to loosen. On Tuesday morning, when I walk into the unknown yet again, at least I'll get to see a familiar face.

Chapter Ten

My first day at Granesville High starts off with a colossal, stress-induced migraine that feels like someone is hammering nails into my skull. Going back to bed isn't an option, so I down a pill with my orange juice and head out, alone, for the ten-minute walk to school.

As I approach the building, I see clusters of kids standing out front, standing and talking or staring down at their phones. The cacophony of voices, coupled with the bright morning sun, makes my head throb even harder. No one looks at me as I make my way to the entrance and go inside. The blast of air conditioning stems some of the nausea churning in my stomach, and I'm able to focus enough to get my bearings. Not that the layout of this school is overly complicated. The entire two-floor building could probably fit ten times over into my last school. I have a feeling it won't be so easy to blend in here.

According to the schedule I received yesterday, my homeroom—and first class—is in Room 114, precalculus with Ms. Fiore. I start in the direction of the classrooms, counting doors to distract myself from my nervousness and pounding head. When I reach 114, I pause outside the door and swallow down a fresh surge of nausea. No matter how many dozens of times I've done this, walking into a room filled with strangers never stops being terrifying.

"Avery."

I turn around and spot Liam, forging a path through the crowded hallway with his crutches. My heart gallops, sending a painful rush of blood to my head. I try not to wince.

"You in here too?" he asks when he reaches me.

I nod, slightly surprised. Seeing as this school only has about a hundred seniors, odds are good that we'd have at least one class together. But for some reason, I never took him for the advanced math type. He told me before that he plans to join the military after graduation…why would anyone take calculus unless they need it for a specific college major? Like actuarial science, for example, the field I plan to go into next year.

Maybe he just really likes math.

"Are you okay?" Liam asks with a note of concern. "You look kind of pale."

I step into the room ahead of him, already scanning for the most unobtrusive place to sit. "Migraine. It's getting better now, though." It is—the pill is doing its job, narrowing the blood vessels around my brain and loosening the tight band of pressure. The nausea is still there though, and now I really need to pee. Another lovely side effect. But I don't want to have to leave and hunt for a bathroom before the teacher even arrives, so I decide to wait.

The classroom is still mostly empty, so I have my pick of seats. I head for a desk in the back row, aware of Liam behind me. To my relief, he sets his backpack on the desk next to mine and props his crutches against the back wall. I try not to stare as he braces both hands on the desk and carefully lowers himself into his seat, sticking his booted leg half into the aisle.

A high-pitched bell rings, aggravating my tender head, and the room begins to fill up.

"What happened, dude?" a tall, blond guy says to Liam as he takes a seat in the next row over. "You get hit by a car or something?"

My stomach drops. I glance over at Liam, waiting for him to say, "Yes, that's exactly what happened, and the driver's name is Avery and she's sitting right here." But he just stares straight ahead and says, "Fell off my bike."

I quietly let out a breath. Liam catches my eye and gives me a little half-smile, and I know he's not going to spread it around school that I'm the one who put him on crutches. Which *would* reassure me, if Kath wasn't a student at this school too. I wouldn't be surprised if she handed out flyers detailing exactly what I did.

The teacher enters the room then, and I force my attention away from Liam and on to her. Ms. Fiore is plump and dark-haired, with an ultra-white smile and glasses perched on top of her head. She moves across the room to her desk, nodding at several students she apparently knows. The first thing she does is take attendance, and I've been the new girl in enough small towns to know my unfamiliar name likely won't go by without comment.

I'm right.

"Avery Bishop," she says, tilting her head at me. "Where are you from?"

I resist the urge to slump down in my seat. Being singled out is the worst. *Nowhere*, I feel like telling her. *I'm from nowhere.* Instead I say what I always do when asked this question: "All over. But my parents are originally from Boston."

"Interesting. And what brings you to Granesville?"

I can feel everyone watching me, probably inwardly snickering at my embarrassment. "My dad's job," I say, hoping she won't ask me to explain further. I remember the hostility from the waitress at First Choice Grill when I mentioned the new bridge, and I'd rather not risk a similar reaction here.

"Interesting," she repeats, and thankfully leaves it at that.

For the rest of class, I'm completely distracted by my aching bladder and barely take in a word that's said. When the bell finally rings, I bolt out of my seat, almost colliding with Liam as he struggles to get his backpack on while balancing on one leg. My need for the bathroom is approaching emergency status, but I can't just leave him to fend for himself.

Wordlessly, I grab hold of the backpack and help him secure the straps against his shoulders. My fingers graze his collarbone, and suddenly I forget all about my bladder as a flood of heat rushes to my face.

"Thanks," Liam says, his voice an octave deeper than usual. We look at each other and then away, Liam turning to grab his crutches while I pretend to examine a scratch on my arm. His face is pink too, making me wonder if he likes standing close to me as much as I like standing close to him.

Flustered, I mumble a good-bye and flee. My next class is upstairs—Room 222, English with Mr. Dyson— and I have exactly five minutes to find a bathroom, pee, and get myself up there.

I arrive just as the bell rings, which means even the teacher—a middle-aged short man with a crew cut—is here before me. The small room mainly consists of three long tables positioned into a U-shape, and I squeeze my way toward one of the last empty chairs. The second I sit down, I notice Kath directly across from me, leaning on the table with her head propped against her hand. Her dark hair is styled into an intricate French braid, and for the first time since I've met her, she's wearing makeup. I try to catch her eye, nod a hello, but she keeps her gaze fixed on the teacher at the front of the room.

Mr. Dyson—bless him—doesn't even pause over my unfamiliar name as he takes roll. With my migraine almost fully gone, I'm finally able to concentrate on my surroundings, and I notice only a few people shooting me curious looks. It's nice to know that not everyone in this town seems to care about outsiders.

By the time lunch hour rolls around, I'm exhausted. And starving, since I barely ate any breakfast. I pause in the emptying hallway to dig out my locker assignment. Locker #186. I haven't had a chance to locate it yet, but I assume it's near homeroom. This school has those annoying half lockers, but with any luck, I'll at least get the top bunk.

For a school so small, the hallways are like a maze. Maybe because they all look exactly alike—plain cinderblock walls, faded gray floors, banks of chipped, brick-red lockers. After five minutes of disorientation, I find my locker exactly where I expected it to be, directly across from pre-calc.

I also find Liam. He's alone in the hallway, right hand gripping the handle of one crutch as he tries to lower himself enough to reach a bottom locker. But he can't crouch with his cumbersome boot, so he keeps losing balance and hopping in place to center himself.

"Need some help?"

He raises his head as I approach. His face is red and sweaty from exertion, and he looks like he's two seconds away from clobbering something with his crutches.

"Thanks." He straightens up and lets out a frustrated sigh. "I managed to get it open and put my books in, but I've been trying to get the damn thing locked for the last five minutes."

I squat down and fasten his lock, then I pick up his now-light backpack and hook it over his fingers.

"Wow," he says. "That took you all of three seconds. I miss the days when it didn't take me an hour to do the simplest thing. I feel so helpless."

"You're not. You have lots of help." I gesture to the locker above his. "I'm sure whoever owns that one will switch with you."

"I don't know who owns it. They haven't been here." He leans his weight on his left crutch and maneuvers his backpack over his other shoulder. "How you liking ol' Granesville High so far? Kath says you got the vacuum for English."

"The what?"

He grins. "Mr. Dyson. Everyone calls him The Vacuum."

"Because of his name?"

"Yeah, and because he sucks."

I laugh. It's a fitting nickname. Even after one class, I can tell Mr. Dyson is going to be one of those teachers who makes even the most interesting material seem dry and dull. I'm about to ask Liam about his other classes when Kath appears, her footsteps echoing off the lockers as she speed-walks toward us.

"Liam." She frowns as she looks him over, taking in his flushed skin and damp forehead. "I texted you that I was on my way here to give you a hand."

"No worries," he says, then nods toward me. "Avery helped."

Kath shifts her gaze to me, looking intimidatingly fierce and beautiful. A few moments pass and then she blinks, her expression suddenly softening, like she's decided that maybe I'm not a total menace, after all. That maybe I *am* capable of being around Liam without causing him some sort of bodily harm. "Thanks," she says tersely, then clears her throat as if the word injured her on its way out.

"Anytime. Really."

She nods and turns to Liam. "Ready?"

"Yeah." He does a three-point turn on his crutches, then glances back at me. I meet his gaze, expectant, sure he's about to ask me to join them for whatever they usually do at lunch. But all he says is, "Thanks again, Avery. See you later."

I force my features into an impassive expression. "See you," I reply, then go to my locker while they head off together down the hallway. As I dump my books, I remind myself that I'd planned to go home for lunch today anyway. I don't need an invitation from them. I don't need a social life, period. I'm here to academically kick ass so I can have my pick of colleges, not make more friends only to say good-bye to them a few months later. Never mind that I'm so bored and lonely, I'm tempted to try yoga with my mother.

Nah. I'm not *that* desperate yet.

Walking home, alone, I try to determine whether the niggling ache I'm feeling is bitterness over not being included, or just plain homesickness for Weldon, and Mia, who was always there to eat lunch with me. Some people think introverts don't require regular human contact, but it's not true. We do need social interaction, but preferably in small doses, and followed by a period of alone time to recharge.

Like now. Three hours surrounded by crowds has left me depleted, and all I want to do is sit in the kitchen, by myself, and eat the leftover spinach pizza that's currently sitting in the fridge.

As I round the crescent to our house, I'm surprised to see my dad's truck in the driveway next to my mom's Corolla. It's her day off, but he never takes one. Oh God. Did something bad happen? Did someone die?

But when I get inside, the house seems empty. Even Hazel is quiet, dozing on the sun-soaked chair in the living room. Too hungry to care, I go to the fridge and extract a cold slice, biting into it as I grab a pitcher of iced tea.

A door suddenly opens down the hall. I freeze, pizza in one hand and pitcher in the other, as footsteps pad across the hardwood. A second later my mother appears in the doorway, her hands frantically tying the belt on her fuzzy green bathrobe.

"Avery," she says, eyes wide. "What are you doing home?"

I swallow the food in my mouth and start to answer her when a second set of footsteps approaches from the hall. My father, his face flushed and his hair mussed like he just got back from one of his three-mile runs. Only he didn't.

Oh God. Were they…*oh God*. Ew. I know they still do these things—I've heard them often enough—but usually I don't have to face them directly afterward.

"I…this morning…I told you I might be home for lunch," I say, my brain struggling to process the situation.

"Oh." Mom smooths down her hair and glances at my dad, who's looking everywhere but at me. "Your father decided to, uh, come home for lunch too."

Dad clears his throat and peers into the still-open fridge. "Any pizza left?"

I almost hand him mine, seeing as I've completely lost my appetite. Instead, I nod and step back, avoiding eye contact.

"How was school?" Mom asks, like it's any other day and I didn't just interrupt their afternoon quickie.

"It was school," I say flatly. She raises her brows at my tone. I'm not usually the snarky type, but I don't feel like being mature at the moment. "I think I'll eat this in my room. I have some research to do."

I have no idea where that came from, or what I could possibly have to research on the first day of school, but my parents don't even question it. They just let me go.

Alone in my room, the bitterness from before seeps in again, eclipsing the horror of the last few minutes. I sit on my bed, lunch forgotten on the nightstand, and try to figure out exactly what it is that's bothering me, aside from the obvious.

I'm pissed, I realize. Not embarrassed. Not disappointed. Not homesick. I'm angry. I'm angry at Kath and Liam for excluding me, even though being left alone is what I thought I wanted. I'm angry at Mia for drifting away, even though it's my fault too. I'm angry at my parents for forcing me to leave a place I loved and moving me to a boring little town with a dumpy little school and nosy people and senile old men who run through intersections. I'm angry at them for being so caught up in each other that sometimes they fail to see me.

Mostly, though, I'm angry at myself, for pretending I don't care about being seen.

Chapter Eleven

My first paycheck arrives on Friday, and for some reason I'm surprised when I log into my bank account after school and find it there. I've been so focused on the idea of paying back Liam, I almost forgot that I'll be the one getting paid.

I use the calculator on my phone to figure out exactly seventy-five percent of the total. Then I bring up my money transfer app and text Liam for his email.

I'd rather cash, he texts back twenty minutes later. *Want to meet at the store next to Sadler's before your shift? They have an ATM.*

I don't question why he prefers cash over a convenient money transfer. All I care is that he gets what I owe him. *Sure*, I reply.

When I pull up in front of the KwikShop convenience store at ten to five, Liam is outside waiting, his back against the brick wall and his booted foot resting on the sidewalk. Seeing me, he straightens up and secures his crutches under his arms.

"You sure you don't want to revisit the seventy-five-twenty-five arrangement?" he asks when I get out of my mom's car. "I mean, twenty-five percent of practically nothing is…practically nothing."

"No, it's something." I open the door and let him go in ahead of me. He's getting good on the crutches now, pivoting smoothly around obstacles. Must be all the extra movement at school this past week. Yesterday I spotted him vaulting up the stairs like it was nothing.

The bank machine is at the back of the store. Liam nods hello to the cashier—a fifty-something woman with poufy blond hair and long red fingernails—and leads the way, carefully moving through the dusty, narrow aisles. The woman watches us warily from behind the counter, like we're about to grab something and hobble our way out of here.

"I think I should get to see what you were paid, so I know you're dividing it up fairly," Liam says as I dig out my wallet.

I look up at him, wide-eyed. "I am not showing you my bank account deposits."

He smiles, making me momentarily forget that we're standing between a sketchy bathroom and a display of shriveled beef jerky. "So, what, I'm just supposed to trust you?"

His tone is light and playful and borderline flirty. Heat fills my cheeks and I fumble with my bank card, almost dropping it on the filthy floor. "Yes," I say, shoving the card in the slot. "We're in the same math class. You know I'm more than capable of figuring out a simple percentage."

I know *he's* capable too. As much as I try to focus in class, I often catch myself watching him instead. He doesn't crack jokes and disrupt class like a lot of the people around us; he actually works. And Ms. Fiore clearly loves him, always beaming her white smile his way whenever he answers her questions correctly, which he always does. My answers are always correct too; I'm just too nervous to volunteer them.

The machine prompts me to put in my code. I glance at Liam, and he courteously turns away, pretending to examine a scratch-and-win promotion sign on the wall. He turns back when the ATM spits out the cash. "Since the machine only gives out twenties, I had to round up," I say, handing over the bills.

He peers at the money in his hand and I can almost see his brain working, tallying the hours I worked to determine if the amount I gave him matches up.

"It's right," I say, interrupting his mental calculations. "I wouldn't cheat you."

Finally satisfied, he slips the twenties into his back pocket, knocking a crutch loose in the process. It tips back and crashes into the beef jerky display, sending two of the packages flying off their hooks.

"What are you kids doing back there?" The cashier's voice is unexpectedly deep and gravelly, and it startles me more than the crutch-jerky collision.

"Sorry, Brenda," Liam calls to the woman as he retrieves his crutch.

I bend down and grab the packages off the floor, returning them to their rightful hooks. Then we bolt for the door, Brenda glaring at us the whole way. I manage to hold in my giggles until we get outside, even though we're still visible through the window. But I can't help it, especially when I see Liam's beet-red face.

"Brenda," he mutters. "She thinks everyone's out to rob her."

I crack up again. Liam smirks, then snickers, until finally, he's laughing too. It feels good to laugh with someone like this. My parents and I don't joke around much, and I'm not sure if Kath even has a sense of humor. Mia and I used to giggle together until our sides hurt, but it's been a while since that happened. Come to think of it, I've barely laughed at all since we moved here.

"What are you guys *doing?*"

We shut up and turn toward Sadler's Subs. Kath is leaning out the door, watching us with a vaguely frantic expression. Oops. I'm supposed to be at work right now.

"Dinner rush," she says to me. "Get in here, would you?"

"Sorry," I tell her, but she's already back inside.

Liam and I exchange a glance, suddenly awkward. The lightness from a minute ago is gone.

"I'll go with you," he says, like he thinks I'm afraid to face the Wrath of Kath alone. Which isn't a lie. "Just to say hi."

I nod and open the door, almost sending a guy crashing to the ground like Liam's crutch. The tiny ordering area is bursting with people, packed together like sardines in a can. I squeeze my way through while Liam gets intercepted near the door by some guy he apparently knows. The area behind the counter is almost as busy, all four Sadlers working various stations to keep up with the demand. Dinner rush, indeed. I've never seen it so busy.

Mr. Sadler catches my eye from the register and gestures toward the assembly area, where Isaac is working the board at lightning speed. I dart past Kath and her mom at the prep counter and grab my apron, securing it as I take my place next to Isaac.

"Wrap and bag," he says, sliding two turkey subs in my direction.

I move quickly, wrapping and bagging as neatly as possible before handing the correct orders to Mr. Sadler. In between, I try to keep the board clean, but it's useless. Isaac is too fast, almost slapdash, and veggies are flying everywhere. At one point, I look up to pluck a piece of lettuce from my hair and catch sight of Liam, still immersed in the crowd. He looks wistful, like he'd enjoy nothing more than to rush back here and help. But I can't imagine how disastrous it would be to add crutches and a hulking walking boot to this chaos.

After about twenty minutes, the crowd starts thinning out. When the place is finally empty, save for the six of us, everyone breathes a collective sigh of relief.

"Good job, guys," Mr. Sadler says, wiping a bead of sweat off his forehead. He heads to the back room while the rest of us put the place back in order.

"Steller wrapping skills, there, Avery," Isaac says, handing me a cloth so I can help wipe down the board. "You should work at one of those gift-wrapping booths at the mall during the holidays."

Kath squeezes between us and switches out the empty onion bin for a fresh one. "Isaac, you're such a dork."

He reaches out to flick her arm and I notice he's wearing the *I Finished the Sizzlin' 48oz Steak at First Choice*

Grill! shirt again. He catches me looking at it and says, "I have eight more at home. I rocked the steak challenge nine times now and I plan to go for number ten in the very near future."

I nod, unsure how to respond. "That's…an accomplishment."

He grins and tosses a discarded tomato slice toward the garbage can. It misses and hits the floor with a wet plop. "Yes. It *is* an accomplishment. I'm glad someone around here recognizes that."

"Please," Kath says, her back to us as she slices pickles. "Consuming five pounds of dead cow in one sitting isn't something to be proud of. It's repulsive."

"Your face is repulsive."

"Enough." Mrs. Sadler shoots them both a look as she pulls off her apron. "Okay, I'm out of here for the night. Behave."

Kath turns her head to grimace at her brother, and he makes the same face back at her, only exaggerated. Their mom ignores them and walks toward the front, where Liam is still stationed, leaning against the menu wall and looking at his phone.

"You need a lift home, sweetheart?" Mrs. Sadler asks him, placing a hand on his forearm.

"That's okay." He pockets his phone and smiles at her. "Mom took Brody and Keira out for pizza. She'll pick me up on the way through."

"Tell Norah I'll text her later, okay?" She squeezes his arm once and then leaves, waving at us as the door eases shut behind her.

I go back to cleaning, their conversation and all these new names swirling in my head. Brody and Keira must be Liam's siblings, and Norah his mother. And she and Mrs. Sadler—Linh—are friends. Not for the first time, I wonder about Liam's father and where he is. Ireland? Is that why he's so determined to get there?

Even though we don't hang out and I wouldn't exactly call us friends—still no lunch invite despite seeing him at his locker every day this week—I'm still curious about him. Maybe my hitting him with a car has bonded us in some weird way. Maybe taking over part of his life has made me feel like I know him better than I do. Or maybe I'm just interested because I think he's cute and I like him.

Oh God. I like him. How did *that* happen? I remind myself about Noah Barnett and how dejected I felt after our break up. *Never again.* Okay, but this is different. I let myself get attached to Noah. I let myself fall in love. But this…this is loneliness and hormones and a misplaced sense of connection. This is just a little crush.

"Excuse me."

I look up to see Kath standing in front of me, a fresh bin of pickles in her arms. My face warms and I quickly step aside so she can deposit the bin with the other toppings. How long was I zoned out, thinking about Liam? And—oh God—was I staring at him while I was thinking about him? To cover my embarrassment, I bend to retrieve the discarded tomato slice from the floor. As I straighten back up, a waft of air conditioning washes over me, making me shiver.

"Ghost?" Kath asks, staring at my goosebumpy arms.

"Either that or a demon."

She snickers. "Quick, get the salt. We'll line the entrances so he can't get in."

"What the hell are you guys talking about?" Isaac says, nicking a sliced pickle from the bin and popping it into his mouth.

I give Kath a tentative smile. "You're a *Supernatural* fan too?"

She looks at me the same way she did in the hallway on the first day of school when I helped Liam with his locker—like I may have some redeeming qualities after all. "Since I was about twelve."

"Oh, *that* show." Isaac rolls his eyes. "The one that made you believe in ghosts."

"I didn't say I believed. I said it was *possible*."

"Right." He adjusts his baseball cap and grins across the counter at Liam. "It's Liam who believes in hauntings."

Liam's mouth falls open. "Dude."

"What? It's true." Isaac turns to me. "There are these abandoned train tracks behind Rite Price Auto where a woman supposedly got hit by a train back in the fifties. Her name was Rosemary. People say they've seen her ghost wandering around the tracks, but I think they were just high and hallucinating or something. Liam believes it, though. We've even gone there a few times, to see if we could catch a glimpse of her, but we never did. Liam said it's because Rosemary is shy."

Liam's cheeks flush and he grips his crutches like he wants to dislocate Isaac's jaw with them. I press my lips together to stifle a laugh.

"Isaac," Kath says in a warning tone, her eyes on Liam. "Ease up, would you?"

"Sorry, sorry." He picks up an onion and tosses it in the air, catching it baseball-style. "Hey, we should go there some night. All of us. You too, Avery. Maybe Rosemary will show herself for an out-of-towner."

I glance at Liam. His head is down, gaze trained on the tip of his right crutch as he taps it on the floor. But I can tell he's listening, waiting to see how I'll respond, if I'll make fun of him for believing in small town folklore. The fact that he cares what I think of him sets off a warm tingling in my stomach.

"Sure," I say with a shrug. At least I'm getting invited to *something*. "I wouldn't mind trying to get a look at her."

Liam flashes me a grateful smile, like he knows I'm just playing along to get Isaac off his back. Which is mostly true. I'm too scientific-minded to believe in ghostly hauntings, but I have nothing against people who do. I think it's brave, in a way, to put your faith in something that you've never actually experienced firsthand.

Chapter Twelve

W hen I walk into English class on Monday, Mr. Dyson already has our essay topic on the whiteboard: *Does social media create isolation?* I sigh quietly. Only a week into school, and this is our third in-class essay. At first I assumed he wanted to check out our writing skills, but he hasn't even handed anything back yet. All he does is stare at his laptop during class while the rest of us scribble away.

The Vacuum is a well-founded nickname for him. He certainly sucks all the joy out of language arts.

I take my seat and dig out a pen. Mr. Dyson is already engrossed in his laptop. No one has ever seen what he does on there, but there are several theories floating around: He's writing a novel. He's playing *The Sims*. He's looking at porn. Personally, I think he's just checked out and doesn't care.

As someone who has moved several times, social media is a great way to help keep me connected to—

Someone lets out a barking laugh. I stop writing and look up, locking eyes with the hulking dark-haired guy

102

who sits at the table diagonal to mine. He's also in my Global History class. I know his name—Damian—but we've never spoken. So I'm not sure why he's glaring at me right now like I've personally offended him.

Surprised, I blink and return my gaze to my paper. A stinging heat creeps up my neck and ears. Unable to help myself, I glance up again. Damian isn't glaring at me anymore; he's whispering to the blond guy next to him, whose gaze keeps flicking to me. Either they're talking about me, or I'm imagining things.

I'm used to this kind of attention, always being new, but the curiosity usually dies down after a few days. And usually no one acts hostile toward me. I've only been in this school for a week and have mostly kept to myself. What is this guy's problem?

I steal a peek across the room at Kath. She's sitting straight up, pen in hand, watching Damian and his friend with a wary expression. I guess I'm not imagining things.

"Less talking, more writing," Mr. Dyson intones, not bothering to look up from his screen.

Damian smirks and goes back to his paper. After a few moments, I do too, but it's difficult to concentrate. I scrawl a bunch of stuff about social engagement and YouTube and then doodle in the margins for the remainder of class. It's not like Dyson cares anyway.

I'm relieved when the bell rings. After passing in my paper, I join the flow of students spilling out into the hallway. I'm almost at the door leading to the stairs when a voice calls out behind me.

"Hey."

I turn around. Damian is standing a few feet away from me, flanked by his blond friend. They're both looking right at me, and not in a friendly way. My skin prickles with uneasiness.

"Your last name's Bishop, right?" Damian asks before I can say anything.

"Yeah?" The end of the word tilts up like a question.

"And your father is Derrick Bishop? From MRT Engineering?"

I nod, baffled as to what he's getting at. "Why?"

Damian steps closer to me. "Why?" he repeats, his dark eyes flashing. "Because that bridge your dad's building? It's gonna put *my* dad out of a job. He operates the ferry. But obviously *your* dad doesn't give a shit about him, or any of the other people whose jobs will be axed in a few months." He leans even closer, so close I can smell the aftershave on his skin. "So why don't you run along home and tell your daddy thanks a fucking lot."

His anger roots me to the floor. I'm frozen, unable to speak. No one has ever confronted me like this before, and I'm not sure whether to shrivel into a ball or fight back. But, as it turns out, I don't get the chance to decide either way, because all of a sudden Kath is between us, forcing Damian to pull back.

"Leave her alone," she snaps at him. "Who do you think you are, talking to her that way?"

People stop to stare at her, this willowy girl yelling at a pissed off, six-foot-whatever guy. I'm staring too, shocked that she's here, that she's actually sticking up for me. Damian steps back a few inches more, his jaw set.

"Did you ever stop to think that the bridge construction is *creating* jobs too?" she continues, crossing her arms. "No, of course you didn't. You're too busy making an ass of yourself and taking your anger out on someone who isn't even at fault. Did it make you feel good, using your size to intimidate a girl? Dickface." She unfolds her arms and tucks one around mine. "Let's go," she says, steering me toward the door.

"I—" Lost for words, I clamp my mouth shut instead. Then, at the bottom of the stairs, I manage a simple "Thanks."

She shrugs and drops my arm as we reach the hallway to my locker. And Liam's locker. I spot him up ahead, leaning on one crutch as he fiddles with his lock.

"Damian," Kath mutters as we approach. "Son of Satan. Suits him."

I let out a snort, causing Liam to look up. When he smiles, all I can think about is how non-devilish he looks in comparison. Angelic, more like.

"What's up?" he asks, his gaze bouncing back and forth between us. He seems surprised to see us together. Hell, *I'm* surprised to see us together.

"Nothing," Kath says, adjusting her ponytail. "Avery's going to eat lunch with us."

I am? I turn to look at Kath, but she keeps her attention on Liam, whose eyebrows shoot up at this piece of news. Mine are probably just as elevated.

"Cool," Liam says, snapping his lock closed. His locker neighbor ended up agreeing to a switch, so he's having a much easier time navigating.

"But," I say as we start walking, "I don't have cash for the cafeteria, and I didn't pack any food."

"Food? Where we're going, we don't need food," Liam says in a deep voice.

I smile. *Back to the Future* is my father's all-time favorite movie. I know Doc Brown's lines by heart. "Great Scott!" I reply.

He laughs. Kath rolls her eyes at both of us. "Come on, nerds."

We walk down another hallway and turn right, where there's an outside exit with sunken concrete stairs leading up to the soccer field. Kath pushes the door open, and I notice a guy and a girl already standing outside. I recognize the pale, auburn-haired girl from my chemistry class, but I've never seen the guy. He's short, with thick dark hair and light brown skin. The two of them are leaning against the iron railing, holding hands.

"Hey," Kath says to them as she holds the door for Liam, then me. "This is Avery. She's new."

I wait for her to add something like *She's the one who did this to Liam*, but she doesn't. Maybe she hasn't told anyone, though I can't imagine why she'd spare me like that. "Hi," I say to the couple, and they both lift their free hands to wave at me.

"Samantha and Ravi," Kath goes on, gesturing to the couple. "They're Granesville lifers, like Liam and me."

"You make it sound like we're gonna live here until we die," Ravi says.

"Like our parents," Samantha adds, reaching behind her to grab a wrinkled paper bag I haven't noticed until now.

"Oh good, you brought some," Liam says as he props his crutches against the low concrete wall and lowers himself to sitting on the steps. Kath takes a seat beside him while I just stand there, unsure of my place.

"Of course I brought some." Samantha opens the bag, releasing the most intoxicating cinnamon scent. She catches me breathing it in and offers the bag to me. "My mom owns Janelle's Bagels over in Keating. These are sticky bun flavor. A little stale, but still good."

I reach in and take one, immediately coating my fingers with the gooey, sugary topping, but I don't care. It looks and smells amazing. Samantha passes the bag around until everyone has one, and then the five of us spend the rest of lunch eating day-old bagels under the midday sun.

After math homework that evening, I slip outside to the back deck, where my parents are soaking up the last of the day's warmth. At the sound of the door, they stop talking and look up, like they're surprised to see me. Like they forgot for a second that I live here too. I've gotten this look from them all my life, and it used to make me feel invisible, like a ghost. Now, it just annoys me. It makes me want to be bigger, brighter, unmistakably noticeable.

I take a seat on the patio chair across from them and say, "So I found out today that the son of the ferry operator goes to my school. He confronted me in the hall about the new bridge and how it'll cost his father his job."

They both stare at me, two pairs of sunglasses glinting in the waning light. Mom crosses her legs and takes a sip out of a sweating glass of iced tea.

"Confronted *you*," she says, setting the glass back down on the patio table. "How did he even make the connection? Have you been telling people that it's your father who—"

"No," I cut in. "This is a small town. Word gets around fast."

Dad leans back and stretches his legs out in front of him. "Just ignore him, and anyone else who says anything to you about the bridge. It's no one else's business."

I don't point out that it actually *is* some people's business, especially the ferry workers and their families. But even though my parents might feel sympathy for them, I know that in the end, they believe obsolete jobs are an unfortunate side effect of progress.

"Well, I hope you did the mature thing and walked away," Mom says.

I nod, even though it was more like I was dragged away, by Kath, after she said all the things I wasn't brave enough to say. "I doubt he'll bother me again."

"Good. It's your senior year, and you need to be focusing on your grades and looking into colleges, not worrying about this nonsense. Let your father and me deal with the bridge detractors."

This makes me wonder if they've been receiving similar reactions around town. Some people really resent change. I get it, though. If I'd lived in one place all my life and some stranger showed up one day and started to change things, I might feel resentful too. Or maybe I'd choose to see the benefits, like Kath.

There's a scratching sound at the door. Hazel, wanting outside. I get up to let her out, and she tears across the deck and down the stairs to the yard. She runs in circles for a minute before pausing at her favorite shrub.

"Speaking of colleges," Dad says once I'm seated again. "Have you given any thought to where you want to apply?"

I have. Now that I'm back into the school routine, I've started to think a lot about college and where I want to be for the next four-plus years. My "top choices" list has been narrowed down to three or four schools, all scattered around the country, but one place consistently rises to the top spot.

"I was thinking about Eckert College."

"Eckert," my father repeats with a trace of surprise. "In Weldon?"

"Yeah."

My parents exchange a look I can't decipher through their sunglasses. When they turn to face me again, their foreheads are in full furrow position.

"But you've already lived there," my mom says, like I've forgotten this.

"I know." I watch Hazel as she gallops back onto the deck and plops down, panting, at my feet. "It wasn't my idea to leave, remember? I liked it there. I made friends there. And Eckert has a great actuarial science program, so I thought…it seems like a good fit for me."

"Well, I suppose," Mom says slowly. "But Avery…your grades are excellent. You could go anywhere you want. After you graduate and we're done with everything here, we're hoping to go to Europe next. You could study in France. Switzerland. Germany. *Anywhere*."

"You could see the world," Dad adds.

A jolt of anger pulses through me. They don't get me. They don't see me. And I'm sick of it.

"I don't *want* to see the world."

My words come out louder than I'd meant, surprising all three of us. We don't yell. We talk things out like mature, rational adults. Only I'm *not* an adult, not yet, and sometimes raising your voice is the only way to be heard. I think of Kath, facing down tall, scary Damian while I just stood there, frozen and mute. She spoke up for me today, but eventually I'll have to start speaking up for myself. Like right now.

"Avery, we're simply presenting options," Dad says in his logical way. "You don't have to make a decision today."

"Since when do you not want to see the world?" Mom asks with a slight frown, like I've personally insulted her. "You've always been up for new adventures."

This shows how little they pay attention. *They're* the ones who are always looking for the next adventure; I'm just along for the ride because they're my parents and I legally have no other choice. But in a few months I'll be eighteen, newly graduated, and finally ready to carve my own path. And unlike theirs, mine will end somewhere instead of running the length of the planet.

My anger fizzles into a dull, thrumming ache. I stand up, suddenly exhausted. "I have some more homework to do," I mumble, stepping over Hazel on my way to the door.

Inside, I close myself up in my room and sit on my bed. The familiar softness of it calms me. The world is vast, filled with infinite possibilities, but all I really want is one little corner of it to claim as my own.

Chapter Thirteen

I saac wasn't kidding about the ghost-hunting trip to the train tracks. Somehow, he convinces his parents to let Kath and me off an hour early Friday night so we can try to catch a glimpse of the elusive Rosemary.

There's not enough room in one car for the four of us plus Liam's crutches, so the boys borrow Mr. Sadler's car while Kath rides with me in my mother's Corolla. I texted Mom earlier to tell her I had plans after work, and all I got in response was a thumbs up emoji. She and Dad have been giving me a wide berth since our college talk on the deck a few days ago. Or maybe they were in the middle of something when I texted.

"You're going to have to give me directions," I tell Kath, trying to erase these unpleasant images.

She's peeking at her phone, like she's been doing all evening at work, and startles a bit at my question. "Oh. Right. Head toward the intersection and go straight."

I turn left out of the Sadler's Subs parking lot and flick on the stereo. Soft music—*not* Ariana Grande—fills the car. But Kath is so distracted, I don't think she'd notice if I blasted speed metal.

"Are you okay?" Normally I wouldn't dare ask, fearing one of her steely glares, but I feel like we've made a lot of progress this week. She stuck up for me at school. She invited me to eat lunch with her friends, not just once but all week. And during our Wednesday evening shift, when the place was completely dead, she ran across the street to the coffee shop and bought us both hot chocolates. She's definitely thawing, and despite my reluctance to get close to anyone here, work and school go a lot faster when you have people to talk to.

"Yeah, I'm fine," Kath says with a sigh. "It's just…I'm being stupid."

I switch lanes and slide in behind a car that seems to be going about ten miles per hour. "Stupid about what?"

She glances at me, hesitating, like she's not sure if she should get into it with me. "Brooke," she says after a few moments. "Since she left, we've been texting each other constantly. But today…I texted her after school and she still hasn't responded. I know that doesn't mean anything. She could be studying or busy or whatever, but for the past couple of days she's been posting these pictures on her Instagram…her and her dorm mates, who are of course all girls, and they always have their arms around each other, and I just…" She makes a frustrated noise and shoves her phone in her jacket pocket. "Like I said, I'm being stupid."

"No, you're not. Long distance is hard. It can make you really paranoid. I'm sure she's just friends with all those girls, though," I add quickly, even though I'm not sure at all. I don't even know Brooke. But Kath looks so defeated, I feel like I should give her *some* hope.

"Yeah, I know." Her hand slides to her pocket, but she leaves her phone where it is. "Thanks."

I nod and brake at the intersection. This is the exact spot I was in when I hit Liam. Or when he hit me. It's hard to believe that was a month ago. In as little as two weeks, he could be getting his boot off. And taking his job back. The thought of leaving Sadler's gives me a weird, empty feeling. My job there got off to a bit of a rocky start, but it's one of the only things that kept me sane during my first few weeks in this town. Even when Kath barely spoke to me.

I glance at her now as the light turns green and we sail through the intersection. A month ago, I never imagined we'd be hanging out on purpose.

"Avery," she says a few minutes later, after directing me past the used car dealership and onto the tree-lined road behind it.

"Yeah?" My fingers tighten on the wheel. It's really dark back here.

"I'm sorry I was such a bitch to you when you first started working. I'm not usually like that. Okay, maybe I am, but sometimes I take it too far."

I'm speechless for a moment. Did she read my mind? "It's okay. I mean, I understand. The accident *was* partly my fault."

"Pull over up here." She gestures to a gap in the trees up ahead. "That's the thing, though," she goes on as I hit my blinker and pull onto the gravel shoulder. "I think it was partly *my* fault, too."

"Huh?" I look behind me to make sure we're not about to be sideswiped by a semi. The boys are nowhere to be seen.

"Liam had a shift that day. He was going to drive his truck to work, but it wouldn't start, so he took his bike instead. When he didn't show up on time, I got annoyed and started texting him. He didn't answer because he was on his bike, but I didn't know that so I kept texting and texting…" Her voice trails off and she swallows. "He denies it, but I think the constant vibration from his phone distracted him and that's why he didn't notice your car until it was too late."

An image flashes through my mind: the first time I saw Kath, standing outside Sadler's with her phone, looking annoyed. Minutes before the accident.

"Anyway, I'm sorry I took all my worry out on you," she continues, fiddling with her jacket zipper. It's clear that apologizing isn't easy for her. "I've never hated you, if that's what you think. In fact, I thought you were kind of cool right off. Mostly because you didn't ask me where I'm *from* from."

I shut off the engine and turn to face her. "Where you're *from* from?"

"It's a question I get sometimes from strangers. They ask me where I'm from, I say here, and then they're like, no, I mean where are you *from* from? Hazards of being biracial in a mostly white town."

"That must get annoying."

"It does. I mean, my mom's lived here most of her life too. Her family emigrated from Vietnam when she was three. After the war." She unbuckles her seatbelt.

114

"I've never even *been* to Vietnam. I was born here and have lived here all my life. I'm a Granesville lifer."

"Next time someone asks, tell them you're from Narnia," I suggest.

Kath laughs. "Or Middle-earth."

We're still riffing off fictional fantasy locations when Isaac and Liam pull up a couple of minutes later. Kath and I get out of the car and wait in the cool, fall-like air while Isaac fetches Liam's crutches and two heavy-duty flashlights from the back of the car. He hands a flashlight to Kath.

"Let's go find Rosemary," he says, flicking on his own flashlight and heading toward an opening in the trees.

Clouds blanket the sky, making the woods even darker. I can barely see where I'm going, even with the beams of both flashlights illuminating the way. Beside me, Liam picks carefully along the uneven terrain, planting his crutches firmly before shifting his weight forward. I tense up even more, waiting for him to hit a pothole and fall.

But he doesn't, and after several minutes, we emerge into a small clearing. Kath and Isaac do a sweep of the area with their flashlights, revealing rotting logs and large rocks and empty beer cans. Rusted railroad tracks cut through the clearing and disappear into the thickness of trees.

I shiver. It's creepy as hell out here and I wouldn't be surprised if we *did* see a ghost.

Kath walks further into the clearing and accidentally kicks one of the beer cans. "Litterbugs," she mutters.

"Big party spot in the summer," Liam says beside me. He's standing so close, I can feel the heat from his arm and smell the fabric softener on his hoodie. I tremble again, for different reasons.

"I bet the police love that," I say as we walk toward Kath, who's standing next to what looks like the charred remnants of a campfire and peering at her phone. She's frowning, which I assume means Brooke still hasn't texted back.

"Cops bust up parties here all the time because of the underage drinking," Isaac says, then reaches into pocket and brings out a silver flask. He twists off the top and takes a long drink.

"What the hell?" Kath charges over and tries to grab the flask from him, but he backs away, out of her reach. "You're driving, asswipe. What's in that thing?"

"Vodka." Isaac takes another swig. "You can drive Dad's car home. I'm heading somewhere else after this."

"Of course you are." Kath crosses her arms, letting the flashlight dangle from her fingers. "Well, don't expect me to chauffer you to wherever you're going."

"Did I ask you to chauffer me, Katherine?"

They go back and forth like this a few more times while Liam and I stand there awkwardly. Or at least I stand there awkwardly. Liam seems used to it. He activates the flashlight on his phone, catches my eye, and gestures toward a log a few feet away. I nod and we make our way toward it, leaving the siblings to their bickering.

At the log, Liam begins the long, slow process of lowering himself to sitting. I'm trying to decide if I should help him when he loses his balance for a second, almost crashing into me. I clutch his forearm to steady him.

"Sorry," he says, his mouth inches from my neck.

He straightens up and I quickly let go of his arm, suddenly grateful for the darkness and its ability to mask my scorching face. I wonder briefly if I still smell like onions.

By the time we're finally settled on the log, a foot or so between us, Kath and Isaac have stopped squabbling and joined us, sitting on another log across from us. The ground at our feet is littered with cigarette butts and empty liquor bottles. Isaac takes another hit from his flask and then offers it to us, though he knows I'm driving and Liam is already unsteady enough on his feet. We shake our heads. Kath checks her phone again. Behind us, there's a low rustling sound in the woods. The hair on the back of my neck goes stiff and I have to resist the urge to jump up and run.

"So this Rosemary," I say to distract myself. "Did the train accidentally hit her or did she jump in front of it or what?"

"Rumor has it she was pushed," Isaac says ominously. "Murdered. Which is why her spirit is trapped here. That's what Liam used to say, anyway."

I can't see Liam clearly, but I'm pretty sure he's glaring in Isaac's direction. "Mrs. Jimenez told me that story when I was a kid. She's lived here since the sixties."

"Mrs. Jimenez?" I ask.

Kath glances up from her phone. "Librarian at Granesville Library."

"She just told you that because she knew you were into those Goosebumps books and liked scary stories," Isaac says, his words slurring together slightly.

I smile. I like hearing about the townsfolk, the long history everyone has with each other. It makes me feel grounded somehow, like I have a foothold in something solid and durable, even though for me, this town is only temporary.

Isaac stands and takes a big swig of vodka. "Let's walk the tracks."

"No, thanks," Kath says, thumbs flying across her phone screen.

Liam knocks on his boot. "I'll pass for obvious reasons."

Isaac looks at me, but I shake my head. I've seen *The Walking Dead* and know what can happen when you walk along deserted train tracks. My courage has a limit.

"This is boring," Isaac says, capping his flask and slipping it into his pocket. "I'm gonna take off."

Kath looks up. "What? You can't walk anywhere from here."

"Sure I can. Devon said he'll pick me up at the car dealership."

"That's like a half hour walk." Kath sighs heavily and turns off her phone. "I'll drive you to whatever party you're going to. Mom and Dad would kill me if you got hit by a car or passed out in a ditch or something." She gets to her feet and turns to Liam and me. "You guys okay for ten minutes?"

Ten minutes. Alone in the dark woods. With Liam. And possibly hungry woodland creatures. In spite of all this, I feel a jolt of excitement.

"Sure," I say, and Liam nods in agreement.

They leave us with one of the flashlights and start toward the road. Once they're out of sight, Liam and I sit in silence for a few minutes. An owl hoots in the trees, and another one, farther away, hoots back.

"It was his idea to come here," I say, mostly just to break the awkwardness.

"Don't take it personally." Liam rests the flashlight in his lap, its beam pointing toward a copse of trees a few feet ahead of us. "Isaac has the attention span of a mosquito."

I noticed. At work, he's always restless, quickly tiring of one job before moving on to the next.

"He makes it hard to love him sometimes," he continues. "Though Kath never stops trying."

"And you?" I haven't been able to get a read on Liam and Isaac's relationship. From what I've seen, it mainly consists of Isaac giving him a hard time and Liam giving him dirty looks.

"I try too. The Sadlers are my second family."

I nod. I noticed that too, and I find the dynamic fascinating. Friends becoming like family seems as foreign and impossible to me as living in one place forever. How comforting it must feel to have all that security.

A heavy, almost wistful feeling engulfs me. I suck in a long breath of cool, piney air, trying to tamp the feeling down. "Do you really believe in ghosts?" I ask, turning to look at him. All I can make out is the shadow of his jaw and a quick flash of his eyes.

"I think so. Not Rosemary, necessarily, but yeah. I believe in the afterlife." He shifts on the log, closing some of the gap between us. "How about you?"

I stay completely still, my senses hyperaware of his proximity. If he moves any closer, I might erupt into flames. "No. I believe more in science, I guess."

He laughs. "You can believe in both, you know. Science *and* the supernatural."

"I know." Flustered, I add, "I have nothing against people who believe in ghosts." Sometimes I wish *I* believed. Ghosts float from place to place, unmoored, longing to settle and be at peace. If anything, I can relate to their goals.

A branch cracks behind us. Liam grabs the flashlight and spins around, pointing it in the general direction of the noise. My muscles tense, images of snarling wolves and hungry bears rolling through my brain. But neither of us see anything, and all is quiet again in the clearing.

"My mom told me about this castle in Ireland," Liam says with a slight tremble in his voice. "Belvelly Castle. Supposedly it's haunted by a lady with no face."

I swallow. "No *face*?"

"That's just one of the stories she told me. Ireland is full of haunted places."

"Is that why you want to go there?"

He's quiet for a few moments, his fingers still tight around the flashlight handle. "No. There's another reason."

Something he said when I visited him at the hospital resurfaces in my head. He was on pain killers at the time, but his words were clear: *Ireland...that's where my parents grew up. My father…This trip is probably my only chance to see it.*

My father.

"Is it because your father lives there?"

"No," he says, surprising me. He lets out a breath. "Not anymore, anyway. He's dead."

Horror washes over me. "Oh my God. I'm so sorry. I didn't—"

"It's okay," he cuts in quickly. "It happened a long time ago. He was killed in a motorcycle accident when my mom was pregnant with me. I never even met him."

"That…that's still horrible."

"Yeah." He clears his throat. "Anyway, my mom wanted a fresh start after he died. Her cousin Aileen lived near here at the time, so she decided Granesville was as good a place as any. We moved here when I was four months old. She hasn't been back to Ireland since. Too many bad memories, she says." He pauses and stretches out his booted leg. "I want to go, though. The senior trip itinerary says we get one free afternoon when we're in Dublin. So I'm going to take a bus to Glasnevin, where my parents grew up. And where my father died. His ashes are in the cemetery there."

I study his profile, hazy in the muted glow of the flashlight, and it finally clicks in. Now I understand how frustrated he must have been over his broken ankle, and why he was so angry at me when I went to visit him in the hospital. I understand why going on this trip, seeing the place where his father lived and died, is so important to him.

A Kath-like protectiveness rises up in me. He'll get to Ireland if I have to charter a plane and fly him there.

"I just need to see the place for myself, you know?" Liam says. "I don't even really know why. It's not like I have any family left there anymore."

"Because it's a part of you. *He's* a part of you. Your dad." I lift my hand to touch his arm, but chicken out at the last second and place it on the rough wood between us instead. "And no thanks to me, you *will* see Ireland this spring."

I can feel, rather than see, his hand moving from his lap and coming to rest on the log, less than an inch from mine. "You mean *thanks* to you," he corrects, his voice low and close. My stomach flip flops, and I forget all about vengeful ghosts and hungry bears. Nothing exists but Liam's hand, lightly grazing mine. And his breath, fanning against my face as he moves closer, and closer again. My eyes slide shut.

"I'm going to *kill* that douchenugget."

Liam and I spring apart at the sound of Kath's voice. She's walking toward us, flashlight shining at our faces, making us squint and raise our hands to block the glare.

"Sorry I took so long," she says when she reaches us. "Isaac couldn't remember where the party was, and no one was answering his texts, so I had to drive him around looking for it. While he sang at the top of his lungs and played drums on the dash with used McDonald's straws. I almost dumped his ass on the side of the highway." She sighs loudly and sits on the log opposite us. "So what did I miss? Did Rosemary make an appearance?"

Liam and I just sit there, hands back in our laps, eyes straight ahead. My entire body is buzzing and I'm sure my face resembles a ripe tomato, but if Kath suspects anything, she doesn't let on. Thankfully. She may have forgiven me for hurting Liam, but I'm not sure how she'd react if she caught us in an almost-kiss. *If* that's what it was. Maybe I misread the whole thing and he was only leaning in to brush a bug out of my hair or something. But that's not what it felt like to me. It felt...exhilarating.

"No," Liam finally answers her, then steals a glance at me. "I guess we'll have to try again later."

Chapter Fourteen

A few mornings later, I find Kath standing near my locker when I get to school. At first I think she's waiting for Liam, but she perks up when I emerge from the hallway crowd, like it's me she wants to see.

"Hey," I say, walking toward her.

"Hey." She crosses her arms and watches me as I open my locker and stuff my jacket inside. Out of the corner of my eye, I notice her foot tapping against the floor. She's making me self-conscious.

"What's up?" I ask. I've never seen her so agitated.

"Nothing." She scowls and flicks a strand of hair off her face like she has a personal vendetta against it. "I mean, it's no big deal. I just wanted to get your take on something."

I stare at her, waiting. "Okay."

She doesn't speak right away, so I turn back to my locker and busy myself with loading up my backpack with extra pencils, giving her time to gather her thoughts.

"So," she says, finally. "You've moved around a lot, right?"

"You could say that, yeah."

She shifts closer to let a kid carrying a giant instrument case squeeze past. "So, like, how do you handle it? Missing your friends and having to keep in touch online and stuff. How do you do the long-distance thing without completely losing your mind?"

"I don't." I close my locker and face her. "This is about Brooke, right? Did she still not text you back?"

She waves a hand. "No, she did. Eventually. But it's like...things are different now. Between us. Maybe it's just me being insecure, but this is a lot harder than I thought it would be, you know? And I wondered if there was some secret to making the long-distance thing less shitty. Since you're the only person I know who has experience in this area, I thought I'd ask you." She pauses and tilts her head at me. "What did you mean when you said *I don't?* You don't know how you handle it?"

"No. I meant I *don't* do the long-distance thing. Not as a rule, anyway. It's never worked out well for me. There's only one friend I've made that I still keep in touch with, and things aren't the same between us, either."

Her face falls. "So you're saying Brooke and I don't have much of a chance, then."

Oh God. What is wrong with me? She comes to me for relationship advice and I end up crushing her hopes. I really shouldn't be allowed to mix with the general public. "No," I say firmly. "I'm talking out of my ass. Don't listen to me. Just because I suck at maintaining relationships doesn't mean *you* do. I'm just jaded."

Her expression lightens, and she gives me a little smirk. "Yeah, I've noticed. Sometimes you look at Liam

125

Rebecca Phillips

and me like you're expecting us to run away from you screaming."

The warning bell rings. I swing my backpack over my shoulder. "To be fair, I didn't exactly make the best first impression on you guys."

"Agreed."

I raise my hand in a wave as she starts off toward her own class. "Wait," I say, realizing something. "Where *is* Liam?" My cheeks warm just speaking his name. Hopefully Kath doesn't notice as she backtracks toward me.

"His mom had to take his brother to an appointment and his sister is sick, so he's home with her," she tells me. "He'll be back at lunch."

"Does he take care of his brother and sister often?" That seems like...not his responsibility.

She shrugs. "Well, yeah. Norah's a single mom working two jobs. She's a receptionist at Granesville Middle School during the day, and she waits tables at Smiley's Pub three or four nights a week. Liam's with Brody and Keira a lot, but he doesn't mind helping out. His mom's amazing. She totally lives for her kids." The bell goes, and she starts backing away again. "But I guess most parents do, right? See you in English."

She disappears into a knot of people as I head toward pre-calc. *Most* parents. Exactly. I can't say that my parents live for me. With me, yes, but not for me.

As promised, Liam resurfaces at lunch, and the three of us meet Samantha and Ravi in the usual spot outside. Today, the bagels are blueberry flavor. I take one and sit next to Liam on the concrete steps. Kath is on his other side, so it's a tight fit. Not that I'm complaining.

"The corn maze at Milner Farm opens this weekend," Samantha says, leaning back against Ravi's chest. They only time I see them physically unattached is when Samantha is in chemistry class with me. "We should plan a day trip for Sunday."

Ravi wraps an arm around her waist. "Remember the time we went there on a school trip in second grade and Joey Culbertson got lost in the maze for an hour?"

Everyone laughs. I bite off another piece of bagel. Whenever one of them gets going on a *Remember the time* story—which happens at least once every lunch period—I'm not sure how to react. In some ways it feels alienating, but at the same time, I wish I shared all these memories too.

"I'm up for Milner Farm," Kath says, finishing the last of her bagel.

"Me too," Liam adds. "If everyone's okay with me slowing them down."

Kath leans across Liam's lap to look at me. "Avery?"

"But won't I have to cover for you at work?" I ask.

"I'll clear it with the parents. They're okay with us having a day off now and then so we can, you know, have a life outside of subs."

Liam grins at her. "There's a life outside of subs?"

She shoves his shoulder and gets up. "Come on, Ravi. Let's kick the soccer ball around."

Ravi's face lights up and he follows Kath to the field. I don't know Ravi all that well yet, but one thing I do know about him is his love for soccer. He plays on the school team. Samantha, on the other hand, seems more artsy. She takes drama and has apparently been in every high school play in the past four years, plus she does an improv class once a week. They're both pretty cool, and neither of them has breathed one word about my dad's dumb bridge. Damian hasn't either, not since Kath told him off, but he occasionally still glowers at me in class.

After a few minutes, Samantha wanders off toward the field too, leaving Liam and me alone on the steps. I furtively wipe my buttery fingers off on my jeans and run my tongue over my teeth, checking for blueberry gunk.

"The corn maze is always fun," Liam says. He leans back, propping his elbows on the stair behind us. His forearm brushes my side, leaving a path of tingles. "We go every year."

"I can possibly drive," I say, willing my voice to sound steady. All I can think about is the other night, sitting with him in the dark, the warmth of his breath on my face as he leaned in. "If my mom doesn't need her car that day."

"We usually go with Samantha. She has her own car." He sits up straight again until his shoulder is level with mine. We're not quite touching, but every inch of my body is aware of every inch of his.

"Oh," I say.

"But I'd rather go with you."

I glance over at him. He's staring at the ground, skin pink from his neck to his cheekbones. "Oh," I say again, softly this time.

"If you want," he adds.

I want. Oh God, do I want. But despite the waves of euphoria coursing through me, my stupid logical brain won't let me forget about the vow I'd taken months ago:

Never again. My heart can't handle a repeat of Noah Burnett. Liam is different than Noah, but I'm a different person now too, and if I'm as smart and jaded as I think I am, I wouldn't be setting myself up for more pain and disappointment.

"Or I can go with Sam," Liam says when I don't respond right away.

"No, it's just—I'm not sure if I can get my mom's car."

He nods, but I know by the way he's avoiding my gaze that I hesitated a touch too long. Damn it. This isn't good, either. I don't want him to think I don't like him, because I do. And I don't want to be the type of person who throws out mixed signals, but that's exactly how I feel. Mixed up.

The bell rings then, saving me. I make an excuse about needing to visit the bathroom before class and quickly escape through the doors.

By the time school ends, I'm bursting to talk to someone about whatever is going on between Liam and me. Get some perspective. Not Kath, of course, because she's Liam's best friend. Not my mom, either, because we don't really talk about boy stuff. Plus I'm still a bit pissed at her anyway. And I don't know anyone else here well enough to ask for advice on personal matters. In fact, there's only one person I can think of to ask, someone my age who knows me and has experience with relationships. Someone I've admittedly been neglecting lately.

Weldon is two hours behind us, so I wait until after dinner to text Mia. *You free for a video call? Need boy advice. 911.*

Her response comes immediately, as I suspected it would. "Boy advice" is Mia's bat signal. *Duh, of course.*

I settle on my bed with Hazel and my tablet and bring up my video chat app. Seconds later, Mia's wide grin and familiar blond curls fill the screen. A wave of homesickness hits me, but surprisingly, it's not as strong as usual.

"You look great," I say, because she does. Full makeup, glossy hair, cute top. Even lounging at home, Mia always looks put together.

"So do you." She leans to the side for a moment and I see the edge of her floral print curtains in the background. She's sitting on her bed too.

"So what's new?" I ask. Now that I'm looking at her, I feel guilty about soliciting advice after barely texting her for days. Like the only reason I'm contacting her is because I'm desperate to unload on someone. It's not exactly true—I *do* miss her—but I'm afraid she'll think I'm only using her for advice, even though she lives to give opinions. She runs a book review vlog in her spare time, recording her opinions on various books and uploading the videos to YouTube. She has over a hundred thousand subscribers.

"Not much," she says. "Just working on my reading wrap-up for September. Oh my God, is that Hazel?"

I tilt my tablet down so she can get a full view of Hazel, who's passed out cold next to me, paws twitching.

"Aww," Mia squeals. "I miss her. I miss *you*. Now tell me about the boy."

I laugh. So much for small talk. I've already filled her in on what happened at the intersection and my temp job at Sadler's Subs, so I go straight to the meat of it: "You know the guy I hit? Liam?"

"How could I forget? It's not every day I get a text from you telling me you hit someone with a car."

"True." I lean back on my pillows. "Anyway. We've been hanging out at school and stuff and I think...well, I like him."

Mia's eyes widen. "Really. And does he like you back?"

"Yeah. I mean, I'm pretty sure. Yeah."

"So..." She draws out the word. "What's the problem?"

I look down at Hazel, run a finger over her ear. "Noah."

"You still have feelings for Noah?"

"No." This, I'm sure of. Any love I had left for him disappeared when I saw his couples selfie with Makayla Cross.

"Oh," she says after a pause. "You're scared that what happened with Noah might happen with Liam?" When I don't deny it, she adds, "That's not a given, you know."

I raise my eyes to the screen again. Mia's watching me, a coil of hair twisted around her finger. "How isn't it? This time next year, I'll probably be back in Weldon and he'll be...somewhere else."

"Yeah, but next year is next year. Now is now."

"But what's the point in starting something that you know has no future? You saw what I was like after the break up with Noah. I was a mess. I can't go through that again. Letting yourself get attached to people when you know you'll have to leave them in a few months is just a form of self-torture."

Mia stares at me for a few moments, not speaking. Then she shakes her head slowly and says, "No offense, Avery, but moving every couple of years has clearly messed with your head."

I shrug. I'm not offended. Much like Kath, Mia tends to be brutally honest. I'm used to it. Besides, she's right.

"You're so afraid of getting close to people," she goes on. "Whenever someone tries to get past the wall you've built up, you panic and pull back. It took *months* for you to let your guard down around me, and that was only because you thought you were finished with moving."

I nod. She's right again. The only time I let people in, *truly* let them in, is when I believe they'll be in my life for the long haul. Which is why I rarely let people in.

"This thing with Liam—if it is a thing—doesn't have to be like it was with Noah, you know. It's possible to date people for fun and not fall in love with them. You don't *have* to get attached. You can just, I don't know, roll with it."

"Roll with it," I repeat, unconvinced. I'm more of a planner than a roller.

"Roll with it." She draws her hands together over her heart, the way Mom does during tree pose. "And see where it leads you."

That's the problem. I'm worried that it might lead me into the exact situation I'm hoping to avoid. But like my dad told me after the accident, avoiding something can be even worse than meeting it head on. Sometimes it's better to take the hit.

Chapter Fifteen

Kath and I are scrubbing down the sub shop after another hectic Friday evening shift when the door swings open, letting in a blast of cool air and two blond children. A blond woman follows closely behind, holding the door for Liam, who maneuvers smoothly inside. It takes me several seconds to recognize the woman—I saw her at the hospital the day I went to visit Liam. His mom.

"Hey!" Kath smiles at them as she wraps up the still-fresh veggies for the fridge.

"Sorry, I know you're about to close," Liam's mom says. "But Keira has a bit of a bathroom emergency and couldn't wait till we got home."

"I really, really, really need to pee," Keira adds. She's about seven or eight, with her mom's strawberry-blond hair and dusting of freckles.

"Of course, chickie," Kath says, gesturing toward the tiny bathroom in back. Keira bolts around the counter and heads to the back like she's been here a million times before.

"Is Linh here?" Liam's mom asks. Her accent makes everything she says sound interesting. "I want to say hello."

Kath nods and Liam's mom moves behind the counter too, carefully dodging the mop I'd been pushing around when they came in. She pauses and catches my eye. "You must be Avery, then," she says, her blue gaze taking me in. For a cold, horrifying moment, I think she's going to yell at me for what I did to her son. But she just smiles and says, "I'm Norah. It's nice to meet you."

"It's nice to meet you, too."

She moves on, and my body loosens in relief.

Kath finishes with the veggies and moves over to the drinks fridge. "Hey, Brody, you want a chocolate milk?" she asks Liam's brother, who's still lingering near the door. He appears to be about ten or eleven, his hair and coloring the same as his mom and sister. He looks up at Kath and blinks.

"Okay," he says, his tone just above a whisper.

When she hands him the bottle, he gives her a tiny, shy smile that's identical to Liam's. But this is the only similarity between them. His siblings' other features must come from their father, whoever he is.

"You guys want to grab a pizza?" Liam asks. His question is meant for both Kath and me, but he's looking at me. My body unravels even more. Since our conversation on the steps the other day, when I hesitated a beat too long about driving with him to the corn maze, things have been different between us, though I can't put my finger on how. We're more reserved, maybe. Like we've reversed back a month or so, when we were still feeling each other out. But him asking me—I mean, *us*—to go for pizza feels encouraging.

"Sure," Kath says.

I meet Liam's eyes across the counter, Mia's words echoing in my head. *Roll with it.* Okay, then. I guess now is a good time to start. But if I end up rolling off a cliff or something, I'm totally going to blame her. "I'm in."

He smiles, which makes me smile, which makes Kath's left eyebrow quirk up like it does when something amuses her. Does she find our awkward flirting entertaining? At least she's not glaring at me, like she used to do whenever I went near Liam. Coming from her, a raised eyebrow is almost like a blessing.

Liam's mother and sister emerge from the back, along with Mrs. Sadler. "You guys can go," Linh says to Kath and me. "I'll finish up here."

Kath wastes no time tearing off her apron. I put the mop back in its bucket and do the same. After saying goodbye to Liam's family—they *all* have chocolate milks now, courtesy of the owners—the three of us step out into the chilly night.

"Which one?" I ask once we're on the sidewalk. I peer down Center Street at the three pizza places, all within throwing distance of each other. This town is so odd.

"Which *one*?" Kath stops and gapes at me, stunned.

"There's *only* one," Liam says.

"But…" Confused, I point in the general direction of the pizza cluster.

Kath sighs like I've broken some sacred, unspoken rule. She holds up a hand and starts counting off on her fingers. "Pizza Ladies tastes like ketchup on a clipboard.

Matty's puts the pepperoni *under* the cheese and I'm sorry, that's just unacceptable." She holds up an index finger. "Primo is by far the least offensive of the three."

I commit this information to memory. I still have a lot to learn about the ins and outs of Granesville.

Primo Pizza's interior is small and utilitarian, with six circular wooden tables scattered along a faded tile floor. The menu above the cash is written in chalk, the specials displayed in different colors and surrounded by little drawings of tomatoes and mushrooms. My stomach growls. Everything smells amazing.

We decide on a large pepperoni with extra cheese, then claim the table by the window. Aside from two people waiting to order at the register, the place is deserted.

"Your brother and sister are really cute," I tell Liam. He's sitting to my right, with Kath on his other side, and every time his knee bumps mine, I liquefy. Soon, I'm going to be a giant puddle under the table.

"Yeah." He grins. "They barely take after me at all."

I want to tell him he's really cute too, in a different way, but I can't. At least not with Kath sitting right across from me. She probably wouldn't even notice, though. The second we sat down, she whipped out her phone and has been texting ever since, her face pinching up more with each ding of her cell.

"Kath," Liam says softly after a few minutes of this. "You promised."

She doesn't look up. "What?"

"You said you were going to stop doing this. Or at least try to stop. Fighting with her over text isn't going to solve anything."

Her thumbs pause on the screen and she throws him a quick, half-annoyed glance. "What, would you rather we fight over Zoom?"

"I'd rather you didn't fight at all, to be honest."

She meets his eyes, and they have a silent best-friend conversation that hovers in the tense air between them. I drop my gaze and stare hard at a scratch on the table, suddenly uneasy.

"Liam—" she begins, but another ding from her phone cuts her off. She glances down at the screen, and a few seconds later her eyes fill with tears.

"Kath?" Liam leans toward her, concerned.

She blinks, releasing the tears down her cheeks, and slowly stands up. Liam and I both watch, frozen, as she turns and dashes toward the bathrooms at the far end of the restaurant.

"Shit," Liam mutters as the ladies room door swings shut behind her. He reaches for his crutches and starts to get up.

"Uh, Liam," I say, touching his forearm. He turns to look at me, his face drawn with worry. "You probably shouldn't go into the women's bathroom."

He watches the door for a second, like he's willing Kath to emerge on her own. Then his expression clears and he sits back down. "Yeah, I guess you're right."

I look at his leg, jiggling nervously under the table, then at the rigid set of his shoulders. He's not going to sit still for very long.

"I'll go," I tell him. "Okay? Just wait here."

He nods, clearly relieved, and I get up and make my way to the ladies room.

The smell of cheap air freshener greets me as I push open the door. Kath is leaning against the single sink, a crumpled piece of toilet tissue in her hand. Surprise flickers across her face when she sees me, making me wonder if she was hoping for Liam instead.

"Are you okay?" I ask, inching further into the room. It's the size of a large closet, with two narrow stalls and a dim, buzzing ceiling light.

Kath dabs the tissue under her eyes and holds up her phone, shaking it a little. "She called me *needy*. Brooke. *I had no idea you were going to be this needy*. That's what she just texted me."

I wince. "Sorry."

"We're only three weeks into this and we're already starting to fall apart. The past couple of days have been like one nonstop argument. All I want is for her to make time for me, you know? Text me once in a while. Call me to say good night every night, like she promised before she left." She sniffles and turns around, bracing her hands on the edge of the sink. "Maybe that does make me needy, but I just…some reassurance would be nice."

She tosses the ragged toilet paper into the garbage, and I slip into a stall to get her some fresh squares.

"Maybe I'm not enough for her now," she says when I hand them to her. "Brooke's freaking amazing. She's talented and smart and ambitious and I'm…well, average. One day she'll be playing music in some concert hall in New York or somewhere and where will I be? Here, in Granesville, taking classes at the community college and working the family business. No wonder she's trying to distance herself from all this."

She gestures around us, but I know she's not referring to the drippy, stinky bathroom. She means here. This town. This life. Herself.

"I only met Brooke once," I say carefully. "But she seemed really into you. Maybe you guys just need some time to get used to being away from one another. And there's nothing wrong with community college and working," I add. "There's nothing wrong with *you*."

Kath leans into mirror and studies her blotchy reflection. After a moment, she sighs and turns to me. "Have you ever been in love?"

I think of Noah, the way my heart raced the first time he held my hand. "Yeah. Once." I decide to leave it at that; now is definitely the wrong time to tell her that our relationship started fizzling the moment we knew we'd have to say goodbye to each other.

"Well, you get it, then. The intensity of it, I mean. Like, Liam could call me needy and I'd probably get annoyed for a minute or two and then move on. But when it's Brooke? It feels like someone's stabbing me in the chest with a hot poker."

I nod. I do get it. When you're in love with someone, everything they say and do holds so much more weight. You're vulnerable. Exposed. Kath puts up a tough front, but the weak spot she has for Brooke is clearly seeping through.

"Liam doesn't really get it," she goes on, pitching her toilet paper in the trash. Her eyes are mostly dry now, so I don't bother getting her more. "He's never been in love. I mean, he dated a couple of girls last year, but neither of them lasted longer than a few weeks. He's got a lot on his plate and some girls don't seem to understand

140

that, so he's been kind of off the whole dating thing. Until now, anyway."

My stomach leaps into my throat. I have to swallow before I can produce sound. "Until now?"

Kath gives me a withering, oh-please-I-wasn't-born-yesterday look. "Just be good to him, okay? The last thing I want is for him to end up like me, crying in the bathroom of the only decent pizza joint in Granesville. Speaking of which…" She takes one last glimpse in the mirror and smooths down her hair. "Our pizza's probably ready. Let's get out of here."

Dazed, I follow her back out into the restaurant area. Liam's sitting exactly where I left him, only now there's a steaming pizza on the table in front of him, untouched. As we approach, his gaze stays locked on Kath.

"You okay?"

We take our seats again and Kath scoops up a slice. "No, but let's talk about it later. I'm starving."

Liam watches her for a moment, unsure, before reaching out to grab his own slice. I grab one too and immediately take a bite, but the taste barely registers. My entire focus has narrowed to two words, currently nestling themselves into a tiny corner inside me, warming me from the inside out.

Until now.

Chapter Sixteen

Mom has a full yoga schedule on Sunday, so I'm not able to get the car for our day trip to the corn maze. Samantha's Volkswagen isn't nearly big enough for all five of us plus Liam's crutches, so I figure either the trip will be postponed or they'll go without me. But at the last minute, Ravi convinces his mother to let him borrow her minivan for the day, and we're back on.

The weather is perfect—sunny and calm, with just enough chill in the air to require a sweater. I wait for everyone outside on the steps, half enjoying the early-autumn sun and half worrying that I've inadvertently horned in on their yearly corn maze tradition, and even though I was invited, they don't *really* want me along and they're only including me because I happened to be there when the subject was brought up.

My brain is an exhausting place sometimes.

I relax a little when the van pulls up to my house a few minutes after eleven, Ravi behind the wheel and Samantha in the passenger seat beside him. I slide open the door to see Liam in the middle seat, his back against the window and his booted leg stretched out in front of him. Kath's sitting in the way back, most of her face hidden behind giant sunglasses. Everyone smiles when they see me, and the last of my anxiety fades.

I step over Liam's crutches and slide in next to Kath. For once, she's not attached to her phone.

"I left it at home," she says when she catches me looking at her empty hands. I swear she can read my mind sometimes, or at least my expression. "Today is all about having fun and relaxing with my friends." She glances at Liam. "How was that?"

He nods, as if judging her performance. "Not bad. I give it a six out of ten."

She sticks her tongue out at him, but she's smiling at the same time, letting us know she's not really bothered by the prospect of a technology-free day. Maybe she even welcomes it.

Up front, Ravi flicks on the stereo, and we're off. After a bit of Google Maps research last night, I know that Milner Farm is an hour-and-fifteen-minute drive from Granesville, in a teensy town called Newcomb, directly off Exit 14. I couldn't find the population, but I'm sure it's in the low triple digits.

The drive goes by quick. When I'm not chatting with Kath and Liam about anything other than Brooke, I'm gazing out the window at the trees along the highway. The leaves are just starting to turn, their green speckled with various reds and oranges and yellows. When I'm not gazing at the trees, I'm secretly watching Liam, fascinated by the way the sun brings out the golden highlights in his hair. By the time we get to the farm, my fingers ache with the effort it took not to reach out and touch it.

"Ho-ly crap," Ravi says when we pull into the grassy parking area. "I guess everyone else in the world had the same idea."

The place is swarming with people. The line for the entrance snakes around a decorative pile of hay bales and pumpkins and out onto the dusty road. To the right of it is an open, grassy field, dotted with concession stands and playground equipment. To the left, tractors pull teeming wagons of families into the woods and to the apple orchards beyond.

"Is it always like this?" I ask as we join the herd of people moving toward the line-up. Ahead of us, a little girl drops her ice cream cone and starts wailing, prompting me to double check my bag for my migraine meds.

"Opening weekend, nice weather…" Samantha says with a shrug.

"Don't worry," Liam says, leaning his shoulder into mine. "I'm really good at clearing paths with these crutches."

Heat blooms at our point of contact and flows down my arm before spreading throughout the rest of my body. I catch my breath and smile, my mind replaying— for the millionth time—what Kath said in the Primo Pizza bathroom. Liam hasn't seemed interested in dating anyone *until now*. Until me. But why? Why am I the one to break his long dry spell? I'm not beautiful and outspoken, like Kath. I'm awkward and quiet and I sweat when I'm nervous and, oh yeah, there's also the fact that our first meeting involved me *hitting him with a car*. Maybe he only likes me because I'm new and didn't grow up beside him like every other girl his age in Granesville.

Maybe I should stop being so damn analytical all the time.

We finally reach the counter, where we pay admission and get our hands stamped with the Milner Farm logo. Then we head toward the various food stands—grilled burgers and hotdogs, fresh buttered popcorn, fresh buttered corn on the cob, ice cream. I'm not sure what to choose.

"Fill up now," Ravi advises before we all branch off to different lines. "Once you enter the maze, you might be wandering around in there for hours."

"We're not Joey Culbertson," Kath says, dodging a small boy as he toddles toward the sand box. "Remember last year? Brooke and I were the first ones out." Her mouth droops at the memory and the mention of Brooke.

"No, I think I was," Liam jumps in quickly, before her good mood plunges south. "I was really fast back when I had two working ankles."

Guilt tugs at my stomach; a Pavlovian response anytime Liam refers to his injury. I glance at Ravi and Samantha, looking for some sign that they know I'm the cause of it, but they're both happily oblivious as they wander over to the popcorn, hand in hand. Kath follows them, while Liam and I make a beeline for the grill.

"Hot dogs," he says with a hint of reverence.

"Yeah." I glance down at his leg. "Hey, it must be almost time for that to come off."

145

He follows my gaze, his expression slightly alarmed, and I mentally rewind my words. Oh God. He probably thinks I meant his actual leg. Or even worse, his pants.

"Your boot," I say firmly, my cheeks flaming. Why am I like this? "It's, um, been about six weeks."

"Oh. Yeah. I have an appointment for an x-ray on Wednesday afternoon to see if the bone healed properly. If it has, I can ditch the boot and start physical therapy to get my strength back."

We shift forward in line. "You know, I've never actually seen you *without* crutches and a boot. I mean, aside from those few minutes I saw you lying in the street."

"Sometimes I have a hard time remembering life before them." He lets go of his right crutch to scratch his jaw. "I do take the boot off at least once a day. Like to shower and stuff. But I feel so weird without it…off balance or something."

I know the feeling.

The grill line is the longest, so by the time we have our hotdogs, our friends are already seated around a recently-vacated picnic table. I sit next to Kath and peer across the field at the giant corn maze. To the right of the marked entrance is a row of bright red flags, rippling in the breeze.

"They're so the staff can find you," Kath explains before I can ask. "You take one with you and hold it up if you get lost. No one really takes them, though."

"Not unless you're a wuss," Ravi adds, digging a hand into a jumbo sized popcorn bag. "Rule number one: no flags."

"Jeez, Rav, dial back the competition beast mode," Samantha says, squeezing his arm affectionately. "This is just for fun."

He finishes his popcorn and jumps up. "Last one out of the maze fills the tank for the drive home."

I can't even imagine how much it costs to gas up a minivan, so I shove in the last of my hotdog and stand up too.

"Rule number two," Ravi says as the five of us enter the maze. "No cheating."

"We're not amateurs," Kath mutters from behind me.

I glance over at Liam. He's crutching along beside me, his gaze trained on the ground so he doesn't get tripped up by a random dead corn cob. The dry stalks rise above us on both sides, their leaves rustling like chimes. It's warm in here, a cozy, mud-scented fortress, protected from the autumn chill. "How do you cheat at corn maze?" I whisper. I've never done this before; I'm not sure if there's some sort of maze etiquette.

Liam smiles and glances back at Kath. "You squeeze through the stalks when you hit a dead end, like Kath did last year."

"Liam! I did *not*."

He laughs and keeps going. We stick close for a while, turning randomly at forks in the maze and occasionally pausing to let groups of people past. After one of these pauses, we lose Ravi and Samantha.

"Damn it," Kath says. "Ravi's going to be insufferable if he makes it out of here first."

I kick a cob out of our path. "Do you guys know any secret shortcuts?"

"No," Liam replies. "They grow the maze in a different shape every year."

I shiver. The path feels narrower now, like the stalks are closing in on us. Or maybe I'm just feeling claustrophobic. To distract myself, I search my brain for something interesting to ask Liam. Finally, I settle on, "So, you mentioned you were joining the military right after high school? You're not doing college first?"

"I'm joining the military because it *pays* for college," he says. "Well, there are other reasons too, of course, but that's a definite plus."

"Oh." That makes sense. For some reason, I've been picturing him on a battlefield, firing rounds at an approaching army. "What field are you going into?"

"I'm not a hundred percent sure yet. Probably something health related. Maybe social work." He brushes a leaf away from his face. "Something that requires a lot of travel."

"You *want* to travel all the time?" After all my moves, it's unfathomable to me that someone would *choose* to live that way.

"I've barely been out of Granesville, so yes. Seeing other parts of the world would be nice." He looks at me, eyebrows raised. "You don't like moving around a lot? I think it would be cool, starting fresh somewhere new every few years."

"It's not as fun as it sounds," I say, and leave it at that. I don't like to tell people how disheartening it is, constantly having to say goodbye to people. And how lonely it feels, always being the new girl. Whenever I do mention it to someone, it feels like I'm complaining. A lot of people would kill for the opportunity to travel the world. People like Liam, apparently.

"Um…" He stops suddenly and turns around. "Where's Kath?"

I turn around too, but all I see are shriveled stalks and a middle-aged man with a baby strapped to his back. No Kath.

"She probably saw Sam and Ravi and went to catch up to them," I say. It's a more logical explanation than what my imagination is telling me—that she got dragged away by creepy people who live in the corn. Isn't there a horror movie about that?

"Oh man." Liam starts moving again, faster this time, making long, smooth strides with his crutches. "I bet they formed an alliance. They did that the year before last. Kath and Ravi and Sam teamed up against me because the last one out of the maze had to steal a pumpkin from the pumpkin patch and they wanted to see if I'd actually do it."

"Did you?"

He grins. "Yes. I picked the smallest one and hid it inside my shirt."

We arrive at another crossroads and I look around, trying to get our bearings. "Well," I say, grinning back at him. "Let's make sure you don't come in last this time."

We turn left, then left again, until I'm pretty sure we've traveled in a complete circle. But without any landmarks to guide the way—just more rows of dry, dead stalks—we're not sure how far we've actually gone or if we're anywhere close to the exit. At one point, I think I see a flash of Samantha's white jacket through the branches, but it's gone by the time we turn the corner.

"I think we're going to be paying for gas," I say after several more minutes of aimless wandering.

"Don't be so sure." He nods toward a small clearing ahead. In the middle of it is a giant map of the maze, an arrow pointing to our current location. We're smack dab in the middle. Liam traces the correct path with one finger, like he's working out one of those maze games on the back of a cereal box. "Got it now," he says, heading right.

I'm completely disoriented at this point, so I just go along with him as he leads us to…another dead end. He comes to a halt and looks around, utterly baffled. I start to laugh.

"I've never been very good with directions," he says, turning toward me. As he does, the tip of his left crutch catches in the grass, causing him to wobble. I grab onto his forearms to steady him, unconsciously pulling him toward me in the process.

Neither of us moves. A patch of clouds passes over the sun, enveloping our little corner in shadows. But it's not so dim that I can't make out Liam's face, slowly inching closer. I swallow and shut my eyes.

This time, there are no interruptions. He touches his lips to mine, gently at first, and then not so gently. Everything falls away—the maze, the people, the world—and I thread my fingers through the back of his hair, like I fantasized about doing in the van. His arms slide around my waist, and I'm vaguely aware of the sound of his crutches falling, two dull thumps in the grass. Then he presses me tight against him, and I'm pulled under again.

Minutes or hours later, we resurface to the sound of footsteps. I detach myself from Liam and turn toward the source. A tiny girl with pigtails and pink rain boots stands a few feet away, watching us in stunned fascination. Our surroundings slip back into focus and I quickly drop my arms and step away from Liam, who looks as dazed as I feel. How long has this kid been standing here? How long have *we* been standing here?

"Hannah!" a woman's voice calls from somewhere in the stalks. The little girl turns and sprints away, disappearing around the corner.

Liam lets out a breath and peers down at his crutches, like he's not sure how they ended up on the ground. I lean over to gather them up, glad for the few extra seconds to compose myself. When I hand them to him, our eyes meet and we both burst out laughing.

"I think we just traumatized a child," I say as we start walking again, this time in the opposite direction.

He looks at me, his steel-gray gaze moving from my eyes to my lips. "Totally worth it."

Somehow, we manage to make all the right turns and find our way out in under ten minutes. But it's not quick enough for the three-person alliance, who are already standing outside the exit, waiting for us.

"An hour and twenty-three minutes." Ravi holds up his phone so we can see the timer he'd set. "A new personal low, Liam, buddy."

Samantha rolls her eyes at him while Kath studies us, eyebrow raised as she takes in our flushed faces and Liam's rumpled hair.

"I guess the bad ankle really slowed you guys down, huh?" she says with a smirk. We ignore her, and Ravi's timer too. Like Sam said earlier, the maze race was just for fun. And like Mia said a few days ago, when it comes to Liam and me, fun is all it has to be. *Roll with it.*

It costs us thirty bucks each to fill the van, but neither of us minds in the least. Totally worth it.

Chapter Seventeen

I wake up the next morning to a barrage of texts from Mia, all sent late last night after I'd gone to sleep:

How's it going with hit-and-run boy?

Any progress?

Please tell me you made a move.

Avery! Wake up!

Squinting down at the screen, I type *It was NOT a hit-and-run, WTF?* Immediately after that, I add *And yes, I did*, followed by several kissing emojis.

A few seconds later, Mia responds with a long line of exclamation marks. *Proud of you, roller girl.*

I smile and flop back on my pillows. Mia and I have spoken more in the past few days than we have since I left. All it took was me developing a crush on a boy.

I stay in bed until the last possible minute, yesterday's moments with Liam in the corn maze replaying on a constant loop in my brain. When my alarm beeps for the fourth time, I drag myself into the shower and then out to the kitchen for breakfast.

Dad's sitting at the kitchen island, spooning cereal into his mouth and staring at his laptop screen. He glances up when I open the fridge. "Morning."

Yawning, I grab the carton of orange juice. "Where's Mom?"

"Teaching an early hot yoga class."

I pour my juice and lean against the island, opposite him. "Going in late today?" I ask. He's in his running clothes and his hair is damp, which tells me he just got back from his morning run. Usually, he's showered and tucked away in his trailer office at the construction site by now.

He takes another bite of cereal, a sugary kind that Mom buys for me but he usually eats most of. *I'll run it off*, he says whenever Mom catches him eating it, and then he'll pat his flat stomach for proof. "Took the morning off," he replies. "I'm meeting with a reporter from the Granesville Weekly at ten."

"The local newspaper? Why?"

He places his empty bowl on the counter. "They're doing an article about the bridge and the controversy it's caused around town. They want a quote from me, and a picture."

An article. Granesville must be really hungry for news. I take a slice of bread from the bag on the counter and pop it in the toaster. "What are you going to say?"

"The same thing I always say—that we have to go where the work is. And that I'm just doing my job and didn't deliberately set out to jeopardize people's livelihoods."

I think of that guy Damian from school, who still gives me dirty looks, though they've died down since

Kath switched seats in English to the one next to me. She's like a human mirror, deflecting his glare. But I'm sure whatever Dad says in the article isn't going to do much to improve his family's view on mine.

"I hope this doesn't make things worse," I mumble as my toast pops.

"At least they're asking for both sides of the story," Dad says, getting up to rinse his bowl. "Besides, we can handle any backlash. We're only here for a year. Even less than a year, maybe." He glances over his shoulder at me as he loads his dishes into the dishwasher. "Your mother and I weren't going to mention this to you until we knew for sure, but I just got a lead on a job proposal. Design starts next fall, but if everything stays on track, we'll be finished here in July or August and we can move right after."

I swallow a bite of toast and eye him warily. "Move where?"

He shuts the dishwasher and turns to face me, his brown eyes shining. "Finland. MRT has a branch there, and they might want me to go and work with the new Chief Designer and oversee placement and construction."

"Finland," I repeat dully.

"I know. Cool, right? You've never lived overseas."

I swallow again, the acid from the orange juice burning the back of my throat. "I'm not going to Finland," I say, finishing my toast. "I told you. I'm applying early to Eckert in November, and if I get in, that's where I'm going."

A flicker of surprise crosses his face. Despite my minor rebellion over the past few weeks, he's still not used to the Avery who pushes back.

"You guys can go," I add, shrugging. I'm amazed at how calm I sound, how strong and sure, despite the slightly shaking fingers on my orange juice glass. "I know you both want to. But traveling the world is your thing, not mine. I can't tag along with you forever, right?"

Dad's expression hardens and he turns away, busying himself with putting the cereal box and cartons away. "You know, Avery," he says with forced breeziness. "It almost sounds like you can't wait to be rid of us."

I almost laugh, because that's exactly the way I've always felt about them. My parents, a team of two, with me on the sidelines.

But I don't laugh. Or cry. Instead, I grab my backpack and swing it over my shoulder. "I'm gonna be late for school," I say, and head for the front door.

I expect to see Liam at the lockers when I arrive at school two minutes before the bell, but he's not there. He doesn't show up to first period pre-calc either, the second class he's missed since school began less than a month ago. I consider texting him, but immediately scratch the idea when I realize how girlfriend-ish it would be. And kissing him once doesn't make me his girlfriend. Which is fine. I was so eager and proud to be Noah's girlfriend, and look how that turned out.

After math, I head directly upstairs to English and spot Kath's black hair in the crowd. I catch up to her outside the classroom door.

"I hear we have a substitute," she says as we walk into class together. "Which means we'll probably have to work for once."

She's right; just as we sit down, a pretty blond woman enters the room and deposits her purse on Dyson's desk. She smiles at us, all perky and bright. When she turns to look through some papers, I lean into Kath and—the picture of indifference—I ask, "Where's Liam? He wasn't in pre-calc."

She shrugs. "I don't know. He didn't text me. Something probably came up with Keira or Brody."

"Oh." I tap my pen on the table. "Does he usually miss a lot of school?"

When Kath looks at me, I see traces of the stony glare she'd given me my first few weeks here. "I'm not here to dish about his attendance habits. Why don't you ask him?"

Heat floods my face and I drop my gaze to the table. She's right again; I shouldn't be probing her for info. Kissing him doesn't make him my business, either. "Sorry," I say.

She's quiet for a moment, then lets out a sigh. "No, I'm sorry. I was up half the night texting Brooke, and Bitchy Kath likes to come out when I'm tired. I know you mean well."

Relieved, I give her a tiny smile. "I kind of like Bitchy Kath."

On cue, we both glance over at Damian, Son of Satan. He's too busy ogling the sub to notice. I wonder if his father is meeting the same reporter from Granesville Weekly today, or if he already has. I can only imagine what *his* quote will be.

The morning stretches into lunchtime, and Liam still hasn't shown up. I linger at my locker, half waiting for him and half still thinking about Damian's dad. And the bridge. And how it'll be finished by summer whether the locals like it or not. And how, after it's finished, my parents are likely heading to Finland without me.

Finland. An entire ocean away. Too far to allow for frequent visits once I'm settled in Weldon for four-plus years. The thought of not seeing my parents for months on end, maybe even years, gives me an achy hollow feeling. We've never been exactly close, but I've been with them, a participant in all these moves and adventures, since I was a bump under my mother's shirt. They're my parents. As much as I want to blaze my own path, I need them. And a tiny part of me was hoping that they'd follow *me* this time, suppress their wanderlust for a few years and stick close to their only child, like I stuck close to them all my life.

But I guess some opportunities are too exciting to pass up.

"Hey."

I startle and whirl around. Liam's standing right beside me, his head edging around my open locker door. I must have been really out of it if he managed to sneak up on me in crutches.

"Hey," I respond, shutting my locker. As I do, my nostrils catch the scent of his soap or shampoo or whatever it is that makes him smell faintly citrusy, and yesterday in the corn maze rushes over me again. "Did you just get here?" I ask, trying not to stare at his lips.

"Yeah. Brody has a stomach bug so I stayed with him until our neighbor got there." His brow furrows as he studies my face. "Are you okay? You look sad."

Well, my parents are ditching me for a cool Finnish adventure and I can't decide whether I want to cry or punch them both in the face. "I'm fine," I say, forcing a smile.

His life isn't my business, and mine isn't his. The trick to remaining unattached to someone is to not delve too deeply into their family and personal lives. I knew way too much about Noah's—like how bitter he felt over his parents' divorce, and how hard he struggled with anxiety, and how he dreamed of becoming an astronomer because he was fascinated with anything galaxy-related. Each chunk of knowledge brought us closer, and I regretted that closeness at the end. Saying goodbye to him would have been much less devastating if I'd kept him at a distance.

I won't make that mistake again. Obviously I can't close myself off to people completely, but this time around, I'm going to be more careful.

"You sure?" Liam asks, unconvinced. "So… yesterday in the maze…you're not, uh, upset about…?

"No," I say, smiling for real. He's really cute when he's stammering. "I liked yesterday in the maze."

"Oh, good. Me too." Pink blotches form on his cheeks and he shifts forward on his crutches, closer to me. "So…my mom took pity on me and offered to pay to fix my truck. It'll be ready this evening. Did you want to go for a drive? I mean, not tonight, because I'm watching the rugrats while my mom's at work. Tomorrow after school?"

I shake my head. "Linh switched my shift to tomorrow. I work at four."

"Damn. Wednesday, then?" He shuts his eyes for a second and frowns. "Oh, shit. My x-ray appointment is Wednesday at three-forty-five. I'm sorry. This went a lot better in my head."

I laugh. "How about I go with you to your appointment, and then we can go for a drive?"

He shifts again, and his boot swings into the bottom locker, making a dull clunking sound. We pretend not to notice. "You want to go with me to my appointment?"

"Well, I was there at the start. May as well be there at the end too."

He nods and smiles, pleased with this. "*Hopefully* it'll be the end. For the boot, I mean."

I smile back at him and try not to think about *our* end, and how it'll arrive in a blink, like dreaded occasions tend to do. The irony of us making out in a literal dead end yesterday is not lost on me.

"Wednesday after school, then." Liam says as he backtracks to his own locker. "Don't eat too many bagels at lunch that day, because there's this place I want to take you."

A mystery location with food. Color me intrigued. "Wednesday after school," I confirm. It's hard to envision the end of something when it's only just getting started.

Chapter Eighteen

When Wednesday arrives, Liam and I meet at our lockers before heading outside to his truck, which is definitely the oldest vehicle in the parking lot. I stare at the flaking gray paint as we walk toward it.

"It actually runs pretty well for a truck that's several years older than us," Liam says with a trace of pride as he stashes his crutches in the back.

I grab the passenger door handle and pull, but nothing happens. I pull again, harder, and the door creaks open. "You must have gotten a good deal on it."

"Oh, I didn't buy it." He braces his hand on the seat and boosts himself up. "It used to belong to my stepfather."

"I didn't know you had a stepfather," I say, settling into the worn passenger seat.

"Well, I don't, anymore. My mom divorced him about six years ago, when she found out he hawked all her grandmother's jewelry to fund his secret OxyContin habit."

I gape at him. "Jesus."

161

"Yeah." He turns the key, and the truck wheezes a few times before rumbling to life. "He moved away after the divorce, and the last we heard, he still hasn't cleaned himself up. He calls to talk to Brody and Keira sometimes, but they barely even remember him. Which is a good thing, I guess." He lets out a breath and looks over at me, his lips turning up slightly. "Anyway, he left this truck behind when he moved, and instead of selling it like she should have, my mom decided to save it for me."

I smile and look around the faded, dusty interior, which smells like a combination of motor oil and old coffee. This conversation definitely falls under the "deep personal life confessions" category, so I lighten the mood with, "I'm jealous that you have your own wheels."

"Beats walking." He taps his boot with his knuckles. "Especially in this."

This reminds me of where we're going, and I glance at the time on the dash. "Isn't your x-ray in ten minutes?"

He looks at the clock too. "Oh, shit."

Liam's appointment is at the hospital, and I get a sense of déjà vu when we pull into the parking lot. The last time I was here, I was visiting him. And getting ripped into for breaking his ankle and ruining his plans. I never thought I'd be back here so soon, especially not with him.

"Should I wait out here, or…?"

Liam kills the engine, and my ears ring in the sudden quiet. "I might be a while," he says. "You may as well come in."

We take the elevator up to X-Ray. Liam checks in while I take a seat in the waiting room across from a middle-aged woman with a wrist brace. Liam joins me a few minutes later, but he's barely seated for two minutes when an x-ray technician calls his name. I watch as he follows her down the hallway, hoping that when he returns, he'll be healed and boot-free.

But today isn't the day. When he reappears in the waiting room a while later, his lower leg is still encased in the boot.

"Two more weeks," he reports when I get up to meet him. His expression wavers between resigned and bitterly disappointed. "The bones are knitting well, but it needs a little more time. Just to be on the safe side."

"The safe side sucks." I touch his arm in commiseration.

He glances down at my hand, pale against the sleeve of his black sweatshirt, and his frown disappears. His gaze rises to meet mine. "Let's get out of here."

At first I think he's taking me to one of the few eateries on Center Street. But he turns the truck in the opposite direction, toward Waterview Drive and the lake.

"Where are we going?" I ask as we drive past the motel—my first Granesville home—and the truck picks up speed.

"You'll see."

As we pass by the site of the new bridge construction, I peer out the window to check on its progress. But all that's visible from the road is the glint of bulldozers and excavators through the trees. I'm just glad there are no protesters. The article was published yesterday, online and in print, and features a full color picture of Dad, wearing his royal blue MRT Engineering jacket and smiling. The online comments section has been a trashfire ever since. I stopped reading them after I came across a commenter with the username *AConcernedCitizen*, who referred to my father as "that greedy, soul-eating bridge troll."

My parents and I may be at odds lately, over college and Finland and whatever else, but that doesn't mean I don't fantasize about tracking down *AConcernedCitizen* and kicking them in the kneecaps.

"Almost there," Liam says, snapping me out of my violent daydreams.

I focus on the road, which is getting increasingly twisty. After another five minutes or so, the trees start to thin, giving us an unobstructed view of the glimmering lake and McMahon's Island in the distance. And halfway between the island and mainland—where we're currently driving—I see the ferry.

"We're going across?" I ask when he heads toward the small lineup of vehicles waiting to board at the dock area.

"The place I'm taking you to is over there, so yeah." He shoots me a smile as we join the other cars. The ferry, which is smaller than I thought it would be, is gliding toward us at a leisurely clip. I can see why a bridge would be more efficient. "You haven't gone across yet?"

I shake my head. "What's even over there? Besides the campground and"—I crane my neck and squint—"is that a church?"

"There's a lot more to it than what you can see from here. For an island, it's actually pretty big."

The cars in front of us start inching forward. Liam shifts into drive while I whip out my phone and Google McMahon's Island. "Wow. It has a population of 25,000."

Liam's focused on getting the truck safely onto the ferry. "Huh?"

"I like knowing populations and statistics."

He leans toward me, and for a second I think he's going to start kissing me and my pulse speeds up, but he's only reaching for the glove compartment. He pulls out what looks like those ribbons of small tickets you get from arcade games, and rips one off before returning the ribbon to the compartment. As he does this, a man appears outside his window, and Liam hands the ticket to him. Oh. In order to cross, people pay with pre-bought tickets.

The ferry takes ten minutes to traverse the lake. I want to get out and look over the edge, but the cars are packed in tight. I wonder if Damian's father is on here with us right now, and what he'd do if he knew who I was. Probably throw me overboard.

The ferry stops and lowers its ramp, and suddenly we're driving onto the island. It *is* a church that I saw from the mainland, a white-shingled little building topped with a silver cross, looking out over the lake. We get on another two-lane road and drive for several more minutes, passing gas stations and garages and more churches, until we come to a little clearing at the side of the road. A bright red van catches my eye. No, not a van, a food truck. *Maryanne's Ol' School Donuts* is painted across the side in bold, blocky lettering.

"Donuts," I say as Liam parks the truck in a small gravel parking lot to the left of the picnic tables. "You brought me across an entire lake for donuts."

He nods and opens his door. "You'll see why in a few minutes."

The overwhelming scents of sugar and fried dough greet me as I step out of the truck. Liam grabs his crutches from the back and we make our way to the donut van. Beside the order window is a sign listing all the available flavors.

"Liam," I say, my voice an awed whisper. "They have bacon donuts."

He laughs. "And they're as amazing as they sound."

After a brief internal debate, I decide on the bacon flavor and Liam opts for Peanut Butter Cup. Instead of one donut, I get ten mini donuts, piled in a checkered-paper lined box and drizzled with maple sauce and bits of bacon. Liam's has peanut butter sauce and bits of chocolate. I'm beginning to realize why he brought me all the way here.

It's a beautiful day, sunny and warm, so we sit at one of the weathered picnic tables. I break off a piece of donut with my wooden fork and pop it in my mouth. It immediately melts on my tongue, and I have to stop myself from moaning.

"Right?" Liam says, smiling at my delight.

The gooey, messy donuts require all our concentration for the next several minutes. When mine are gone, I slouch against the table top, slightly nauseated but content. "Thanks for bringing me here."

He scrapes his fork through the stuck-on peanut butter sauce on the bottom of the container. "I thought you might want to get out of Granesville for a while. I know I did."

I nudge his booted foot with mine. "It's not that bad, you know. Granesville. I mean, I prefer cities, but I've definitely lived in worse places than there."

"I've only ever lived there, so I have nothing to compare it to." He looks away, up at the sky. "Are you going to stick around, then? After the bridge is finished?"

I sit up straight and open one of the bottles of water we'd gotten along with the donuts. All that goo has made me thirsty. "No," I say, taking a drink. "I'm probably going back to Weldon for college."

He looks at me. In the waning sun, his eyes are stainless-steal silver. "The place you lived before here?" When I nod, he averts his gaze again, this time downward, at the splintery table between us. "Oh."

My heart thumps. There was definitely some disappointment in that *Oh*. His reaction makes me wonder where exactly his head's at in all this. I think about his behavior over the past few days, since we kissed—waiting for me at my locker, walking me to my classes, smiling at me in pre-calc, saving me the seat next to him on the steps at lunch. And today, ferrying me to an island just to buy me special donuts he knew I'd like.

Oh crap. Is he starting to get attached?

"Liam," I begin, unsure what to say. I decide on the truth. "You know I, um…you know I'm not looking for anything serious, right? Because I went through a bad break-up a few months ago, and I don't want—"

"I'm not, either," he cuts in quickly. "Looking for anything serious, I mean. I tried before, twice, and it didn't work out. I take care of Brody and Keira three or four nights a week. When I'm not with them, I'm working. Or I will be, when I take my job back. And when I'm not working or babysitting the kids, I'm studying. Not much time left over to devote to a serious relationship."

I nod, relieved. Maybe he's not getting attached. Maybe he just really wanted these donuts.

"But this doesn't mean I want to stop hanging out with you," I say, picking at the label on my bottle. "I just…I want to be upfront with you about how I feel."

"And I feel the same. I still want to hang out with you too, even if it's only for a few months. Besides, nothing lasts forever, right?" He smiles. "Unless you're Linh and Doug, I guess."

Or my parents. But I don't want to think about them and their secure, infinite future together without me. I pick at my bottle label again, peeling it off the plastic. As I do, the stamped-on expiration date catches my eye. *Nothing lasts forever.*

A bizarre idea hits me.

"An expiration date," I say, looking up at Liam.

"What?"

"This. Us. Maybe we need an expiration date. And when it comes, we just end it. No more kissing, no more…" I wave my hand back and forth between us, indicating this donut tryst we're currently on. "We'll go back to being friends, and no one gets hurt."

Liam stares at me, completely bewildered. "I'm not sure I'm following."

I push my water to the side and lean toward him. "Let's look at this logically. A fixed end date would totally take the pressure off. Say we decided on, I don't know, October thirty first, for example. Halloween. We're together for a while, and when Halloween comes, we just…stop."

He's nodding slowly. "I get it now. Like a dating deadline."

"Right. Exactly. That'll keep things from getting too serious, and it can just be, you know, fun. No pressure, no expectations."

He turns to the side and props his booted leg up on the seat in front of him. "That could work. Not sure I'm on board with October thirty-first, though. That's only a month away. Like, what would be the point? How about sometime next Spring instead?"

I laugh. "But we're going to need a few months to get over each other before we have to say goodbye forever, right? Spring doesn't give us much time."

"True." He drums his fingers on the table, deep in thought. "How about February fifteenth? Give me Valentine's Day, at least."

I shake my head. A far-away end date means more time to become close. "November thirtieth."

"January thirty-first," he counters.

"December fifteenth."

"*January* fifteenth."

I'm having flashbacks of our paycheck negotiation. "December thirty-first. Start the new year with a fresh slate."

He considers this for a moment, then nods. "Okay. Deal. December thirty-first."

"Okay." I lean back, pleased. I wasn't sure if he'd actually agree to this—a lot of people wouldn't—but Liam is like me in this way. Practical. Logical. Able to make decisions with the brain, instead of with the heart. Even decisions about dating. And after Noah, I'm totally fine with letting my brain take the lead this time.

"Where I come from, deals are sealed with a handshake," Liam says, raising his brows.

I hold out my arm, but he shakes his head and motions for me to come around to his side of the table. When I do, he stands up, drawing closer toward me until there's barely enough room between us for air, let alone a handshake. So we seal the deal with a sweet, sticky kiss instead.

Chapter Nineteen

I'm lazing in my room on Saturday night when a knock sounds on the door. A few seconds later, my mother pokes her head in.

"You're not still reading those comments, are you?" she asks, seeing the tablet in my hands.

"No." I press pause on what I'm really doing, which is watching *Supernatural*, and look at her. "Why, are there more?"

The bridge controversy article is four days old now, and has since been eclipsed by a bigger story—the upcoming Granesville Annual Pumpkin Festival. Samantha's mom is one of the organizers, and apparently it's a big deal in this town.

Mom waves a hand to dismiss my question and steps into my room. I put down my tablet and sit up. The too-bright expression on her face tells me that she's about to say something I don't want to hear.

"How's everything going?" she asks in her usual perky way. "I'm surprised you're even home right now. I thought you'd be out with your friends on a Saturday night."

I know what this is. Small talk to soften whatever's coming. "They're busy," I say warily. It's true—Kath's working, and Liam's watching his siblings tonight. Mom knows I've been spending time with Liam, but she doesn't know about the kissing. There hasn't been any more of it since the donuts—between school, work, and Liam's babysitting schedule, we've barely seen each other this week, let alone made out—so there's not much to tell, anyway.

"I see." She crosses her muscled arms over her chest. Even in loose pajama pants and a T-shirt, she looks ready to slip into downward facing dog at any moment. "Anyway, your dad and I are thrilled that you've made some nice friends here."

I shrug. "Just making the best of things while we're here, like you always say."

She smiles, but like the rest of her face, it's like an overexposed photograph. She hesitates for a moment, then uncrosses her arms and perches herself at the foot of my bed. Time for the main feature.

"So. I was just doing some internet research, and I found out a couple of very interesting things," she begins, still smiling. "Did you know that Finland has some of the best universities in the entire world?"

I squeeze my eyes shut for a second and sigh. "Mom."

"All I'm saying is, if we decide to move there—if *we all* decide to move there—you'd get a top quality education. And there are a lot of science-based universities to choose from." She nods to my tablet. "Did you even Google it?"

I glance at my tablet too. The screen is frozen on a close up of Dean Winchester's beautiful face—an excellent distraction from my mounting rage. "No," I say with measured patience. "I didn't Google it, because I'm not going to college in Finland. I don't know how many times I have to say it."

"We should at least *discuss* this, Avery. We're not even sure we're going yet and you've already made up your mind."

"Of course you're going. You've been talking for weeks about how you want to move to Europe next. You've just been waiting for me to graduate so you and Dad can start traveling the world again, like you did before you had me."

Her sunny expression falters, and she blinks at me like I've deliberately betrayed her. "Yes, we want to travel, but we want to travel with *you*. We're a family, and families should stick together."

Her words should be comforting, but for some reason, they feel kind of hollow. To me, it seems like they've spent the last seventeen years counting the days until they could be free of parental responsibility. "Really?" I say, leaning back against my pillows. "If you believe that, then why did you and Dad leave Boston and your families the second you finished college and haven't looked back since?"

Mom opens her mouth, then closes it, her body perfectly straight and still on the bed. "That was different. I've told you about my parents, how suffocating they were. They barely let me go anywhere or do anything. They tried to convince me to stay at home forever, but I didn't want that. I wanted to experience the world, not settle in one place for the rest of my life."

"Well, I *do* want that. To settle in one place." I swallow and shift my focus to a loose thread on the hem of my shirt, wrap it around my index finger. "People always ask me where I'm from, and I don't even know how to answer them, because I'm not from anywhere. I don't have a hometown filled with family and old friends that I can go back to and visit. The only place that felt even remotely like that was Weldon, but then we had to leave there too, so it wasn't really my home either. But I want it to be."

Mom doesn't respond for several moments. When I glance up at her, she's running her palm over her pajama pants, smoothing out the wrinkles.

"You know, Avery," she says, finally, "home isn't always a place. Home can mean a person too. Or people. Your father—and you—have always been *my* home." She stands up and looks down at me, not quite meeting my eyes. "I'm heading to bed now. Good night."

"Good night," I say, a lump forming in my throat as she slips out the door and closes it gently behind her.

I always thought it would feel good, finally telling my parents how I feel and what I want for my future, but so far, all I've felt is guilty.

Lately, Sadler's has been sort of a peaceful reprieve from the pressures at home. But when I arrive for my shift the next day, the onion-scented air is thick with tension and

Mr. Sadler is pacing the tiny space, his face the same shade as the ripe batch of tomatoes sitting next to the rotary slicer.

I sidle up to Kath, who's restocking the drinks fridge. "What's going on?" I whisper. Mr. Sadler paces his way into the office, and a few seconds later, a loud, clattering noise filters out into the prep area, followed by muttered cursing. It sounds like he dropped a cup filled with pens.

"Isaac," Kath says dully, like that explains everything. She grabs a can of Coke from the box next to her and places it in the fridge. "He was supposed to order more bread the other day, and he forgot. So we only have one flat of buns for the entire day, which obviously won't be enough. And the bakery is closed today, so we're screwed. It'll be wraps or nothing."

Mr. Sadler suddenly reappears, his gaze trained on his cell phone. "The kid just doesn't *think*," he growls to no one in particular before disappearing into the office once again.

"Where's Isaac now?" I ask, handing Kath two more cans. "Hiding?" I certainly wouldn't want to be on the receiving end of Mr. Sadler's thundering, red-faced fury.

"At home. Probably still sleeping off his hangover." She shakes her head and peers toward the office. "Just watch. Any second now he's going to come out here and—"

Before she can finish her sentence, her father comes out and says, "Katherine, why didn't you double check the bread order? You know how easily distracted your brother can be."

Kath blinks, unperturbed. "Hey, don't pin this on me," she says without looking up from her task. "I'm not Isaac's keeper. If he can't handle his responsibilities, then maybe you shouldn't give him any."

I bend down to get the last of the cans, studiously avoiding looking at either of them. If I said that to my dad, he'd probably reprimand me for talking back. But Kath's dad just sighs heavily and retreats to the office again without comment. I let out a breath.

"Told you," Kath says, standing up and shutting the fridge. "They're way too soft on him. No wonder he doesn't bother to try."

I'm starting to see the benefits to being an only child. "It's not fair to blame you, though," I say, low enough that Mr. Sadler doesn't hear.

"I'm used to it. I *am* the responsible child, after all. The one they're banking on to take over the business one day. Which is why I practically live here while Isaac wastes his life partying and sleeping in." She breaks down the box and folds it flat. "But someone has to step up, right?"

She doesn't sound sad or bitter about it—only matter-of-fact. Like this is her destiny, and she's accepted it because it's all she's ever known. "You don't *have* to give in to your parents' expectations, you know," I say, one eye on the office door. "It's your life."

"Exactly." She moves over to the bread racks and runs her fingers along the packages of tortillas, silently taking stock. "This is my life."

With practiced ease, she turns, picks up a knife, and starts cutting the tomatoes in thick, symmetrical slices. Watching her, I can easily picture her standing in the same spot a couple of decades from now, when this place is hers. Maybe some people *are* meant to follow their parents' paths.

By the time the lunch rush dies down at around one-thirty (most people didn't seem to mind the lack of sub buns), Mr. Sadler's anger has died down too. He thanks us for our proficiency and gives Kath a kiss on the forehead before he retires to the office again.

"Brooke calls that his 'grizzly to teddy mode'," Kath says, half-smiling as she wipes down the counter. "One minute he'll be angry and intimidating, and the next he'll be soft and harmless."

I smile at the aptness of this description. "How's it going with her, anyway? Brooke?" Kath hasn't mentioned her much lately—only that they've been texting a lot, which I take as a good sign.

"Okay, I guess." She grabs a fresh cloth and helps me scrub the prep area. "I mean, neither of us want to fight, so we've just been sort of pretending that we're not six hundred miles away from each other and things are the same as always. She says she's looking forward to coming home in December, so…" She trails off with a shrug.

"That's good news."

"Yeah. Hey, speaking of news…" Her left eyebrow goes up, and I brace myself for what I know is coming. "You and Liam."

Knew it. I shake lettuce bits off my cloth, avoiding her gaze. "What about me and Liam?"

She glances at the door, checking for approaching customers, then turns back to me. "A dating deadline, Avery? Really?"

Heat prickles up my neck. Mia said those exact same words, in that exact same dubious tone, while we were FaceTiming the other day. She also said *When I told you to roll with it, I didn't mean toward a brick wall.* "He told you?"

"We're best friends. We tell each other everything."

Now my entire face is on fire. What else has he told her? Does she know the specifics about our first kiss in the corn maze? Does she know about the entire donut date, including the short make out session in Liam's truck during our ferry trip back to the mainland? Exactly how detailed is "everything"?

"How's that supposed to work?" she goes on, folding her arms across her chest. "So the end of December hits and you're both supposed to turn off your feelings like a light switch?"

I don't want to tell her that the whole point—for me, at least—is to *not* develop feelings. She'd probably think I'm just out to use him and then toss him aside like trash afterward, and that's not how it is at all. I'm only trying to protect us both from getting hurt, and aside from avoiding each other altogether—which would be virtually impossible in this town—setting a deadline is the most practical way I can think of to do it.

"We both agreed on it," I say, slightly defensive. "He didn't have to."

"No, he didn't have to, but he did." She pauses, waiting for me to meet her eyes. When I do, she adds, "Because he really, really likes you."

Emotions erupt like fireworks in my chest—joy, excitement, embarrassment, uncertainty. He really, really likes me. Did he only agree because he wanted to please me, and not because he thought my suggestion made sense? No. He seemed just as on board with the idea as I was. Unless Kath knows something I don't.

"For the record…" She drops her gaze and rubs at a smudge on the counter, her movements quick and sure. "I forgave you for breaking his ankle, but I won't be nearly as merciful if you break his heart."

I don't argue, or even respond. There's no point. Kath and I may be friends now, but Liam is her family, and she means every word.

Chapter Twenty

O ver the next few days, the only time I see Liam is at school. I'm starting to understand what he meant when he said he didn't have much time to devote to a relationship. It's hard to date someone who's unavailable most nights.

"What about tonight?" I ask him Friday after school. We're sitting in his truck outside my house, trying to settle on a time to get together. He's driven me home all week, even though I live close enough to walk. But a few minutes of actual alone time is better than none. "We could meet somewhere after I get off work."

He shakes his head. "My mom's covering someone's shift tonight at Smiley's and I told her I'd stay home with the kids. I'd ask her to get a babysitter, but she already spent a fortune on my truck, and it's also kind of short notice, so—"

"It's okay," I cut in, seeing his agitation. "I understand."

He sighs and reaches for my hand, weaving his fingers through mine. "Sorry. I'm really bad at this."

I'm not sure if he means bad at making plans or bad at relationships in general, but a small part of me melts anyway. He's open and honest in a way that I rarely allow myself to be. I squeeze his hand. "You're doing fine. We'll hang out when we hang out, even if it's just at lunch and in your truck after school. We don't need to be joined at the hip."

Like Sam and Ravi, for example. If Liam and I were together as much as they are, constant fixtures in each other's lives, making a clean break in December would be that much harder. And a clean break is important, because the cleaner it is, the faster it heals.

"No," Liam says, smiling now. "I don't accept that. I'd like us to be at least *partially* joined at the hip. Fifty percent, maybe."

I return his smile. "Twenty-five."

He laughs and bends over to adjust one of the Velcro straps on his boot, using his left hand because his right one is still entangled with mine. When he straightens up again, he says, "You could come over."

"What?"

He's gazing out the windshield, not looking at me. "Tonight, after work. You could come to my house."

I stare at his profile, unsure what to say. We've only ever seen the exteriors of each other's houses. I've met his family, but not on their own turf. His invitation makes me feel slightly panicked, as if simply being inside his house, among his personal belongings, will add an unwanted layer of closeness to our relationship.

"My mom's working late," he adds when I fail to respond. "And Brody and Keira go to bed at ten."

On the other hand, I'd really love to spend some time with him outside of school. Does it really matter where we are? "Okay," I say, then lean over the gearshift and plant a quick kiss on his lips. "I have to get ready for work now. See you around nine-thirty?"

His smile is wide and luminous. "Yeah."

I hop out of the truck and head for my house, not looking back until I reach the front door. Liam's still smiling as he drives away.

Several hours later, I'm standing on his doorstep and sniffing at my hair. Luckily, it smells mostly like the Moroccan oil I'd spritzed on in the parking lot after work, and only a tiny bit like onions.

After several knocks, the door finally swings open to reveal Liam, looking vaguely harried. "Sorry," he says, shifting his weight onto his left crutch so he can hold the door open for me. "I was just trying to convince Keira to get ready for bed, which is always a fun time. Come on in."

As I step into the entryway, Keira appears on the staircase in front of us, dressed in blue Darth Vader pajamas. Seeing me, she pauses halfway down the stairs. "Hi."

I wave at her. "Hi. I'm Avery."

"I know. I saw you at the sub store."

I nod, unsure how to proceed. I haven't spent much time around little kids and I never know what to say to them. Their candidness unnerves me.

"Did you brush your teeth?" Liam asks, looking up at her.

Keira meets his gaze straight on. "Yes."

"So if I go up there and check your toothbrush, it'll be wet?"

She bites her lip and starts retreating backwards up the stairs. "Yes," she says again, then turns and races to the top.

Liam glances at me and shakes his head. I give him a thin smile. He sounded like a parent just now, and I can't decide if it's appealing or off-putting.

"You got here at kind of a hectic time," Liam says, motioning for me to follow him. "I'm still working on cleaning the kitchen from dinner. Everything takes ten times as long in this stupid boot."

This, I can relate to. Cleaning up after dinner is one of my jobs too. As I trail him into the kitchen, I take a look around. The inside of the house is more updated than the outside, its shiny oak floors and big windows making the space seem larger than it is. The presence of kids is evident everywhere—various toys littering surfaces, small sweaters hanging off chairs, artwork on the refrigerator door. Unlike my house, which changes every few years, this house feels lived in. Like a home.

"How was work?" Liam asks as he finishes loading the dishwasher, his crutches leaning against the wall by the trash can.

His question fits the whole domestic vibe going on in here. "Chaotic. I was working with Isaac."

He shuts the dishwasher and turns toward me, holding the edge of the counter for balance. "Oh God, you didn't tell him you were coming here after work, did you? He'll tease you mercilessly."

"No. Of course not. I know better than that."

He lets out a breath. His obvious relief—coupled with his concern over Isaac's treatment of me—is adorable, and I can't help myself from going over to where he's standing and kissing him on the cheek. In response, he places his hands on either side of my waist and kisses me on the lips. My arms circle his neck, and we melt into each other as the dishwasher hums beside us.

A loud thumping noise distracts us. It's Keira again, galloping down the stairs and toward the kitchen. Liam and I jerk apart, and I wonder if we're forever destined to have our kissing interrupted by a small child.

"I brushed them," she reports as she bursts into the kitchen. "You can check my toothbrush. It's wet."

Liam clears his throat and reaches for his crutches. "Okay. I believe you."

"Why is your face red?"

I look down at the tile floor, struggling to hold in my laughter.

"Keira, it's time to go to sleep."

"But I want to show Avery my room."

Unable to think of a reason to refuse, I follow her to her room. Liam trails behind us, his boot and crutches expertly navigating the stairs. At the top, Keira leads me into a small bedroom liberally decorated with stuffed animals. She heads straight for an IKEA-type shelving unit near the window, which is home to dozens of assembled Lego structures.

"Did you build all these?" I ask her, moving in for a closer look. The structures range from easy-to-assemble mini sets to large, intricate sets comprised of hundreds of blocks. There are buildings, boats, cars, and even a working Ferris wheel.

"Yeah," she says, straightening a blocky little robot on the shelf closest to her. "I always ask for Legos for presents. Sometimes people get me the pink kind, but my favorite is Star Wars." She points to an impressive Millennium Falcon on the top shelf.

"Star Wars is cool," I say, glancing at her pajamas.

Keira grins, revealing several missing teeth. It's impossible not to smile back.

"Okay," Liam says from the doorway. "It's really time for bed."

Satisfied now that she's shown off her most prized possessions, Keira goes to bed without complaint. Back in the hallway, Liam leans into the door across from Keira's and says, "Ten more minutes, dude."

When he steps back, I see a slightly bigger bedroom, with two twin beds separated by a dresser. Brody sits on one of the beds, a game controller clutched in his hands. He stares at me with wide, blinking eyes, and I get the feeling that—unlike his sister—he has no interest in showing me his room, or even speaking to me in general.

As I move closer to the stairs, something in Brody's room catches my eye. A familiar stuffed bear sits on top of the dresser, propped up by its little wooden crutches. The bear I'd given to Liam in the hospital. It clicks in then—this is Liam's room too. He and Brody share. And he still has the bear, displayed where anyone could see it. For some reason, this discovery sets off a warm, buzzing feeling in my veins.

Back downstairs, Liam gets me a glass of water and we settle on the living room couch. As soon as I sit

185

down, something sharp pokes into the back of my thigh. I lift my leg and dig around underneath for the source, which turns out to be a gray Lego brick.

"Keira," Liam says, depositing the brick on the coffee table.

"Her Lego sets are amazing."

"I know." He flicks on the TV. "She's always been into building things."

"She'd probably love my dad. He can talk for hours about structural design." I take a sip of water and then place my glass on the table. "I bet he'd even give her a tour of the bridge construction site."

Liam's face light up. "Really? That sounds awesome. She'd be thrilled."

I make a mental note to bring it up to Dad. "Bring your brother too, if he wants."

"Nah. Brody's more into video games than construction."

Right after he says this, we hear the sound of a door closing upstairs. Liam watches the staircase for a moment, but when no one comes flying down it, he relaxes and goes back to hitting buttons on the remote.

"He doesn't seem very cool with me being here," I say quietly. "Brody, I mean."

He glances at me, surprised. "Oh. No, that's just Brody. He's really reserved around most people, especially people he doesn't know. He was diagnosed with Tourette's a couple of years ago, and he's still kind of self-conscious about it."

Now it's my turn to be surprised. "I had no idea."

"Well, it's not always like what you see in movies or whatever, with people randomly yelling out curse words. With Brody, it's mostly motor tics. Like blinking."

I nod. That, I did notice.

"He was bullied in school last year because of it," he continues, his eyes on the TV. "My mom put him in karate a few months ago, to help him with his confidence. Things are a bit better this year."

"Good."

The Netflix logo appears on the screen, and we both settle against the back of the couch. Earlier, we'd decided to watch a movie, but sitting here together in this dark living room, our shoulders touching, the warmth from his body soaking into mine, I can barely even think straight, let alone follow the plot of a movie.

After several minutes of browsing, we put on some Will Smith movie neither of us have seen before. I try my best to focus, but by the time we get half way through it, I still have no clue what's going on. Liam is quiet beside me, so quiet that I steal a glance at him to check if he's fallen asleep. He hasn't. Instead, I find him watching me too, his eyes dark in the muted light. He reaches up and touches my hair, smoothing a strand between his fingers, and that's all it takes. I lean in and kiss him.

Just like in the corn maze, everything else falls away and I completely lose track of time, my surroundings, and myself. By the time we resurface, the movie has ended and Netflix is recommending a few more titles for us. I blink and look around for a clock, but there's nothing. Just the dull light from the screen and the streetlights outside.

"What time is it?" I whisper.

Liam reaches across me to the coffee table, where he'd put his phone earlier. "Twelve-fifteen."

I relax again. My parents aren't the type to set curfews—as long as they know where I am and when they can expect me back—and Liam said his mom won't be home until one-thirty. So I don't have to leave just yet.

"You're not going to tell Kath about this, are you?"

He settles against the pillow again, his face inches from mine. "What?"

I look down at our tangled limbs, the twisted hem of my shirt. "She said you guys tell each other everything."

"Uh, not in graphic detail."

I laugh and pull back a few inches, accidentally banging my foot against his boot. Suddenly, I'm reminded of what I'd seen upstairs earlier—my get-well present to Liam, its fuzzy leg encased in a cardboard cast.

"You kept the bear."

Liam blinks at me. "I'm having a really hard time following your train of thought right now."

"The teddy bear on crutches. The one I gave you in the hospital. I saw it upstairs when you were talking to Brody."

"Oh. Yeah." He leans up on one elbow. "Of course I kept it. It's not every day that a cute girl brings me a gift."

I smile. "It's not every day that a cute girl hits you with a car, either."

"Well, I'd rather a cute girl hit me with a car than someone like Old Man Jenkins."

"Agreed. You do not want to get hit by Old Man Jenkins. Been there. Do not recommend."

He slides his hand across my stomach to my hip. "Just think—if it weren't for Old Man Jenkins, you would've missed out on the incredible privilege of replacing me at Sadler's Subs."

"Oh! That reminds me." I reach around to the back pocket of my jeans and bring out a folded wad of twenties. "I got paid today. My second last paycheck."

He takes the money—his seventy-five percent—and flips through it. "You know how sketchy this seems, right? You paying me right after we made out on my couch?"

I give him a small shove. "Do you have enough yet? For the trip?"

"Pretty much. I think I'm only a couple of hundred short, but I can make that up when I start working again."

Happiness churns through me. All of this—my bizarre plan to make amends, my rough first couple of weeks at Sadler's, Kath's stony glares, the incessant guilt—it all seems to mean something now. We did it. *I* did it. He won't miss out on Ireland—and seeing his father's final resting place—because of me.

"You know," I say, tracing his collarbone with my finger. "You never did tell me why you prefer cash over a money transfer."

He smiles and averts his gaze, as if embarrassed. "Honestly? It's just another excuse to see you."

His words wash over me, then settle like a glowing ember in my chest. A part of me wants to let it burn, but a bigger part of me knows I should probably dampen it, and fast, while it's still early. Because the more glimpses I get into his life, the more I want to curl up inside of it and stay.

Chapter Twenty-One

T he trick is," Isaac says, carefully adding another pickle slice to the toothpick in his hand, "you need to line the edges up perfectly, or it'll just look like a bunch of pickles slices on a toothpick."

I double check the topping bins to make sure we have enough for the impending dinner rush. "It *is* a bunch of pickles slices on a toothpick," I remind him. Since I got here thirty minutes ago, he's been painstakingly reconstructing a pickle he'd just sliced, sliding each portion onto a long toothpick so they'll stay in place. Why he's doing this, I have no clue. I've learned not to ask too many questions when it comes to Isaac's motivations.

"Now it's entirely whole." He grins and holds up the assembled, fully formed pickle, its edges lined up flawlessly. The guy has some strange talents.

"Nice," I say as the door opens and Kath comes in, here to relieve him from the day shift.

191

"Oh God, not the vegetable reassembly again," she says when she sees the pickle-on-a-stick. "Isaac, you need a new hobby."

He nudges the pickle slices into his mouth and tosses the empty toothpick in the trash. "At least I'm capable of doing *something* around here. You all should be proud."

She rolls her eyes as she scoots around the counter. "Sorry I'm a few minutes late," she says to me. "I was talking to Brooke."

I search her face for clues as to how the conversation went. They've been alternately fighting and making up for weeks, sometimes both within the span of a day. But she just looks vaguely annoyed, which is her default expression. Especially when Isaac's in the room.

Just as I'm about to ask her if everything's okay, Mrs. Sadler pokes her head out from the back and catches my eye. "Avery, can I talk to you for a moment?"

"Sure." I put down the package of buns I'm holding and follow her into the office. Linh perches on the edge of the cluttered desk while I stand in front of her, unsure what to expect. Did I do something wrong? I've never been called into an office in my life.

"So," she says, running a hand through her sleek dark bob. "Liam comes back to work next week."

I nod, slightly relieved. He told me this a couple of days ago. Tomorrow he'll get his boot off, then he'll take a few days to get some strength back in his ankle, and then he'll ease back into work with a quiet Wednesday evening shift. Which means I have exactly one week left of gainful employment before I have to start the impossible process of finding a new job in a town where job openings are about as common as unicorn sightings.

"I've spent the last few days trying to come up with a way to keep both of you—you *and* Liam—but unfortunately, the funds just aren't there." She gives me a sympathetic frown. "I'm sorry, Avery. You're a fantastic addition around here and I hate that we can't keep you on."

I nod again, this time with sadness. I'd love to stay on, too. Over the past two months, this job went from an act of penance to something that I actually enjoyed. I even got used to the permeating onion stench. "I understand," I say.

She straightens up and moves behind the desk. "Do you have any leads on another job?" she asks, sinking into the creaky desk chair.

"Not yet."

"I'll ask around, see if anyone is planning to hire soon. If they are, I'll make sure to put in a good word for you."

I smile. It's easy to see why Liam thinks so highly of the Sadlers. "Thanks."

Back out front, Kath is ringing up a customer while Isaac half-heartedly pushes a cloth over the sub prep board. When the customer leaves, Kath gives me the same sympathetic frown I got from her mother. "She officially gave you the boot, huh?"

I shrug. It's not like I got fired. It's not like this was ever really my job, anyway. I was always just temporary. "It's fine."

"You can take my spot," Isaac offers, loud enough for their mom to hear.

Kath crosses her arms and looks at him. "You work mostly day shifts, dorkwad."

Not in the mood to listen to one of their bickering matches, I move closer to Kath and ask, "Is everything okay with Brooke?"

A cloud passes over her face. "Oh. Yeah, I guess. I mean, I don't know, it's just—" She lets out a heavy sigh, like simply talking about it irritates her. She digs her phone out of her back pocket, taps the screen a few times, then turns it toward me.

I lean in, expecting to see something scandalous, but it's just a selfie of Brooke, her face expertly made up with winged eyeliner and blood red lipstick. Before I can comment, Kath swipes her finger across the screen, revealing another picture—Brooke, in the same bold makeup, only now there's a gorgeous girl with long black locs posing beside her. They're both smiling, teeth white against bright lipstick.

My gaze flicks up to Kath's stormy face. "One of her dorm mates?" I ask, my tone hopeful.

"Yeah. But this is what I took issue with. Look." She points to a comment under the picture. Someone had written *cute couple*, followed by two red hearts. "She says she barely even knows the person who wrote it, and they probably only *assumed* they were a couple because she and Kali have become such good friends and spend so much time together. But damn, look at this girl." She brings the phone close to her face so she can stare at the beautiful stranger who now spends more time with her girlfriend than she does.

"I'm sure they really are just friends," I tell her. What else can I say?

Isaac comes up behind her, cloth slung over his shoulder, and peers at the phone screen. "Wow. Kali's hot."

"Isaac," I say, my tone a low warning.

He ignores me. "You know, I never really got the whole long-distance thing. The jealously, the paranoia, not seeing each other for months at a time…How is that healthy? Someone always ends up getting hurt."

Even though I secretly agree with him, I still shoot him a you're-not-helping glare, for Kath's sake. He continues to ignore me.

"Who needs that shit?" He pulls the cloth off his shoulder and flings it toward the prep counter. "There are plenty of hot girls right here in Granesville."

Kath slips her phone back into her pocket. "You would know," she says, heading for the slicer. "You've dated most of them."

Isaac grins, his First Choice Grill T-shirt straining against his puffed-out chest. "If you want, I can tell you which ones are bi."

She picks up an onion and stuffs it in the slicer. "One, it's a dick move to expose another person's sexuality, and two, I wouldn't share girls with you even if I were single and desperate, which I'm not."

He shrugs and lopes toward the door. "Suit yourself. Bye, ladies." With a cheery wave, he leaves Sadler's and walks off into the autumn sunshine.

I look at Kath, who's busy churning out a pile of regulation-thin onion slices. "He really *is* an assclown," I say.

She laughs, but then a few seconds later, it turns into sniffling. It could be just a side effect of the onion fumes, but I don't bother checking to make sure. Instead, I hug her right there in front of the rotary slicer.

The next day at lunch, I'm sitting outside with Kath, Sam, and Ravi, soaking up the last of the decent weather, when the door swings open and Liam appears. Just Liam. No crutches, no boot. We all start cheering.

"How's it feel, man?" Ravi asks as Liam moves toward us, red-faced from our celebration and limping noticeably.

"Weird," Liam says, settling in next to me on the steps. "Like my foot isn't really my foot."

"Maybe it isn't," Kath says on his other side. She reaches down and lifts up his jeans cuff. "Are you sure they didn't actually transplant a new foot onto you during your surgery? I think that happened on *Grey's Anatomy* once."

Liam jerks his leg away from her. "It didn't *fall off*."

"Thankfully," I say, glancing at Ravi and Samantha. I'm still not sure if they know about my involvement in Liam's injury. Someone *must* have told them by now. Maybe they're just too tactful to mention it.

"We must celebrate your bootlessness," Samantha declares in her rich theater voice. "When's everyone free this weekend? We could go see a movie."

"I work Friday night and Sunday afternoon," I say.

"I babysit Sunday night, but otherwise I'm free," Liam says.

"I have a game on Saturday, but I should be home by six," Ravi says.

Sam nods. "So Saturday night, then. Is that good for everyone? Kath?"

Kath picks at a loose thread on her jacket, not looking at any of us. "I work Saturday night, but it's okay. You guys go without me."

"No," Liam says, bumping her shoulder with his.

"Really." Her gaze flicks from his hand—which found its way to my knee during the movie night planning—to Ravi's arm, wrapped loosely around Sam's waist. "You four go. Make it a double-date-couples thing."

"Why can't it be a five-friends-hanging-out thing?" Liam asks. "Like we do every day at lunch?"

Kath doesn't answer. Luckily the bell rings then, breaking through the sudden whiff of tension, and we all make our way to the door. Once inside, Kath says goodbye and sprints off to her locker before anyone can say another word. Ravi and Sam head in the opposite direction, and then it's just Liam and me. He takes my hand, which he couldn't do when he was walking on crutches, and we start toward our lockers.

"You seem taller," I say as we walk, slowly, down the hallway.

"It's because the crutches made me hunch a bit." He flashes me a smile. "You seem shorter. And cuter."

"Why cuter?"

"I'm not sure. Maybe the joy of walking on my own without seven pounds of plastic attached to my leg is making everyone seem cuter."

"Even Ms. Laskaris?" She's the oldest, most crotchety teacher in the school, if not the entire world.

"*Especially* Ms. Laskaris."

I laugh, but my thoughts are still on Kath. The way she looked at us outside, so sad and wistful. Did our display of affection remind her of what she had with Brooke, or is she resentful because I've been taking up all of Liam's limited free time lately? The last thing I want to do is encroach on their friendship. Or make her miss Brooke even more than she already does.

"Kath will be okay," Liam says, reading my mind. Or maybe my distracted expression. "She's just having a rough time with Brooke being away."

"I know." I haven't told him about our shift at Sadler's yesterday, how she cried against my shoulder for a minute before rallying and getting back to work. Unlike Kath, I don't tell Liam everything. "I don't blame her for not wanting to go out on a Saturday night with two couples, though," I add as we reach our lockers. "I think she's been feeling like a third wheel lately. Or a fifth wheel, in this case."

Liam stays close to me as I open my locker. "Is that what we are?"

"What?"

He leans in closer, his steel-gray eyes welded to mine. "A couple."

My heart dips, then races, and suddenly it's hard to breathe. I look away, pretend to search for something in my backpack. "Um. Yeah. I mean, we are until the deadline, right? December thirty-first?"

"Right," he says quietly. "The deadline."

Something in his tone makes me look up at him, just in time to see a ripple of emotion cross his face. Sadness? Uncertainty? I can't quite place it.

The second bell rings then, and we each go to separate classes. Global History is half over by the time I figure out exactly what it was that I saw on Liam's face. It was regret.

Chapter Twenty-Two

I'm in my room slogging through endless calc homework when I receive a text from Mia.

You free for a chat?

I gratefully drop my pencil and immediately text back *yes!!!*

When she appears on my tablet screen, I let out an exaggerated gasp. For once, she looks like I do when I'm hanging around at home—T-shirt, no makeup, tired eyes, hair in a messy bun. "Are you sick?" I tease. "Or is this your Avery cosplay?"

She sticks her tongue out at me. "I just got back from a run."

Right. That's another difference between Mia and me—she exercises. By choice. She even used to take my mom's yoga classes once in a while when we lived in Weldon. My parents loved her.

"How's it going?" I ask. It's been over a week since we've talked.

"Oh, it's going." The image shakes as she flops on her bed. "What's new in Granesville? How's the dating deadline working out? Still on track to part ways in the new year, or have you fallen deeply in love and vowed to stay together through all of eternity?"

Heat creeps up my face. "It's working fine," I say firmly. Then I think about two nights ago, sitting with Liam in the movie theater, how right it felt being one half of a couple as we shared popcorn and laughed with Sam and Ravi. Still, just because I like being with him doesn't mean we have any kind of future together.

I decide to change the subject. "How's the booktubing? You haven't uploaded a video in a while."

"I've been too busy with school," she says. "Oh, and guess what? I got a job at Jitters!"

Jitters is the coffee shop we used to go to after school sometimes, a funky little place with chalkboard menus and the best hot chocolate in the universe. A wave of homesickness washes over me, swift and unexpected. I thought I was over missing the city. Once I decided to go back for college, I thought my longing would start to fade. But September seems like a million years away.

"That's awesome," I say, smiling through the ache. "I'm jealous. There's only one coffee shop here, and I don't think they've hired anyone new in the past thirty years."

Mia frowns. "Are you looking for a job again? Is the sub gig over now?"

"Yesterday was my last shift," I say, dropping my gaze. It was harder than I expected, walking out of there for the last time as an employee. Most things in my life are temporary—jobs, towns, schools, friends—and I've learned to harden myself against the inevitable loss and leaving. But for some reason, handing in my apron after my shift yesterday gave me a sad, hollow feeling, the same feeling I get whenever I think about my impending separation from my parents, my only constant in life.

"You'll find something else soon," Mia assures me.

"I hope so. I'd like to have some money saved up before college."

Her face suddenly brightens. "Oh! That reminds me." She disappears from the screen, leaving me staring at her bedroom wall. "Okay," she says, appearing again. She's holding what looks like a stack of magazines. "There was this college fair thing at school today. You know, when a bunch of college reps visit and pass out catalogues and answer questions and stuff?"

I nod, even though we haven't done anything like that at Granesville High yet. I remember it happening at Thompson High, though.

"So I was talking to the representative from Eckert," she goes on, flipping through the catalogues until she gets to the correct one. She opens it and shows me a page of what looks like course offerings. "Did you know they have an amazing English program? Because I didn't."

Excitement stirs in my stomach. I think I know where she's going with this. "You're considering Eckert now? I thought you wanted to go away to college." She always said she'd probably end up at some small, artsy school where she could study literature and creative writing and eventually wind up as an editor for a big publishing house in New York.

She shrugs. "I did, but then I thought about it some more. There's a better chance of my getting a scholarship if I go somewhere local."

"Mia," I say slowly. "Are you saying we might be going to college together next year?"

"I'm saying it's entirely possible." Her grin shines through the screen. "I talked it over with my parents, and they even agreed to me living on campus so I can have the full college experience. Hey, maybe we could be roommates!"

My enthusiasm grows as I imagine us a year from now, sharing a dorm room. Walking the city together like we used to. Hanging out in coffee shops and libraries like my year away never even happened. Just the idea of it feels foreign to me. I've grown so accustomed to leaving people behind forever, it never occurred to me that I could have a friendship that actually survives.

Now that I'm unemployed again, I'm around more often at dinnertime. On Wednesday, both my parents get home late and no one feels like cooking, so we decide to take advantage of First Choice Grill's "Hump Day Special"—half-price wings.

"When are we going to meet this boy you're seeing?" Mom asks when we're almost done eating. "It would be nice if you brought him around once in a while."

I concentrate on getting all the meat off my chicken wing. "I will soon," I say, even though I probably won't. Liam only knows the basic facts about my family life— my parents' jobs, our moves, Hazel. He doesn't know about the tension that's been brewing between my parents and me since we moved here, or our disagreements about college, or Finland. These things feel personal, and sharing them with him would mean exposing my biggest weak spots and vulnerabilities. I guess I *do* have a wall around me, like Mia said, but it's there for a good reason—to protect myself, and to keep people at a distance. The more I let Liam in, the harder it'll be to let him go.

"This is the kid you hit with the car, right?" Dad asks, his hand wrapped around his beer glass. When I nod, he adds under his breath, "Forgiving guy."

"His name is Liam," I remind them. Not that I talk about him much, but you'd think they'd at least remember his name after everything that's happened. "And yes, he's forgiving. And nice. And smart."

Mom takes a bite of salad. "He sounds like Noah."

I drop a chicken wing, splattering the table with hot sauce. "He's not like Noah." But as I'm saying the words, I realize Liam *is* a lot like Noah. Sweet, intelligent, responsible. I clearly have a type. Of course, Noah didn't turn out so sweet at the end, when he moved on to one of my friends before I was even out of the city.

Mom continues to grill me, asking about Liam's family. I tell them what I know, leaving out the part about his Oxy-addict stepdad. Instead I stick to wholesome things, like his sister's Lego building skills, which reminds me of the offer I made a couple of weeks ago while I was at their house. I totally forgot to ask Dad about giving Keira a tour of the bridge construction.

"I don't know," he says when I bring it up. "It's not the safest place for little kids."

"Especially now," Mom adds.

I wipe my fingers on a napkin. "Why especially now?"

They exchange one of their loaded glances. Mom picks up her water glass and takes a sip before answering. "There's been some vandalism."

"Vandalism?"

"Just some idiots throwing empty beer bottles at the equipment," Dad says, like it's an everyday thing. "We have a security company coming in on Monday to set up some cameras."

The comment section for that Granesville Weekly article pops into my head. *Soul-eating bridge troll.* I doubt this vandalism is a random act.

"It was probably just a one-time thing," Mom says. She waves a hand, as if brushing the subject away, and then refocuses her attention on me. "How's the job hunt going? Any calls for interviews yet?"

I push aside my plate of wing bones. "I just started looking." Liam drove me around town yesterday after school, waiting in the truck as I dropped off resumes to almost every business in Granesville. Most of them said they weren't planning to hire anytime soon, but they'd keep me on file.

"I'm sure something will come up."

Sometimes I wish I'd inherited my mother's unwavering positivity. "Hopefully I find something soon, because I want to start saving up for a car."

"A car." She says it like she's referring to some kind of outlandish contraption, like a spaceship. "But everything in this town is within walking distance. And you can use my car whenever it's free."

"I know." I take a sip of diet Coke. "I was thinking more about later, when I leave for college. If I had my own car, I could drive it to Weldon. That way, I'd have a reliable mode of transportation while I'm living there. You know how awful their public transit system is."

My parents stare at me across the table, their foreheads in full-on furrow mode. I haven't gotten that look in a while. "What?" I ask.

"Don't you think you should wait?" Mom asks, putting down her fork. "Until you know for sure that you're going there?"

"You haven't even applied yet," Dad reminds me. "It might be a good idea to keep your options open. Just in case."

"Right. And there's no point in spending all that money on a car if you might have to get rid of it in a few months anyway."

The spicy wing sauce burns in my stomach as I sit there, pinned to the scratchy fabric of the booth. I can't believe them. After all the conversations we've had, after all the things I've said, after expressing my own wants and needs and goals for the first time in my entire life, they still think I'm going to change my mind and trail along with them on the next whatever.

No. Screw that. I'm done with seeking their approval. I'm done with listening to their opinions on the choices I'm making for my own damn life.

I look each of them in the eye and will my voice not to shake. "My mind is made up, and you'd probably know that if you bothered to listen to me for even a second."

Mom frowns, her forehead creases deepening even more. "Avery."

The burning has spread to my eyes, and I know if I don't get out of here right now, I'm going to end up bawling in front of the entire restaurant. I slide out of the booth, avoiding my parents' gazes. "I'll walk home," I say, and then I leave before they try to dispute *that* choice too.

The old-fashioned street lamps lining Center Street flick on as I walk, hands stuffed in the pockets of my jacket. It's starting to get cold, but I can stand it for a few minutes. Like my mother said, everything in this town is within walking distance of everything else. I pick up my pace.

"Avery?"

I look up and see Kath, crossing the street toward me and gripping a to-go cup in each hand. Hastily, I rearrange my features into an expression that I hope looks casual and normal. "Hey," I say, pausing on the sidewalk.

She stops in front of me and peers at my face. "Why are you walking downtown in the cold by yourself?"

There's no way I can even begin to explain, so I shake my head and say, "Aren't you working tonight?"

She nods and holds up the cups. "Yeah. It's pretty dead, though. I just popped out to get some hot chocolate for Liam and me. " She studies me again, making me wonder if my puffy eyes are visible in the dark. "But you look like you need it more. Here."

I shake my head again as she offers me one of the hot chocolates. "No, it's yours."

"Actually, it's Liam's. Take it."

I take it, but only because my hands need warming. Satisfied, Kath tilts her head, motioning for me to follow her. As we head down the sidewalk toward Sadler's, I take a few quiet breaths, trying to calm myself before walking into its bright interior.

Liam looks up at the sound of the door, knife poised above the tomato he's cutting. It's weird seeing him behind the counter, even though he seems completely at home there. His face lights up at the sight of me, and the lingering anger inside me starts to fade.

"I found her wandering the streets, so I gave her your hot chocolate," Kath says as she slips behind the counter.

Liam puts down the knife and moves toward me, his expression shifting into concern. "Are you okay?"

For a moment I want to spill everything, talk and vent until there's nothing left to say, but I don't. That's the worst thing about hiding behind walls—sometimes you have to stay quiet in order to keep people from looking too closely.

"I'm fine," I say brightly. "Just out getting some air."

They both look at me expectantly, like they're waiting for more. But my urge to unburden myself is gone. It's enough just to be here with them, in this onion-scented closet that somehow feels more like home than my own house.

Chapter Twenty-Three

"We should do something tonight," Ravi says, propping his feet up on the seat in front of us.

It's Halloween day, and the five of us are lounging on the gym bleachers because it's too chilly to sit outside anymore. No one minds if we hang out in the gym during lunch, as long as we don't bother the basketball team, which is currently practicing below us.

"Like what?" Kath asks without glancing up from her phone. I know without even peeking over that she's still studying Brooke's Instagram pics of the campus Halloween party she went to on Saturday night. She'd dressed up as a nineteen twenties flapper girl, and Kali, drop-dead gorgeous in a skin-tight cat costume, appeared in almost every picture. "TP someone's house? Smash pumpkins?"

Samantha tucks her head against Ravi's shoulder, almost dislodging her bumblebee antennae. She's the only one of us who wore a costume to school. "Smashing pumpkins is mean."

"I thought it was a band from the nineties," Liam says, and Sam leans across Kath and me to poke him. "I can't do anything tonight," he adds. "My mom got called in to work, so I'm taking Keira and Brody trick-or-treating."

"Such a good big bro," Sam says, nestling into Ravi again. He wraps his arm around her, and Kath shifts a couple of inches closer to me, as if distancing herself from their shameless PDA. "Are you going with him, Avery?"

I glance at Liam. Walking the streets with him and his siblings sounds a lot more fun than staying home and handing out candy to the neighborhood kids. He smiles and nudges my knee with his, an invitation. "Yeah," I say, returning his smile. Things have been generally light and easy between us since the night Kath found me wandering down Center Street, which is more than I can say for my relationship with my parents. Or lack of relationship. I've been actively avoiding them for the past twelve days, because avoiding them is preferable to having the same argument fifty times.

Basketball practice ends, and the five of us gather up the remnants of our lunch and leave the gym. Sam and Ravi head upstairs while Kath, Liam, and I shoulder our way through the crowded hallway. Liam slips in front of me for a moment, and I gaze at the smooth slope of his neck, remembering the warmth and feel of it under my lips a couple of days ago in his truck. The memory is so distracting, I don't notice that I'm about to walk into a door frame until it's right in front of me. I sidestep at the last second, accidently treading on someone's foot in the process.

I turn to apologize, but the words catch in my throat when I see who it is that I stepped on. It's Damian, Son of Satan (and ferry operator). When he meets my eyes, his expression hardens.

"Of course," he says, glaring down at me. "Anything else you want to crush for me?"

Kath is there in a flash, edging between us. "Run along, Damian."

"I wasn't talking to you, Lucy Liu."

"How original," she hurls back at him. Several people pause to stare at her. "Is she the only other Asian woman you know of offhand?"

Liam, who'd inadvertently kept walking without us, looks back to see what's holding us up. When he sees Damian, wariness flashes in his eyes and he doubles back to us quickly.

"What's going on?" The question is for Kath and me, but his gaze stays locked on Damian.

"Nothing," Kath says, wrapping her hand around Liam's forearm. "Damian was just apologizing for getting in Avery's way."

Damian laughs in his snide way, and a thought suddenly occurs to me. Maybe *he's* the one who vandalized the construction site. It hasn't happened again, not since the cameras were installed, but I can picture it: Him and his friends, drinking beer after beer and throwing the empties at the expensive machines and equipment. Of course, with zero proof, I can't make any accusations.

"Maybe she should apologize for getting in *my* way," Damian says with a smirk. A few more people pause, sensing drama.

"Maybe you should keep walking," Kath tells him.

"Maybe *you* should mind your own damn business."

Liam takes a step toward him, but Kath's hand tightens on his arm and she pulls him back again. "Liam, your ankle."

"Yeah, Liam, your ankle," Damian echoes. "Wouldn't want to break it again."

Liam stays put, his entire body tense. "My fists are working fine."

Damian laughs again. He has at least four inches and thirty pounds on Liam. He could break more than a newly-healed ankle.

The bell rings then, but no one moves. A small crowd has gathered in the hallway, watching us and waiting. I want to sink into the floor. This fight—or whatever it is—is happening because of me. Because of my father, and Damian's. Kath and Liam didn't do a damn thing. This is my problem, my fight, and I won't let them get dragged into it anymore. If I can manage to stand up to my own parents after years of quiet compliance, I can certainly handle standing up to a tall, scary stranger with an unfair grudge against me.

A burst of anger thrusts me forward. "Look," I say, raising my face to Damian's. "Your problem is with my dad's job, not with me. I'm not my dad's job. I'm not my dad, either. I didn't ask to move to this town. You think I *want* to be here?"

Surprise flickers in his eyes. I can't tell if he's shocked by my words, or because I'm speaking for myself for once. In any case, it shuts him up. He regains his composure and goes back to glowering at me. "Whatever," he says, then turns and continues on his way. The gawkers disperse shortly after, until it's just Kath and Liam and me standing in the emptying hallway.

"Wow," Kath says after a long pause. "I gotta say, Avery…I was not expecting that."

I realize I'm clenching my fists. I loosen them, my fingers throbbing from the release of pressure. "Me either."

She looks at Liam next, who's staring at the floor, jaw twitching. "And as a bonus, we got to witness a rare appearance of Liam's Irish temper."

"I wasn't pissed at him because I'm Irish," he snaps at her. "I was pissed at him because he was being an asshole."

She shrugs, unbothered by his tone. "Hey, I'm not exactly mild-tempered myself."

The second bell rings, letting us know that we're all late for class. A teacher appears in a nearby doorway, her eyes narrowing at the sight of us still lingering in the hall. "Get to class, you three," she calls, then crosses her arms like she's going to wait there until we do.

The three of us start walking. Kath parts ways with us in the lobby area and Liam and I keep going toward our lockers. We're both unusually quiet, processing what just happened.

"You okay?" I ask softly.

He doesn't look at me. "Yeah."

I reach for his hand, but he swiftly pulls it away, reaching up to adjust his collar. I can't tell if he did it deliberately or not, but something about his demeanor warns me against reaching for him again, so I don't even try.

At our lockers, we quickly gather our things for the class we're currently missing, both of us silent the entire time. Why won't he look at me? Is he annoyed at me for something, or is this just leftover anger from Damian?

"Liam…"

He hoists his backpack onto his shoulder and glances at me once before averting his gaze again. "I'd better get to class," he says, and then leaves without another word.

My heart sinks. What just happened?

Then it hits me. I replay the words I'd spat at Damian, oblivious in the heat of anger. *You think I want to be here?*

Oh God. I basically told about two dozen people—including the guy I'm dating—that I don't want to be here. In this town. With them. With *him*. No wonder he left so quickly.

If anyone is an asshole in this situation, it's me.

I walk to Liam's house after dinner. On the way, I pass several trick-or-treaters, mostly young families carting around hyperactive toddlers with plastic pumpkin buckets. The older kids don't go out until a bit later.

My stomach clenches when I reach the doorstep. Liam skipped last class today to pick up Brody and Keira from school, so I haven't seen him since he walked away from me after lunch. When I texted him earlier to ask what time I should be here—more to feel him out than anything—he responded with a terse *6:30* and that's all I've heard from him since. He didn't rescind his invitation, though, so here I am.

The door swings open before I can knock. Keira stands in the threshold, dressed in brown Ugg boots and a full-on Chewbacca onesie. Her smile fades at the sight of me. "Oh," she says. "I thought you were a trick-or-treater."

"Maybe I am," I say.

She looks me up and down, her eyes partially covered by her furry onesie hood. "You're not wearing a costume."

She has me there. My parents started suggesting I was "too old" for Halloween and trick-or-treating when I was about ten. I don't get really into it like some people do.

"Keira, who's at the—" The door opens wider to reveal Liam, wearing a dark brown vest over a white, collared shirt. "Oh," he says, echoing his sister's greeting. "Hey. Is it six-thirty already?"

The lukewarm reception I'm getting doesn't exactly make me feel welcome. I study Liam's face, trying to gauge his mood. He doesn't look as happy to see me as he usually does, but he doesn't look *un*happy either. After what happened today, I decide to take that as a good sign.

"We're just about ready to leave," Liam says. "Come on in."

I step inside the warm house. Brody sits on the couch, blinding in a bright yellow Pikachu costume.

"You guys look awesome." I smile as I look them over. To Liam, I add, "Are you…?"

He nods and places a hand on his sister's furry head. "Keira insisted."

"Chewie needs Han Solo," she says, flinging her arms around Liam's waist. "They're best friends."

The doorbell rings, interrupting the sweet moment. Keira lets go of Liam and almost trips over herself in her rush to answer the door. After handing out candy to a Disney princess and two fire fighters, she yells "I'll be right back!" in our direction and then bolts up the stairs.

I look at Liam, who—with his brown hair, broad shoulders, and slim build—actually makes a great Han Solo. Suddenly I wish I were Princess Leia.

"She's just a little excited," he says as Keira comes tearing back down the stairs, something white and glittery in her hands.

"Here," she says, handing it to me. "This is from my costume last year. It's the only part I could find."

I look down at the object I'm holding—a white headband with a plush, sparkly unicorn horn attached. I glance up at Liam, who's watching me with a tiny smile on his face, like he doesn't believe I'll actually wear it.

Buoyed by that smile, I shake out my hair and put on the unicorn headband.

"Can we go now?" Brody asks. His forehead is damp with sweat. He must be cooking in that bulky costume.

Liam places the bowl of candy on the steps for the trick-or-treaters, and then we're off. Keira speed-walks down the sidewalk, her giant Halloween bag flapping against her legs.

"Don't get too far ahead of me," Liam calls to her. Then, to Brody, "Keep an eye on her, okay?"

Brody nods and hurries to catch up with his sister. Now it's just Liam and me, a starship pilot and a mythical beast. An unlikely pair.

"Liam," I say after we've been walking in silence for a few minutes. "What I said to Damian in the hallway this afternoon…"

He keeps his gaze on Keira as she skips toward a brightly-lit house a few yards away, Brody trailing behind her. "I remember."

"I didn't mean it the way it came out. I don't—it's not that I hate Granesville or something. I actually do like it here. I just…I liked Weldon more, and if I had the choice, I wouldn't have left it. That's all."

Liam is quiet for a few moments, digesting this. Around us, sugar-fueled children race up and down the streets and sidewalks, parents strolling leisurely behind them. Up ahead, Keira and Brody hold open their candy bags for a woman wearing a pointy witch hat. I shiver in the chilly breeze and straighten my horn, heart pounding double-time as I wait for Liam's response.

Finally, he stuffs his hands into his pockets and half-turns toward me. "Is it because of the guy you dated while you lived there? Is that why you didn't want to leave? And why you want to go back there for college?"

I pause to stare at him, confused. "What? You mean Noah?"

He shrugs. "You didn't tell me his name. Or anything else about him. Just that you had a bad breakup."

"No," I say, resuming my pace. "It has nothing to do with him. We broke up weeks before I moved, and he has another girlfriend how. I haven't spoken to him in months, and I have no desire to reconnect with him next year. Or ever."

"Well, you can't blame me for wondering. You never talk about him or your past or anything personal, so most of the time I'm left guessing." He kicks a rock out of his path. "You didn't even tell me about Damian giving you a hard time about the bridge. Kath mentioned it to me a few days ago. She assumed I knew."

I focus on the dry leaves skittering along the road beside us. "I'm sorry. I guess I'm just a private person."

"I don't think that's it, though," he says in a softer tone. "I think you want to open up to people, but you won't let yourself. And I'm not sure why."

I know why. It's because when I do open up to people—like my parents, for example—I end up feeling vulnerable and trying to justify everything I say and think and want. I give them the power to hurt me, and I then I wind up getting hurt, every time. When you've moved around as much as I have, sometimes it's easier to just drift along the surface, never venturing too deeply below it.

"I think you need to feel in control of your life," Liam goes on, psychoanalyzing me on the street in front of dozens of mini super heroes and princesses and ghosts. "And in control of yourself. That's why you're so selective about what you tell people. And why you wanted to do this dating deadline thing with me. You set up parameters because you feel like you can control what happens within them. Right?"

Sweat beads on my neck. Either he's really perceptive, or I'm much more transparent than I thought. Everything he just said is true, though the thought of admitting it out loud makes me feel itchy and exposed. "I'm not sure what you want from me, Liam."

He frees his hand from his pocket and reaches for me, wrapping his warm fingers around my cold ones. "I want you to trust me."

Trust. Such a simple thing to ask for, yet so hard to give. I grip his hand, keeping my gaze trained straight ahead. Keira and Brody are a few houses away, lugging their half-filled bags up yet another driveway. Brody sees us and waves, his bright yellow costume still visible in the growing darkness.

"I do trust you," I say. It's the truth. I trust him as much as I'm able to trust anyone whose existence in my life is dwindling by the day. "And I do want to be here. In Granesville. With you."

He glances behind us to make sure no one's coming, then stops walking and faces me. "I want you here, too." He reaches up to remove my unicorn horn, carefully untangling it from my hair. When it's free, he hooks an arm around my waist and pulls me tight against him. "And here."

I press my forehead against his Han Solo vest and shut my eyes. Right now, in this moment, with our bodies pressed close and the early traces of winter in the air, I'm exactly where I want to be.

Chapter Twenty-Four

I survey the items spread out on my bed: two sealed envelopes (one containing last year's transcript and the other my midterm grades), laptop opened to the Eckert College online application, and Hazel for moral support. I'm all set.

Originally, Mia and I agreed to apply at the same time, but Thompson is on a different marking schedule and she won't receive her first set of grades until next week. I offered to wait for her, but she insisted that I do this today. Maybe she thinks I'm going to change my mind, too.

"Okay," I tell Hazel, who is lounging in the middle of the bed and looking bored with the whole process. "Here we go."

Everything goes fine until I get to the end of the application, where there's a section about payment options for the application fee. Right. I forgot about the fee. It can be paid online with a credit card (which I don't have), or by mail with a check (which I don't have), or in person with cash (which is impossible).

Great. I'm going to have to involve my parents.

Dad's out at some birthday dinner for one of his coworkers, so Mom it is. I find her in the kitchen, brewing her customary evening cup of green tea. She greets me with a tight-lipped smile and then goes back to poking at her teabag. It's like she's grown so accustomed to my cold shoulder over the past few weeks, she's completely given up on trying to engage me in normal conversation.

"I need some help," I say, leaning against the breakfast bar.

She lifts the spoon out of her cup and places it in the sink. "Oh?"

I explain about the fee, and how my application won't be processed without it. "I was wondering if I could use one of your credit cards. Or you could write me a check and I'll mail it along with my transcripts. Whichever." I keep my voice calm and unemotional, like I'm talking about the weather and not my ticket to the future I want.

Mom clears her throat, and I brace myself for another lecture about keeping my options open and not locking myself into anything until I feel completely sure and so on and so on. But it doesn't happen. Instead, she says, "I'll write you a check."

My body lightens in relief and I force myself to act normal, though I'm wondering if she's had some sort of yogic epiphany or midlife crisis. "Okay. Thanks. So, the fee is fifty dollars. I'll pay you back."

She moves toward her purse, which is hanging on the back of one of the breakfast bar stools, and digs out her check book and a pen. Not wanting to break the spell, I watch silently as she opens the check book and flattens it against the counter, then uncaps the pen. She pauses for a second, blinking as she stares at the blank check in front of her. It's only then that I notice the tears in her eyes.

My relief fades in an instant. "Mom? Are you—?"

"I'll just sign it," she cuts in, her voice strained and wobbly. "You can fill in the rest."

She scribbles her name on the signature line and rips out the check, the sound loud in the quiet kitchen. I'm frozen, unsure how to deal with this perplexing reaction. I expected lectures. I expected arguments. I did not expect tears.

She slides the check across the breakfast bar, keeping her face turned away from me. "Here. Don't worry about paying me back."

"Mom," I say again, but she already has her tea and is swerving past Hazel as she trots into the kitchen. A few seconds later, I hear the door to the guest room click shut behind her.

I pick up the check and look at it. Guilt lances through me at the sight of her hasty signature, and I put the check back on the breakfast bar, face down. Then I look at Hazel, who's now whining at the patio door, eager to get out.

I go to open the door for her, then change my mind and grab her leash instead. I need to get out too.

As Hazel and I walk, I think about all our moves over the years.

In spite of the chaos surrounding each transfer, there was a predictability about them too. Dad would move first, to meet his crew and secure housing for us, while Mom and I stayed back to tie up loose ends. Then, after a few weeks, we'd join him in our new location, and he'd say, without fail, *I missed my girls*. And then my parents would both beam with the joy of their reunion, because for them, being apart is torture and being together means their worlds are complete.

I always thought this feeling existed more between them as a couple, rather than us as a trio. I thought I was the third wheel, an accessory to be towed along as they moved on to the next adventure. But now, when I think back on all those separations and reunions, I wonder if I'm wrong. Maybe I was more essential than I thought. Maybe the joy came from the *three* of us being together, our little family complete once again.

But our next move will be different. There will be no joyful family reunion at the end. No *I missed my girls*. By choosing a different path, I've changed the game. And my parents can't seem to deal with that.

It's sad that my applying to college is what it took for me to realize they might want me around after all.

The leash strains against my hand, and I look behind me to see Hazel sniffing furiously around the base of a utility pole. I didn't even notice that she'd stopped. As I backtrack toward her, a white car pulls up to the curb beside us. My muscles automatically tense, preparing my body to run, but then the driver's side window slides down and I realize it's just Isaac.

"Where you headed?" he asks.

I look down at Hazel. She's now peeing on the pole, unaffected by the presence of this guy who, for all she knows, could be trying to abduct me. Some protector she is. "Home."

"Kind of a long way, isn't it?"

I reach for my phone to check the time, but it isn't in my pocket. I left the house too quickly to grab it. It feels like we've been walking for only a few minutes, but going by my current location—I've practically taken us all the way to Waterview Drive—it's been at least a half hour. The sky is almost completely dark.

"Hop in," Isaac says. "I'll take you home. You look like you're frozen."

"But…" I gesture to Hazel, sitting on the sidewalk and panting.

"Dogs are cool with me."

It *is* pretty damn cold out here. I bend and scoop up Hazel, then circle around to the passenger side door. Once inside the car, I settle her on my lap to minimize the spread of dog hair. This is Mrs. Sadler's car, and she probably doesn't take kindly to animals shedding on her upholstery.

"I'm just coming from work," Isaac says, pulling back out onto the street. "Had to stay through the Friday evening dinner rush."

I nod. I knew I smelled a hint of onion in the car, mixed in with Isaac's cologne.

"What's the dog's name?"

"Hazel."

"Hey, Hazel." He reaches over to pet her, and she stands up on all fours on my lap, tail wagging. She's not usually this friendly with strangers. Maybe she's just grateful to be out of the cold, like I am. "Do you always take her for walks in the dark when it's practically cold enough to snow?"

I shrug. "Had to get out of the house."

"I feel that."

He doesn't say anything else or ask any questions, which I appreciate. We drive in silence for a few moments, passing long rows of houses with glowing, curtain-covered windows. I picture the families tucked behind them, watching TV or eating or working, blissfully unaware of the world outside.

"Hey, Isaac?"

He reaches over to turn down the radio. "Yeah?"

"If you had a chance to go to college in Finland, would you do it?"

"Well," he says as we turn into my neighborhood, "that depends on if this is a serious question or a hypothetical question. Because with my GPA, I'd probably be turned down for clown college."

"Hypothetical, then."

He grins. "Okay, then yes. Absolutely. I'd jump at any chance to get out of this dump."

"What if you don't really want to go to Finland, but you feel like you should because it would be such a great opportunity or whatever?"

"Why do I get the sense that this isn't actually hypothetical?"

"Because it's not." I run my hands over Hazel's ears and sigh. "My dad's probably getting transferred to Finland this summer, and my parents want me to go with them and go to college there. But I'm so done with traveling and moving around...I just want to go to college in a place I love and settle there for a while."

I'm not sure why I'm saying this to *him*, of all people, when I haven't mentioned a word of it to Liam or Kath. But maybe that's *why* it feels so easy to talk to Isaac about it. We're barely even friends. Half the time, I'm not sure I even like him. He doesn't care about me the same way Kath and Liam do, so I'm not worried about his reaction like I would be with them. We're not close, so his opinion of me doesn't hold as much weight.

"If you don't want to go to Finland, then don't go to Finland." He slows down and peers out the window, trying to get his bearings. He drove me home from work once, but that was weeks ago and Isaac doesn't have the best memory.

"The white one with the red shutters," I remind him, and the car lurches forward. "It's not that simple, though. My parents are upset that I don't want to go with them. They make me feel like I'm abandoning them or something."

He pulls into my driveway and idles next to the Corolla. Hazel lets out a high-pitched *yip* and scrambles to get off my lap, but I hold her close against me.

"It's your life," Isaac says. "You think I live up to my parents' expectations of me, like, ever? Hardly. They wanted me to get a business degree and eventually take over the store, but the thought of being chained to that place forever makes me want to hurl. I'm not my sister."

I have a flash of Kath at Sadler's, her brow knit in concentration as she does inventory and slices vegetables. *She'd* follow her parents anywhere.

"Sometimes I feel like a horrible daughter," I say, gazing out at my house. Mom's in there somewhere, probably meditating her sadness away.

He nods. He knows what it feels like to disappoint parents. "You get used to it after a while."

Hazel wiggles in my arms, impatient to get inside to her food and water dishes. I turn to Isaac. "Thanks for the lift."

"No problem. And hey," he adds, giving me a rare serious look, "do whatever makes you happy. Screw everyone else."

I almost laugh. *Screw everyone else* is exactly the type of advice I expected from Isaac.

"But damn," he goes on, shaking his head. "If you *do* end up moving all the way to freaking Finland? Liam will be *crushed*. You're aware that he's in love with you, right?"

My heart leaps into my mouth. "Did he tell you that?"

"He didn't have to. It's totally obvious." He places his hand on the gear shift, ready to reverse his way out of here. "See you around, Avery."

Feeling numb, I clutch Hazel to my chest and get out of the car. Isaac waves once and then backs away, his headlights sweeping across the yard. Once the driveway is clear, I put Hazel down and let her lead me to the front door.

Inside, all is quiet. Dad's still not home, and Mom must still be in the yoga room. Or maybe she went to bed early. I unclip Hazel from her leash and she bolts for the kitchen. Our walk has left me parched, so I follow right behind her. The first thing I see when I walk in is that check, still face down on the breakfast bar, right where I left it. I get my glass of water, then grab the check on my way out of the room.

The incomplete Eckert College application is still up on my laptop. I put my glass and the check on the bedside table and then sit down on my bed, pulling the laptop closer. Three minutes later, the application is filled out and ready to send.

It's not until I click *submit*, placing the trajectory of my future in someone else's hands, that I allow myself to think about what Isaac said in the car. *He's in love with you.*

Clearly, I can't control everything, no matter how many parameters I put in place. *Love* is a complication that I hadn't really anticipated.

Chapter Twenty-Five

When I get to school on Monday morning, Kath and Liam are huddled together at his locker, deep in conversation. I hang back for a moment, reluctant to intrude, until Liam catches my eye and nods briefly, indicating that it's okay for me to join them.

"It could be anything," he's telling her as I sidle up to them. "Don't assume the worst."

Kath throws me a quick glance and then looks back at Liam. "How can I not assume the worst? It's pretty clear, if you ask me."

"I'm just saying…maybe you should wait and see what she says before you freak out."

Unconvinced, Kath turns to me. "Okay, let's see what Avery thinks."

"See what Avery thinks about what?" I ask, my first contribution to whatever is happening in this conversation.

"So last night," she begins, her features tense, "Brooke texted me to say she'll be home the first week of December, which is earlier than she thought."

"Awesome," I say. "That's only three weeks away."

She continues as if I haven't spoken. "Then she says she wants us to have *a talk* when she gets here. I asked her what kind of a talk, and she said *a talk about us*. Then I asked her what that meant, exactly, but she kept saying she wanted to wait until we were face to face to discuss it. So naturally, I assume she's either going to tell me she cheated on me, or she's going to break up with me, or both. I mean, what else is *a talk about us* supposed to mean?"

"Um." I glance at Liam for help, but he just shrugs. What am I supposed to say here? That I agree, and it's entirely possible that Brooke *is* getting ready to dump her? That I'm actually surprised that it's taken this long? But naturally I can't say that, so I settle on, "It could just mean that she wants to discuss your relationship and how you can improve on handling the long distance aspect?"

"Exactly," Liam says, giving me a grateful look. "Brooke's in love with you, Kath. It would take a lot more than a three-month separation to change that."

Anxiety squirms in my stomach. *In love with you.* Between Liam's work and child care, I saw him for a total of two hours this past weekend—and those were spent eating ice cream at Cherries with Sam and Ravi—so I haven't had a chance to bring up what Isaac said about him in the car on Friday night. Not that I have any clue what to say, anyway. *Please don't be in love with me because that just makes things more difficult? Because knowing you feel that way about me makes me wonder if I might feel the same way about you?*

"I appreciate you guys trying to make me feel better," Kath says, her voice quivering. "But I knew from the moment she told me she was going away to college that she'd eventually move on from me. I mean, let's face it—the reason she was drawn to me in the first place was because Granesville isn't exactly a hotbed of out-and-proud lesbians. Now she probably has her pick of hundreds, so it's no surprise that she wants her freedom."

"Kath…" Liam reaches out to touch her arm, but she turns away, swiping a tear off her cheek. He drops his hand and winces, like it literally pains him to see her cry.

First bell rings, and Kath sucks in a breath and runs her fingers through her hair, smoothing out the tangles. Her eyes are sad and exhausted. "I'll be okay. Don't worry about me." She straightens Liam's shirt collar and gives him a fair approximation of a smile. "Focus on your good news, okay? See you in English, Avery."

She spins on her heel and walks away. Liam and I watch after her until she's swallowed up by the hallway crowd.

"Good news?" I ask as we cross the hall to pre-calc.

"Oh," he says, the fog lifting from his face. "I finally saved up enough money for the senior trip. Paid the fee last night."

I smile and squeeze his hand. "That's great. You must be relieved to have that behind you. Now you can start saving toward spending money and souvenirs."

"Yeah," he mumbles.

We enter the classroom and take our seats at the back. I watch Liam as he digs out his math book, confused by his lack of excitement. He's been working toward this moment for months; I thought he'd be ecstatic.

I lean across the aisle toward him. "What is it?" I ask in a low voice.

The fog settles onto his face again, and he gazes down at his desk. "The teacher organizing the trip, Mr. Rothman? He tweeted this morning that if more people don't sign up within the next two weeks, the trip might be cancelled. Apparently these group tours need a certain number of people."

"Oh no." I move back, sit up straight in my seat. Wow, this morning has just been loaded with sunshine. "How many more do they need?"

"A couple, I think. But the deadline to sign up is the end of this month, so…" He shrugs and taps his pencil on the desk. "I've tried to convince all our friends to go, but none of them have the funds. Actually," he adds with a slow smile in my direction, "the only person I haven't tried to convince is you."

"Me?" I laugh. "I don't have the funds either. I'm still jobless, remember? Besides, I don't like traveling."

"Even if it's with me?" His smile fades, and a flash of vulnerability crosses his face. "You know, it might be kind of nice to have you with me when I go to the cemetery. Just for moral support. What do you think?"

Several different emotions flood through me, paralyzing my vocal chords and pinning me to my chair. Go on the senior trip? I know I probably *could*, if I wanted to. My parents have always encouraged travel and seeing as much of the world as possible, and even though we're on the outs right now, they'd likely give me the money, or at least lend it to me.

But Ireland with Liam? It's his birthplace, his origin. This trip means so much to him. Everything about it is personal, from seeing where his parents grew up to visiting the remains of the father he never got to meet. But experiencing all that with him, watching him do something so hugely meaningful and emotional, would connect us on a level much deeper than this safe, surface level I've kept us on since September. Growing even closer to him just weeks before I have to tell him goodbye seems totally counterproductive to me.

Also, there's the fact that the senior trip is in May, months after our December thirty-first end date. Has he forgotten about that? Does he think *I* have?

Liam is still watching me, expectant and hopeful. I'm about to say something—I'm not even sure what—when the teacher comes in and tells us to take out the homework she'd assigned over the weekend. I turn and face the front, silently thanking Ms. Fiore for buying me some time to come up with a logical response.

I'm still struggling six hours later, when I meet up with Liam at his truck after school. We couldn't exactly have a private conversation at lunch while surrounded by our friends, but now we're alone for the first time in days.

I finally work up the nerve once we're idling in my empty driveway. "Liam, I—"

"Hey, is she okay?" His words drown out mine; I'd spoken so softly, he didn't even hear me. "She looks kind of frantic."

I follow his gaze and see Hazel in the living room window, barking her head off and pawing at the glass. Usually, she just stares suspiciously at us when we're sitting out here.

"Oh," I say. "She must really need to go out. Do you want to...?" I motion toward my house, and Liam's eyes widen a bit. I've never invited him inside before.

He shuts off the engine and we make our way to the house. As soon as I get the door open, Hazel spins in circles and jumps on my legs. She must be busting, because all she does is sniff Liam once before charging toward the back door. I follow her into the kitchen and let her outside.

"Winston would've just peed on the floor," Liam says behind me.

I laugh and shut the door. Winston is the Sadlers' old cocker spaniel. I met him once, when I picked Kath up for work one day. They live in a nice split-level house close to the lake. "Hazel's too dignified for that," I say, even though she's used the floor as her bathroom more than once. "Usually," I add, rubbing my twitching jaw. A migraine started coming on about an hour ago, probably triggered by stress.

Liam looks around, taking in my mom's minimalist décor. "This is nice."

"Yeah." I lean against the counter. "We like it. Not as much as our last house in the city, but..."

"What was your house in the city like?" he asks as my sentence trails off.

"Old, but modernized. Renovated. I loved it." Thinking about that house makes me sad, so I guide us back to the subject at hand. "So about this morning—"

This time, I'm interrupted by a muted bark on the other side of the garden door, followed by frenzied scratching. Oops. Hazel must be freezing. I let her back in, and she shakes her fur at me before sauntering over to her food dish. I turn back to Liam, who's closer than he was a few seconds ago. He must have moved while I was letting Hazel in.

"Um," I say, distracted by his nearness and how cute he looks standing in my kitchen, his hair tousled from the wind outside and his shirt collar crooked once again.

"About this morning?" he prompts.

I reach up to straighten his collar, like Kath did earlier today, and then, somehow, my arms are around his neck and we're kissing, right there next to the water cooler. And then, somehow, I'm leading him to the living room couch, where we sink down and kiss some more.

For a while, I forget about everything—this morning, Ireland, and even my budding migraine. But the last one roars back into focus when I lift my head off the pillow and the entire left side of my face throbs with the movement.

I let out a sharp gasp, and Liam jumps back like I'd kicked him. "Sorry," he says.

"No, it's…" I sit up, which makes the pounding even worse. It feels like a bird pecking at the inside of my skull. "My head. Migraine. I need to go take my meds."

"Oh, you should've said something."

I refrain from commenting that my mouth was too occupied to speak, and go swallow one of my triptan pills. When I return to the living room, Liam's sitting up at the end of the couch and Hazel's nestled in the chair opposite, watching him.

"Stretch out for a few minutes," he says. "I'll rub your head."

He doesn't need to ask me twice. I lie down and rest my head in his lap. He strokes my hair, his fingers gently digging underneath to massage the tender areas of my scalp. My eyes drift closed.

"About this morning," he prompts me again, his voice as soft as the worn denim of his jeans under my cheek. "Do you mean what happened with Kath, or when I asked you to go on the senior trip with me?"

"The senior trip." I try to focus, but it's not easy when his thumb is kneading my neck.

"And? Do you? Want to go with me?"

I hesitate, not sure how to put this in a way that won't hurt him or make him hate me. The thought of doing either of those things makes my head ache even more, not to mention my heart. What am I supposed to say? *I can't go to Europe with you because it's too much of a commitment and I'm afraid it will bring us closer? And oh, remember how we said we were going to stop dating after New Year's? Sorry, but that still applies.*

No. My brain is too muddled for that right now.

"I'll have to ask my parents," I hear myself say instead. Because apparently I'm commitment-phobic *and* a coward.

"Really?"

I don't need to look at him to know that he's smiling. Guilt prods at my stomach, but before I can warn him not to get too excited yet, we hear a car door slam out front.

Oh God. My mother. She's home early. I spring off Liam's lap, setting off a pulsing in my head so severe that it makes me see stars. By the time Mom walks in, Liam and I are two feet apart on the couch.

"Hello," she says, surprised. She's still dressed in her yoga gear and carrying her rolled up mat. "I was wondering who—" She pauses, glancing over her shoulder toward the driveway, where Liam's truck is taking up half the space.

I stand up and Liam, just as surprised as my mom, does the same.

"Hi, Mom," I say through another wave of pain. "This is Liam Kavanagh, the guy I…" I'm about to say *hit with the car*, but I change my mind and finish with, "Replaced at Sadler's."

"Of course." Mom steps forward, a strained smile on her face. I can tell she's not exactly thrilled to find us alone in an empty house, Hazel our only supervision. I'm just glad she didn't walk in twenty minutes earlier. "Liam Kavanagh," she repeats, holding out a hand. "That's a very Irish name."

"I have a very Irish mother," Liam replies as they shake hands.

Mom smiles for real this time. "Avery didn't mention that."

I squirm a little. I haven't mentioned much of anything to her about Liam.

"It's so nice to finally meet you," she continues, propping her yoga mat against the wall. "I've been telling Avery for weeks that she should bring you around."

She mentioned it once, almost a month ago, during the First Choice Grill dinner that I stormed out of in a fit of frustration, but I'm too woozy to correct her. My meds are starting to kick in, adding to the surrealism of the moment.

My mother keeps talking, smoothing over the awkwardness in the room. "You'll have to come over for dinner one night. Maybe this weekend?"

An image of the four of us sitting around the dinner table flashes through my sluggish brain. Having your boyfriend over to dinner is such a relationship-type thing. Noah used to join us for meals all the time, and I loved how he fit in so well with my family. He made us feel more rounded, a complete circle rather than a triangle with me at the farthest point. But involving him in all aspects of my life made it that much more difficult to lose him.

"Liam works, Mom," I quickly put in.

Liam glances at me and nods. "Yeah, Fridays and Saturdays are a little chaotic for me."

Mom's smile doesn't budge. "Well, how about Sunday? Avery always used to get off at seven, and it's your shifts she was covering, right? We could have a late dinner."

Liam throws me another glance, but I avoid his eyes this time. There's nothing I can say here, no excuse I can make to stop my mother from her quest to get to know him better. So I say nothing, even though everything in me is resisting the idea.

"Uh, sure," Liam says after a pause. He sounds hesitant, and slightly confused over my lack of enthusiasm.

"Wonderful," Mom says, and just like that, it's settled.

This is what I get for inviting him into my house this afternoon. If I hadn't, I probably could have made it all the way to the end of December—to the end of us—without ever introducing him to my family. I'm supposed to be gradually extracting him from my life, not pulling him deeper into it.

Chapter Twenty-Six

After much deliberation, my mother decides to roast a chicken for Sunday dinner. She doesn't eat meat, but she isn't totally opposed to cooking it now and then, since Dad and I are both carnivores. I've assured her that Liam is too, but this doesn't stop her from asking a million other questions.

"Does he like broccoli?" she asks, peering through the oven window to check on the chicken. "Maybe I'll throw some in the steamer."

I keep my eyes on my knife as I slice perfectly symmetrical carrot rounds. Two months at Sadler's has taught me something, at least. "I don't know," I say, irritation prickling down my spine. I'm even less in the mood for conversation than I am for this dinner. It's weird—for years I've wanted her to show an interest in my life, and now that she is, I just want her to stay out of it.

"How about peas? Does he like peas?"

My knife slams down on the cutting board with a loud crack. "I don't *know*, Mom."

She straightens up and stares at me. "What is *wrong* with you? You've been on edge all week."

She's right, I have been, and it isn't just because of this dinner. It's everything—the months of tension with my parents, the dating deadline, the senior trip, Kath's angst over Brooke, waiting to hear from Eckert about whether I've been accepted, Isaac's declaration about Liam being in love with me…

It's no wonder I've had a low-grade headache since Monday.

"I'm sorry," I say, sweeping the carrot circles into a pile. "I just…I wish you'd asked me before you invited Liam to dinner, that's all."

She goes back to peeling potatoes. "Why? Is there some reason you don't want us to get to know the boy you're dating? Is there something wrong with him?"

"No." If anything, there's something wrong with *me*. Twice this week, Liam asked me if I was sure I wanted him to come over, and twice, I assured him that yes, of course I do. He gave me an out, and I was too chicken to take it. Our meal tonight is appropriate.

My father enters the kitchen then, saving me from this line of questioning. He sidles up to Mom and kisses the side of her neck. "What can I do?"

She smiles and gestures toward the peeled potatoes. "Chop."

The doorbell rings, sending Hazel into a barking frenzy. I put down my knife and leave the kitchen before either of my parents have the chance. I shoo Hazel away from the door and pull it open. Liam stands there, his cheeks red from the cold.

"Hey," I say, too brightly. I'm nervous. Why am I nervous? Because I'm afraid they won't like each other? Because I'm afraid of what they might say to each other?

"Hey." Liam steps inside, his gaze immediately shifting to the couch, the scene of our make out session the other day. His cheeks turn even redder. "Your dad's not going to punch me or something, is he?"

I smile, some of my nervousness dissolving. "No. I don't think my mom even told him about catching us here." Surprisingly, her only reaction was to ask me if I was being careful. I assured her I was, even though I meant it in an entirely different way. Careful, for me, means a limited level of intimacy, which means slamming the brakes when things get intense. "Hazel, quit it," I snap over her persistent barking.

Confident that our guest isn't here to kill us, she shuts up and flounces back to the kitchen. Liam and I follow her, and I introduce him to my father, who's still chopping away.

"How's the ankle?" Dad asks after everyone's greeted each other.

Now it's my turn to blush. Does he have to keep bringing up the car/bike collision?

"It's fine," Liam replies. "No lasting damage."

"Thankfully," Mom says as she takes the chicken out of the oven.

"Yeah," Dad adds, "or else Avery might be indebted to you for life."

Oh my God. Why is he being so embarrassing? "When will dinner be ready?" I ask.

Mom pokes the boiling potatoes with a fork. "Ten minutes? We'll let you know."

I seize Liam's hand and pull him into the living room before my father can humiliate me any further. We sit on the couch, thighs touching.

"How was work?" I ask, distracted. All I can think about is that I should have cancelled this dinner days ago, when I had the chance. We haven't even made it to the table yet and already I want the night to end. He shouldn't be here, hanging out with my parents, folding himself into my family as if he'll have a place here in the future. As if *we* have a place in the future.

"It was…interesting. I was on with Isaac." A small frown appears on his lips. "I mentioned I was having dinner with you and your parents tonight, and he asked me if—"

"Avery, I don't think you offered Liam anything to drink," my mother calls from the kitchen.

I look at Liam, who shakes his head. "I'm good."

I wait for him to finish his comment about Isaac, but he doesn't. "You were saying?"

"Oh, it's nothing," he says, the forced breeziness in his tone suggesting otherwise. "Let's talk about it later."

Before I have time to ruminate on this, Dad appears and tells us that dinner is ready.

Once we're at the table, I start worrying about what to talk about. Dad used to talk to Noah about baseball, which they both follow, and Mom usually asked him questions about astronomy, which Noah loves and Mom finds fascinating. But Liam isn't into sports and I don't think he knows any more about stars than I do.

Luckily, my parents don't seem to be in a third-degree grilling type of mood, so the vibe is casual and neutral. At least at first.

"Have you applied to any colleges yet, Liam?" my dad asks when we're about halfway finished eating.

"Not yet," he says, taking a sip of water. Going by his stiff posture, he's just as nervous as I am. "I'm not sure where I want to go, and there's still time before applications are due. I want to research some more before deciding."

"That's very smart," Mom says, tossing me a meaningful glance.

The food in my mouth turns to cement. Oh no. Please don't let her start in on my college choices again. Not now. I thought we were starting to move past this.

The topic shifts to Granesville and the new bridge, and I relax. My food goes down and I scoop up a forkful of mashed potatoes, listening as Dad rambles on about the big controversy, which of course Liam has heard all about. But once Dad gets going on something, there's no stopping him.

"This is one of the more...*vocal* towns we've lived in," my mother says when Dad finally runs out of steam. "Have you lived here all your life, Liam?"

"Since I was a baby."

She nods and spears a piece of carrot. "And your mother is from Ireland, you said?"

"Yes." He clears his throat. "So was my father. He died there, before I was born."

"Oh, how sad."

Dad drains his wine glass and reaches for the half-empty bottle. "Have you ever been back?" he asks Liam. "To Ireland?"

"No. I mean…not yet." He looks at me for a moment, and my fingers tighten around my fork. "I'm going in May for the senior trip."

Shit. I put my fork down, the food in my stomach tightening into a dense ball. Even though I told him I would, I still haven't mentioned a word about the senior trip to my parents. Why? Because there's no point. Because if they knew, they'd probably just add to my pressure. Not that Liam has been pressuring me about going, or about anything else, for that matter. That's not his way. In fact, he hasn't even mentioned the trip again. Until right now, anyway. At the dinner table with my parents. Who are supposed to know about it, but don't.

"A senior trip!" my mother says, beaming. "To Ireland!"

"And Scotland," Liam adds, and my stomach clenches even more.

"How fun." Mom turns to me. "Avery, you never mentioned it."

Now all three of them are looking at me, my parents with interest and Liam with surprise, and I resist the urge to slide under the table. "Oh," I say, gazing at my placemat. "I meant to."

"What a great opportunity," Dad says, holding up his wine glass. "I went on a European tour with my parents when I was sixteen. Had my first sip of beer at a little pub in London."

245

Liam smiles politely. "At least I *hope* I'm going. There's still a chance it might be cancelled if more people don't sign up."

I know he's not saying these things with an agenda or in a manipulative sense. I know he's just making conversation. I know this. But damn it, I wish he'd stop talking.

My mom grins at my dad. "Might make a good Christmas present for Avery, huh?"

Okay. That's it. I can handle the cracks about college and Liam's ankle, but I can't handle being coerced into going to yet another country that I don't want to go to. "I'd rather a car," I say.

My mother's smile fades, and I immediately regret opening my mouth. I sound like an ungrateful brat, lobbying for a car over a trip to Europe. What is wrong with me?

"I'm kidding," I tack on quickly, but it's too late. The damage is done and I've made everything awkward again.

Dinner continues, and somehow I make it through the rest of it, plus dessert. By the time we're done eating, it's almost ten o'clock and time for Liam to go home. He says goodbye to my parents and I walk him outside to his truck. Neither of us says anything as a hint of tension crackles between us.

"Want to get in for a sec?" Liam asks, looking at my bare, goosefleshy arms. I'd gone outside without my jacket.

We climb into the truck and he starts the engine. The tension is more pronounced in here, filling the cab, constricting my chest and throat. One evening in my house with my parents has knocked down a chunk of my protective wall, leaving me exposed and vulnerable. And there's nothing I can do to build it back up.

"You didn't ask them," Liam says. The words punch through the silence and settle around us.

"No."

He reaches over and cranks up the heat. "Why not?"

I shiver as the warm air hits my skin. As usual, there's nothing I can say that won't make him hate me, so I keep quiet.

"Were you even planning to mention it to them at all?" Liam asks when he realizes I'm not going to answer. His tone is calm, matter-of-fact, but I can hear the hurt simmering underneath. "Do you even *want* to go on the trip?"

I peer out the window at my house, the place that isn't my home and never will be, and feel a jolt of anger. I'm not sure if it's anger toward my parents, myself, Liam, or all three. All I know is, everything feels like it's spinning out of my control and the only thing preventing me from spinning away too is the slow, steady burn in my stomach.

"The trip is in May, Liam," I remind him, my gaze still trained out the window.

"So?"

Is he willfully ignoring it, or has he seriously forgotten our conversation over donuts two months ago? I turn to look at him. "We agreed on December thirty-first. Remember?"

"Yeah, our deadline. How could I forget?" He turns the heat down, his movements quick and jerky. "But that was a while ago. When I agreed to it, I didn't know I was going to…" He trails off, and before I can ask what it is he didn't know, he finishes with, "Anyway, things change. Feelings change. It's not like we signed a binding contract or something. We can do whatever we want."

I feel another jolt, but this time it's not anger. It's betrayal. Setting a deadline on a relationship was probably a doomed idea from the start, but still. We both said we weren't looking for anything serious. We both know nothing lasts forever. We made an agreement, and here he is breaking it like it's nothing.

"I told you," I say, impatience creeping into my voice. "I'm done with traveling the world. I'm not going to take off to Ireland with you just because you want me to."

"But you'll go to Finland with your parents just because *they* want you to?"

I freeze, the fight draining out of me. Liam's chest rises and falls underneath his jacket as he stares at me, eyes dark in the faint light of the dashboard.

"Isaac told me," he says, and there's no mistaking his hurt this time. It's all over him. "When I mentioned I was coming here after work, he asked me if you'd made a decision about moving to Finland yet. He thought I knew all about it. You know, because it's something you probably would've told your boyfriend."

Crap. "Liam, I—"

"*Am* I your boyfriend? Because sometimes I'm not sure." He grips the steering wheel, squeezes his fingers around it. "What exactly are we to you, Avery? Some kind of side project to make the time go faster while you're stuck in this town for a year? Something you can stick an expiration date on so that once our time runs out, you can walk away like it never happened? Well, it doesn't work that way. *Life* doesn't work that way."

"I'm not moving to Finland," I cut in, like that matters. But I'm desperate to clarify *something*. "My parents want me to, but I'm not. That's why I didn't bother telling you."

"But you told Isaac? You trusted him with it, but not me?" He rakes a hand through his hair and sighs, his frustration seeping out with his breath. "You know, I thought I could do this, but I'm not so sure anymore."

My heart thumps. "Do what?"

"Be with someone who constantly has one foot out the door. Someone who opens up to a guy she barely knows but refuses to open up to me." He waves a hand toward the house. "And tonight…I could tell you didn't really want me there. It's like you want to keep me in a box, separate from the rest of your life. You only show me what you want me to see, and it's not enough. I need more."

And that's it—that's exactly what it boils down to. He needs more from me than I'm willing to give. To see more than I'm willing to show. He wants all of me, and the mere thought of letting him in like that scares the hell out of me.

Never again, I told myself after Noah. When I moved to this town, I was adamant about not forming attachments or making ties. Yet here I am, sitting next to a boy who fell for me even after I hit him with a car. A boy I'm pretty sure I fell for too, somewhere along the way. In spite of my promise to myself, I ended up making the exact same mistake all over again. I let myself get attached.

Liam's right—I can't pretend we never happened. But I *can* change the path we're currently on, just like I changed my own. After all, our little dating experiment was supposed to be for fun, and right now it feels like just the opposite.

"I'm sorry," I tell him. I wrap my arms around myself, wishing I had something to count, some figures to tally up to make me feel calm again. But there's nothing. "Maybe we should…take a step back."

"Maybe we should," he says, staring straight ahead at the darkened windows of my house. "I mean, your deadline is coming up soon, anyway. There's no point in prolonging this, right? May as well call it now and go back to being friends."

Friends. Where we ever just friends? Is it even possible to hit reset like that? Still, he's right. "Okay," I say softly.

He doesn't look at me or say anything else, so there's nothing left for me to do but leave. I want to kiss him good night, but I don't. The kissing is over, along with so much else. Instead, I tell him I'll see him tomorrow and get out of the truck, my eyes stinging with tears and my legs unsteady beneath me. I pause at the front door and watch him go, the glow from his headlights blurring and distorting as he drives away.

I thought keeping him at arm's length would assure a clean break. But instead, all it did was cause a huge, jagged mess.

Chapter Twenty-Seven

I have pre-calc first period the next morning, so there's not even any time to psych myself up before facing Liam again.

But when I walk into class, he's not there. He's still not there after the bell rings, so he's either avoiding me by skipping class or one of his siblings needed him again. I can't decide if I'm disappointed or relieved to have an extra hour of peace before what's sure to be one of the more awkward days I've spent here. And that's saying a lot.

The brief moment of calm is quickly replaced by dread when class ends and I have to go to English. I may have escaped facing Liam this morning, but I still have to face Kath.

Last night, while I was trying unsuccessfully to fall asleep, her words from a few weeks ago passed through my head on a scrolling news ticker: *I forgave you for breaking his ankle, but I won't be nearly as merciful if you break his heart.*

Did I break his heart? It was his idea to bump up the deadline, though I was the one who suggested stepping back in the first place. All blame aside, I think we're both feeling pretty heartbroken this morning. At least I am. Liam is still nowhere in sight when I get out of math. If he *is* around here somewhere, he's probably upstairs at Kath's locker, telling her everything.

And now the second period bell is about to ring, so I have no choice but to go upstairs too.

I count floor tiles on the way, trying to ground myself and soothe my anxiety. For once, it doesn't really help, and by the time I walk into English and see Kath already sitting at our table, my palms are so sweaty I have to wipe them on my jeans.

"Hi," I say as I sit down next to her. At least she hasn't gone back to her old seat, across the room from me.

"Hey." She takes out a pen and a notebook, not looking at me. She's wearing her default expression—bored with a hint of irritation—so it's hard to tell if she's mad at me or not. Dyson arrives then and tells us to get started on our latest essay, so I don't have a chance to find out.

By the end of class, I've managed to scribble a page and a half of semi-coherent sentences, and Kath still hasn't spoken to me beyond *hey*. Something is definitely up, and it's clear what that something is. They really do tell each other everything.

My suspicions are confirmed when we're packing up our things and she turns to me and says, "I don't like to say *I told you so*, but I told you so."

My palms immediately get moist again, along with my neck and underarms. "What?"

She zips her backpack and stands up. "The ridiculous deadline you came up with. I knew it wouldn't work."

I stay seated and stare at my paper, the messy cursive wobbling on the page. I thought I was immune to Kath's contempt, seeing as I lived through it my first few weeks here, but maybe not. It cuts way deeper now that I've experienced the warmth of her friendship too.

"He's not a term paper or a tax form, you know. He's a person, with feelings. And a heart." She flips her hair over her shoulder and hoists up her backpack. "As for you? I'm not so sure."

She passes in her paper and leaves the room, leaving me pasted to my chair, throat aching with the effort not to cry in front of half the class and the teacher. Slowly, I gather up my things and bring my essay to the front of the room, handing it to Dyson without looking at him or anyone else. As I shuffle to the door, I pass Damian and accidently bump him with my shoulder.

"Sorry," I mumble.

To my surprise, he barely even looks at me. He just keeps going like I don't even exist. I watch him as he walks down the hall, smiling at people he knows as they pass. I don't blame him for ignoring me. No, he shouldn't have taken his anger out on me, but I understand why he's mad. My father's company swooped into town—*we* swooped into town—and turned his life upside down. And in the summer, when everything's done, we'll swoop right back out again while his family—and all the other families—stay here to deal with the fallout.

It isn't fair. No wonder people are pissed. Our time here is only temporary, but the impact we've made will last forever.

I'm not brave enough to head to the gym bleachers at lunch and possibly get rejected by all my friends, so instead, I walk home alone.

As I push through the icy wind, I think about what Kath said in English class. Maybe she's right—maybe I am cold and unfeeling. Maybe that's what happens when you try to follow your brain instead of your heart: your logical side takes over and you end up closing yourself off to anything real. Or maybe, after growing up as third wheel to my parents and leaving friends behind every couple of years, my heart eventually developed a hard shell around it. Noah managed to crack through it, but after we broke up, the shell grew back tougher than ever.

Or so I thought. It doesn't feel very tough right now. I guess Liam—and the friends I've made, and this sleepy little town—somehow snuck past it after all.

Hazel is the only one home when I arrive. She's excited to see me, jumping and barking and spinning in circles. I scoop her up and carry her to the kitchen, where I grab a yogurt from the fridge, the only food I can possibly get past my tight throat. The last time I felt like this—sad and lonely and sick to my stomach—was when we first moved here, before I knew anyone and was living in a cramped motel room with my dog. Before I went job hunting in my mother's Corolla and hit an unsuspecting cyclist, shoving us both off course and sparking a chain of events that led me to here, alone and lonely again, standing in the quiet kitchen with my dog.

But this what I wanted, isn't it? To be alone? To keep my head down, focus on school, make it to graduation without any ties or attachments getting in the way? Granesville is only a pit stop, after all. Transitory. Not the place where I'm supposed to plant myself. At least that was the plan before I moved here.

But I'm starting to realize that plans, not matter how logical and carefully constructed, rarely play out the way they're supposed to. Like Liam said, life doesn't work that way. Something always intervenes.

Like a broken ankle, for example. Or a broken heart.

When I arrive back at school after lunch, Liam is standing in front of his open locker. He's alone. My heart leaps, then races, making me feel lightheaded. At least he's actually here and not avoiding school and me, like I thought he might be this morning.

He turns his head toward me as I approach. His eyes light up for a split second before quickly going flat, like he forgot for a moment that last night happened but then it came rushing back.

After a pause, I go to my own locker and open it, my body tense and hyperaware of his, stationed just a few feet away. Neither of us says a word as we gather our things, the cacophony of voices and laughter and slamming locker doors echoing around us, and I wonder if this is how it'll be now. Not talking. Barely looking at each other. Sharing classrooms and streets and places for the next several months while trying to pretend like the last three never happened.

No. I wouldn't be able to stand it.

I shut my locker and walk toward him. "Liam."

He looks up and meets my eyes. His are a dusky gray today, like the clouds right before a rain storm. "Yeah?" he says, sounding tired and slightly wary.

Now that I'm standing here, inches away from him, everything I want to tell him seems to dissolve in my mouth. Like how sorry I am about everything, and how grateful I am that he welcomed me into his world despite our disastrous beginning, and how he's made my first few months here better and brighter than I could have ever imagined. Like how I fell for him too, and that I miss him already, and that I want us to forget about the stupid deadline and just make the most out of the time we have left before we part ways for possibly forever. But at the same time, the thought of doing it all over again, growing more and more attached only to watch everything fall apart at the end, scares me so much that I want to lock myself in my bedroom and stay there until August.

I want to say all this, to explain, but I can't. At least not here, in a congested hallway seconds before the bell. So instead, I swallow the words back and look away. "Nothing," I say, and then I turn around and bury myself in the crowd.

Chapter Twenty-Eight

"**H**ey, Avery."

I shut my chemistry book and look up. Samantha is making her way toward my desk, dodging people as they file out of the classroom after the dismissal bell. I instinctively tense up. Sam and Ravi haven't exactly been ignoring me, but they haven't sought me out, either. I figured they were either pissed at me, like Kath, or keeping me at a respectful distance, like Liam.

"Hi, Sam." I stand up and glance at the teacher, who's erasing the whiteboard at the front of the room. If Sam plans to lecture me or something, I hope she doesn't do it right here in front of Mr. Caldwell.

She hugs her textbook to her chest. "How are you? We missed you at lunch this week."

Okay, so she's not pissed. Still, I didn't expect to hear this. "We?" I ask, raising my eyebrows.

She flushes a bit. "Well, I can't speak for anyone else."

Thought so. I doubt Kath or Liam care that I've gone home for lunch every day this week, and walked home after school instead of meeting Liam in the parking lot for a drive. They're probably glad. Kath, especially. She told me this deadline idea wouldn't work, that it was stupid to assume we could turn off our feelings like a light switch, and she was right. My feelings for him are still there, burning as bright as ever, even now that we're just friends. Though we're not even that, unless *just friends* means exchanging terse hellos at our lockers, barely looking at each other in pre-calc, and nodding like acquaintances as we pass in the halls, the two of us constantly surrounded by a cloud of awkwardness. If that's the case, I'd rather be nothing.

"It's sad," Samantha says as we leave class together. "You and Liam are such a cute couple."

Were, I correct silently.

"Kath will get over it, you know," she goes on. "She's just being…Kath. You'd think she, of all people, would understand where you're coming from with your whole aversion to long distance relationships, right? She and Brooke haven't exactly mastered it."

I glance at her as we move down the hallway. I didn't realize how much she knew about me and my attachment issues. "She's really protective over Liam, that's all."

"Oh, I know." She stops and pulls me out of the stream of traffic, then turns to face me. "Liam dated my friend Maddie for a couple of months last year, and when she broke up with him? Kath gave her the evil eye for weeks. They're good now, though. She *does* get over things, no matter how prickly she seems."

It occurs to me then that I've never asked about the girls Liam dated before me. Not because I didn't care, but because past relationships definitely fall under personal history, which I tried to avoid. And I knew, if I asked him about his exes, he'd ask me about Noah, and talking about him would have exposed all the weak spots I work so hard to conceal.

"I think I get it, though," Sam says, giving my forearm a squeeze. "A couple of summers ago, Ravi went to India to visit his grandparents. He was gone for six weeks and I swear I almost lost my mind, I missed him so much. No wonder you're so reserved, Avery. I can't imagine getting close to people and then having to move away and never see them again."

Unexpected tears spring to my eyes. Her situation isn't exactly comparable—even with Ravi away in India for six weeks, she knew he'd be back and that their relationship would continue like always—but it's nice to know she understands. "Thanks, Sam."

She smiles. "I have to go meet up with Ravi. See you later!"

With a wave, she turns and heads right, toward the lobby area. I continue to my locker. By the time I get there, the school has practically cleared out, the hallways quiet and empty. There's no sign of Liam, but that's okay. Sam's words have buoyed me enough that his absence doesn't sting as much as usual.

I gather what I need for the weekend and slip into my coat. As I'm zipping it up, my phone chirps with an email alert. I dig it out of my backpack, expecting spam or yet another Old Navy sale announcement. But it's neither. My pulse thuds when I see the sender's address. Eckert College.

With a shaking finger, I click it open.

We are very pleased to inform you that your application has been accepted…

There's more, but I don't read it. Not yet. For now, I have all I need to know.

It's official. I'm going back to Weldon. I'm going home.

The one person I'm dying to tell is Mia, but I know I need to tell my parents first. Even though they've been against this from the start, they're still my parents. And while I don't need their blessing, I feel like they should at least acknowledge my plans before I go ahead with them. Deep down, I guess I've never stopped craving their acceptance.

Dad doesn't get home until after eight. When I hear him come in, I hit stop on the *Supernatural* episode I'm watching and leave my room. As I approach the living room, I hear my mother ask why he's so late getting home.

"I was talking to the police," Dad says as I slip into the room. Neither of them seems to notice me. I sink into the chair and watch my father as he takes off his boots by the door.

"The police?" Mom sits up straight on the couch and turns the volume down on the TV. "Why?"

"The vandals were back again the other night, and this time the camera caught them. The police came by to give us an update. The guys were identified and charged with public intoxication and destruction of property."

"Were they teenagers?" I ask.

Both of them look at me, startled, like I'm a piece of furniture that suddenly started talking.

"No," Dad says, stepping into the living room. Hazel runs up to him and sniffs him once before hopping into my lap. "They were older, in their twenties. Just some punks with nothing better to do than get drunk and vandalize construction sites."

For some reason, this makes me feel better. It might not have been personal, and even better, it definitely wasn't Damian.

"Well," Mom says, arranging a blanket over her legs. "I'm glad that's over."

Dad takes off his MRT Engineering jacket and hangs it on the coat rack. "I don't know about you guys," he says, his voice tired, "but I'm not going to mind leaving this town behind."

My phone, and the email living inside of it, burns in the pocket of my sweater. This seems like as good an opening as any.

"Speaking of leaving," I begin.

They both turn to me again. I nudge Hazel off my lap and stand up, digging out my phone. I bring up the email and hand my cell to Mom. She looks down at the screen, her brow creasing as she reads, then back up at me. "You got in," she says, sounding almost surprised.

"Yeah." I sit back down, and Hazel immediately resumes her position on my lap. "I mean, the acceptance is dependent on my final grades, of course, but yes. I got in."

Dad sits beside her on the couch and leans in to read too. After a moment, Mom places my phone on the coffee table and leans back, snuggling into Dad's side. He wraps his arm around her. They're both unnervingly quiet.

"I know it's not what you wanted," I blurt into the silence. Unable to look at them, I focus on Hazel instead, stroke her little ears between my fingers. "But it's what *I* want, and I'm not going to change my mind. For the past seventeen years I've gone everywhere with you guys, but I'm sorry, that's over now. It's time for something different."

I glance up at them, just to see if they're listening. They're both watching me, but not with the furrowed-eyebrow concern I'm used to seeing whenever I voice my dissent. They look almost...happy?

"We're proud of you, Avery," my mother says, smiling.

"Really?" I ask, unable to hide my shock. I expected at least a perfunctory attempt at resistance.

"Absolutely," Dad confirms. "You got accepted early to a college that happens to be really tough to get into. You worked hard for what you wanted, and you succeeded."

I feel like I'm in some kind of bizarre alternate timeline. "But I thought...You were so against it before."

They exchange a look, then Mom places her hand on Dad's knee before turning to me again. "We've done a lot of talking over the past few weeks," she says. "Your father and I."

"About what?"

"About *you*." She drops her gaze and brushes some dog hair off the blanket. "Remember a couple of months ago when I came into your room to talk about colleges in Finland?"

I nod. How could I forget?

"Well, something you said that night stuck with me. You told me you felt like you weren't *from* anywhere and all you wanted was to stay in one place. And I realized we never really thought about it before, how all this moving around may have affected you. We just kept dragging you along on all these different adventures without even bothering to ask how you felt about it."

I'm glad she didn't bring up the obligatory "family vote," which was useless considering they always voted as one. "It wasn't *all* bad," I say. It's the truth. I think about all the places I've seen, the different kinds of communities I've lived in, the people I've met. My feelings about nomadic lifestyles aside, there *are* some advantages to seeing the world before settling into a tiny part of it. At least I know what else is out there, which is more than a lot of people can say.

"Our point is," Dad says, placing his free hand over Mom's, "while we don't share your views on this matter, we understand where you're coming from. Or at least we're trying."

"We're a work in progress," Mom adds with a little laugh. "And we know you don't need our permission or blessing or whatever to go to Eckert, but we want you to know that you have our full support. Truly."

"Our financial support too," Dad says. "We have some money put away."

263

I haven't cried in front of my parents in years, but their nice words combined with my past week of misery is suddenly too much, and I'm overwhelmed with a rush of emotion. "Won't you need that to get set up in Finland?" I ask, blinking back tears. Hazel tips her head back and licks my hand, her way of comforting me.

My parents do their silent-conversation thing again before Dad says, "I haven't accepted that job yet."

This is news to me. I thought it was all set. "What do you mean?"

"We were thinking," Mom says slowly. "You know, the Finland job isn't mandatory. There are other engineers who can go, if they need someone that badly."

Dad nods. "I've been looking into a few different projects coming up, and I found a couple within a few hundred miles of Weldon."

"Close enough for us to drive in and visit you about once a month or so," Mom puts in. "Or you could drive to us, once you save up enough for your own car."

"And you'll have somewhere to stay during holidays and summers. I mean, until you're able to move out on your own, of course."

"But," I say, my mind spinning with all this startling new information. "But you guys *want* to go. You should go."

Mom waves a dismissive hand. "Finland will still be there a few years from now. And families should stick together, right? We'd like to be near you for a little while longer." She untangles herself from my father and sits up straight, angling her body toward me. "What do you think?"

What do I think? I think all three of us got things wrong. They shouldn't have assumed I was on board with a transient life, and I shouldn't have assumed they didn't care about my opinions. They should have paid better attention, and I should have spoken up sooner. But it's time to move past it now. We're all works in progress. What counts is that they're willing to follow *me* this time, payback for all my years of following them.

"I think…" I cross my legs beneath me in a comfy-chair version of Sukhasana, a pose I've seen Mom do a million times, one that promotes alignment and peace. "I think I'd like that."

Chapter Twenty-Nine

When I walk out of school a few days later, it's snowing.

Okay, so it's not exactly snow. More like damp, dreary, last-week-of-November sleet. Either way, it's freezing cold and coming down fast.

I flip up my hood and cross the parking lot, eyes on my boots as they track through the slush. Up ahead, a car spins out on the slick pavement, leaving behind an arc of dirty water. I dart to one side to avoid it, not realizing that there's another vehicle coming up behind me until the front bumper is literally inches from my body. I jump out of the way, almost slipping on a patch of ice, and spin around to mouth an apology to the driver. But my *sorry* evaporates in my mouth when I realize that the driver is Liam, and the vehicle that I narrowly escaped colliding with is his old, decaying truck.

You have got to be kidding me. Is this the universe's messed up idea of karma?

Liam rolls down his window and leans out, his face as white as the sky. "Are you okay? I thought you saw me."

I yank off my hood, the reason for my lack of peripheral vision. Locating my voice again, I say, "Sorry. I wasn't paying attention."

"Well, at least nothing's broken," he says, his color returning. He peers out at the rain-snow for a second, then looks back at me, wet and shivering in the road. "Want a lift home?"

My heart spasms. "Oh. It's…you don't have to. It's a short walk."

"I know I don't *have* to." He nods toward the passenger side, where I haven't sat for what feels like forever. For days I've been avoiding him after school, walking home alone rather than waiting around to see if he's still willing to drive me. "I want to," he adds, giving me my answer.

A few seconds later, I'm sitting beside him and dripping all over the frayed upholstery. Liam cranks up the heat to maximum, which produces a half-hearted whine from the vents instead of more hot air, and carefully maneuvers us out of the parking lot. The sleet has turned to full-on snow.

"One thing I can say for this truck," Liam mumbles as he pulls smoothly onto the street. "It has really good tires."

I turn to look at him for the first time since I sat down. There's a smudge of pen ink on his cheek and the collar of his jacket is turned the wrong way. Everything in me aches to tidy him, to touch him, but I've lost that right. Instead, I squeeze my hands together and try to

267

pretend that sitting here, breathing in the truck's familiar smell—old coffee and dusty vents, mingled with a hint of Liam's citrusy scent—is enough. And in a way, it is. This truck holds some fond memories—driving around together, laughing, making out. I try to focus on that instead of the persistent miasma of awkwardness.

I search my brain for something to say. Finally, I come up with, "I heard the senior trip is officially on."

"Yeah. Student council put on a movie night in the gym last weekend and it raised a lot of money." He brakes at a stop sign. "Just in time, too. The last day to sign up is tomorrow."

"That's great. I'm glad you get to go. I know how important this trip is to you."

He nods, and silence descends again. The truck cab is warm now—almost too warm—and beads of nervous sweat form on my neck.

"So what's new with you?" Liam asks, his hands tightening on the steering wheel. He's clearly feeling uneasy too.

"Oh. Um." I adjust my seatbelt just to have something to do with my hands. "I got accepted to Eckert."

He glances at me, a ghost of a smile on his lips. "Yeah? Congratulations. That's awesome. Are you definitely going?"

I nod again. "My friend Mia is going too." She announced the news to me yesterday by sending me a screen shot of her acceptance email—which looked exactly like mine—with the word *Roomies?* scrawled across the top. "My parents even said they'd help with tuition."

He turns left onto my street. "Aren't they disappointed that you're not going to Finland with them, though?"

"No, because they're probably not going either."

"What? Why?"

I consider giving him a vague non-answer, or changing the subject like I always do whenever conversation veers toward the personal. But for once, I don't want to have to censor myself. Being on guard all the time is exhausting, and I'm sick of trying to control what people see and don't see. Sick of this wall around me, which not only keeps people out, but also keeps me in. I don't want to hide anymore. Even if we never speak again after today, I want him to see the real me.

So, I tell him everything. My shaky relationship with my parents, how moving around affected me more than even I realized, and why I feel the need to protect myself from people who venture too close. I even get into my relationship with Noah, and how my experience with him sealed off a part of my heart. And how hesitant I've been to open it back up again, especially to someone who has the power to destroy it completely.

Liam, who'd been quietly listening to my speech up until now, shakes his head and says, "I get that you're scared, but it doesn't have to be that way with us. I'm not Noah. I wouldn't tell you I was on board with staying together and then back out before you were even gone."

I shake my head. We're parked in my driveway now, engine idling, Hazel watching from the living room window. "Both of us backed out. It wasn't all his fault."

"Still. I wouldn't give up without even trying, and you shouldn't either."

"I've read that only about five percent of high school relationships last through freshman year of college," I say, rubbing at a damp spot on my jeans. "Those are horrible odds. That's why I suggested the dating deadline. Breaking up was inevitable, so I thought I'd at least try to minimize the damage."

"Not everything has to be scientific, you know," he says, the words laced with frustration. "I can believe in ghosts, and I can also believe that it's possible for relationships to beat the odds and last. We're people, not statistics."

"But look at Kath and Brooke," I counter, my voice trembling. "Kath's been miserable since Brooke went to college. They fight all the time. Do you really think they'll last the year?"

He reaches over to flick off the heat, his face flushed. "It doesn't matter what I think. Besides, we're not Kath and Brooke. Of course I'd miss you after you left, but I think I could handle it. Some people *can* handle being apart for long periods of time."

I swallow hard. "I don't think *I* could."

"How do you know?"

His question hits me in the gut. He's right. I *don't* know for sure, because I've never tried. The minute I found out I was leaving Noah, I began to pull away. Hardened myself to it. My cracked shell fused together again, and I let it happen. Let us drift apart. The struggle to stay together wasn't worth it since we were doomed anyway, at least statistically.

And here I am doing it again—calculating probability like I'm in math class instead of real life.

"I don't," I reply, watching the snow as it gathers on the windshield. "All I know is that I'm tired of leaving. I feel like it's all I ever do."

Liam sighs. "Getting left isn't much fun, either."

I look over at him. He's staring out at the snow too, his head tipped back on the seat and his eyes dark and sad. I've never really thought about it, what it's like being the one left behind. Liam lost his father, and then his stepfather, yet still believes relationships can last. And me? I've lost people too, but only because I assumed distance would wreck any relationship I tried to hold on to. Maybe it's time I stopped assuming things and find out for myself.

"Liam," I say quietly.

"Yeah?"

"I'm really sorry about everything. Especially the senior trip…I wasn't really saying no to *you*. It's just— agreeing to go felt like such a big commitment and I was too focused on that stupid deadline to see past it." My hands tremble with the urge to touch him, but I'm not sure how he'd react if I did, so I pull my sleeves over them instead. "I never meant to hurt you. Physically or otherwise."

He peers down at his foot, resting against the floor mat. "Well, my ankle healed fine. Jury's still out on the rest of me, though."

He smiles after he says it, a sad smile, and I return it with one of my own. "I miss hanging out with you guys," I say around the lump in my throat.

"You should start eating lunch with us again. We miss hanging out with you too."

"We? Even Kath?"

271

The snow has changed back to sleet again. Liam flicks on the wipers, sending heaps of slush flying. "Well. Kath is…Kath."

Sam said almost the exact same thing. I can't help but laugh. Liam smiles in response, then turns serious again.

"I'm sorry too," he says. "If I made things harder for you."

"You didn't." Quite the opposite, in fact.

Liam's phone beeps in the cup holder. He picks it up and looks at the screen. "Shit," he says, putting it back. "I'm late for work. I forgot that my shift started at four today. Doug's wondering where I am."

"Oh." I quickly unbuckle my seatbelt and reach between my feet for my backpack. "Sorry for keeping you so long."

"Don't be sorry."

We lock eyes for a moment, and the space between us contracts, drawing me toward him. Then his phone beeps again, and the spell is broken.

"Hey," he says as I'm about to open my door. I turn back to him. "Isaac's eating the steak on Saturday."

I blink at him, confused. "What?"

"The seventy-two ounce steak-eating challenge at First Choice Grill. He finally doing it."

"Oh," I say, the pieces clicking in. Isaac and his quest for free meals and T-shirts. "Well, good for him."

Liam runs a hand through his hair, suddenly nervous. "This is his tenth time and he hasn't failed yet, so it's a pretty big deal. The local news is going to be there and everything."

As usual, I'm amazed by what passes for big news in Granesville. I can see the headline now: *Local Youth Five Pounds Closer to Consuming the Equivalent of an Entire Cow.*

"You should stop by, if you can," he goes on. "The more people cheering him on, the better."

"Oh," I say again. "Okay. Yeah. I'll be there."

He smiles for real this time, and I simply can't resist anymore. I reach over and fix his collar, letting my hand linger for a moment on his shoulder before pulling away again.

"See you at school tomorrow," I say, then quickly get out of the truck.

I'm halfway to the door when I hear Liam say my name. I turn around, and before I can even process what's happening, he's out of the truck and his hands are in my hair and he's kissing me right there in the driveway.

I kiss him back, my body melting into his. Icy water drips down the back of my neck, but I barely even notice. All my focus is on Liam, the warmth of his mouth, the feel of his thumb brushing against my jawbone. Right now, I can't believe I thought I could just quit kissing him once December thirty-first arrived. Like it's that simple. Like it's possible to suddenly stop wanting this— wanting each other—once some arbitrary date on the calendar arrives. I thought we were being logical, setting that deadline, but in reality, we were just being foolish. I hope we never have to stop.

But then we do. Too soon, the kissing ends and Liam pulls away. Then, without a word, he turns and walks back to his truck, which is still idling in the driveway, the driver's side door open wide and letting in the rain. He gets in and backs away, his face obscured by the rain-smeared windshield. But I can only guess that he feels the same way I do—cold, confused, and cautiously hopeful.

Chapter Thirty

L iam wasn't kidding. When I get to First Choice Grill on Saturday afternoon, there's an actual news crew there. A tall guy with a giant camera on his shoulder follows a brunette woman with a microphone around the restaurant while another woman, a photographer, snaps pictures of everything. You'd swear it was the news story of the year.

The place is jammed. I step around a cluster of people standing by the door and immediately spot Mrs. Sadler near the hostess booth, talking to Mrs. Jimenez, the town librarian. Mrs. Sadler spots me too and smiles, then say something to Mrs. Jimenez before heading in my direction.

"Avery," she says when she reaches me. "I was hoping I'd see you here."

"Hi, Mrs. Sadler."

"Can you believe this crowd?"

I glance toward the tables, looking for Isaac—and Liam—but there are too many people. "Are they all here to see Isaac eat the steak?"

She shrugs. "Word gets around. Anyway," she adds, squeezing my forearm, "I was going to call you if I didn't see you today. Yesterday I ran into Mike Coombs, the manager over at FoodValu, and apparently he's losing one of his stock clerks in a couple of weeks. He hasn't advertised the open position yet, and I told him not to." Her smile widens. "Because I already have the perfect person for him."

It takes a moment for her words to sink in. "He's hiring me?" I ask, shocked. Stock clerk, a job dedicated to my favorite pastimes: tallying and organizing.

"Well, he'll want to interview you, of course. But you have a fantastic reference from Doug and me, so I don't see why he wouldn't offer you the job." She digs something out of her purse. "Here's his card. Call him to set up the interview."

I take the card and wrap my fingers around it. Maybe I'll get to save up for that car, after all. "Thanks, Mrs. Sadler…Linh. Really."

"Don't mention it." She pats my shoulder and walks away, back to Mrs. Jimenez, who's still near the hostess booth, now talking to Brenda, the cashier at KwikShop. Half the town seems to be here.

I slide the card into my pocket and continue to weave through the crowd toward the seating area. Suddenly, a loud cheer rises up somewhere ahead of me, and I burst through the wall of people just in time to see Isaac, sitting alone at a table, baseball cap on backwards and a gigantic smile on his face. In front of him is a steaming platter of food—a dripping steak the size of a Frisbee, surrounded by a side salad and a fully-loaded baked potato. It's enough food to feed my entire family, including the dog, and he's planning to finish it all on his own. In under an hour.

An older woman I've seen around here before—the manager, I think—appears with one of those old-fashioned oven timers with the dial. She holds it up for everyone to see and twists the dial to sixty minutes. "Time starts…now!" she calls, placing the timer on the table.

The crowd cheers again and Isaac, totally in his element with all this attention and adoration, makes a show out of taking his sweet time, sipping his water and then dabbing his mouth with a napkin before picking up his fork. Finally, he digs in, starting with the quicker, more easily digestible salad.

Someone squeezes in beside me. It's the woman with the camera, trying to get a good angle for the photo that will surely appear on the front page of the Sunday Edition Granesville Weekly tomorrow. I shift to the side to make room for her and inadvertently jab the person behind me with my elbow. Before I can turn and apologize, I find myself wrapped in a peach-scented hug.

"Avery!" The hugger pulls away and I catch a glimpse of dark-framed glasses and dark red hair.

"Brooke," I say, surprised. I knew she was getting home this week, but I wasn't expecting to see her here. I wasn't expecting such an exuberant greeting either, since we barely know each other. I feel like I know her, though, and she probably feels the same about me, if Kath ever talked about me. "When did you get back?"

"Last night." Another raucous cheer rings out, and she shakes her head, laughing. "This place hasn't changed a bit. It's good to be home."

I peer through the horde of people surrounding us. "Is Kath…?" I almost to ask if they're here together, but I don't want to pry. Maybe they're broken up and avoiding each other.

"Yeah, she's here," Brooke says brightly, and I breathe an inward sigh of relief. "She's at the bar getting us some lemonades. I was just heading over there. Come on."

I glance back at Isaac, who has demolished the salad and is now into the steak. He still has at least fifty ounces to go, so I figure I won't miss much if I step away for a few minutes. I want to talk to Kath.

Brooke and I shoulder our way to the bar area where, as advertised, Kath is buying two glasses of lemonade. Her face brightens at the sight of Brooke, then dims again when she notices me trailing behind her.

"Hi," I say, instantly nervous. We haven't spoken beyond necessity since she told me off in English class almost two weeks ago. I miss her.

"Hey." She hands one of the lemonades to Brooke and takes a sip from her own. "Looking for Liam? He's helping out my dad at the store. He should be here any time now."

Well, I *am* looking for him too, but he's not the person I want to speak to right now. "Can we talk for a sec?"

She regards me silently, straw between her teeth, then nods. Brooke gives her a quick kiss, then waves at me before disappearing into the crowd again. I step closer to Kath and lean against the bar.

"So she didn't dump you," I say, even though it's obvious she didn't, unless they're the kind of exes who kiss and make heart-eyes at each other.

"No. It was all a misunderstanding." She looks at me again, and the frost in her eyes melts a little bit, like she just realized she misses me too. "The *talk about us* thing she mentioned?" she goes on, friendlier now. "It had nothing to do with Kali—who she really is just friends with, by the way—or us breaking up. She only wants us to write up a love contract."

"A what?"

"You know, like, promises. We talk about what we need to make our relationship work, then we write a list of promises to each other and sign it. Apparently it's something her parents did when they went to marriage counselling last year."

"Oh." Whatever helps, I guess. "Well, I'm glad you guys are good now."

She pokes at an ice cube with her straw. "I wouldn't say we're *good*, exactly, at least not like before. I think we'll be okay, though. The past three months have been hell, but..." Her lips twitch into a tiny smile. "It was worth it."

I think about a few minutes ago, how her face lit up when Brooke emerged from the crowd. All that time spent missing her, the countless arguments and jealously and crying, all put to the side the minute they saw each other again. Love is a resilient thing sometimes.

"What did you want to talk to me about?" Kath asks, draining her lemonade.

I look at her. I've never had a friendship like this before, one that started out hostile and turned into something I cherish. "I just...I hope we can be friends again."

Her eyebrow shoots up. "Again? I hadn't realized we'd stopped." She puts her empty glass down on the bar. "Liam told me about the other day. About how you apologized to him and explained to him the reasons why you're...the way that you are. I understand it better now, so...sorry if I was a bitch."

I smile. "I like Bitchy Kath, remember?"

She laughs. "Me too."

Brooke reappears then, her glass still half full. "He only has about fifteen ounces to go," she reports.

Kath checks her phone for the time. "Wow. It's only been twenty minutes. Usually he finishes in about thirty. He must not have eaten this morning."

The three of us maneuver through the crowd to the front. When we get there, Isaac sees us and grins around a mouthful of meat. Beads of sweat roll down his face, and he looks faintly green. Hopefully all those ounces will stay down.

"Would you look at this asshat?" Kath mumbles, shaking her head at him. She's smiling, though, like she's secretly proud.

"Where the hell is Liam?" Brooke asks. "He's missing the whole thing."

Seconds after the words leave her mouth, Liam comes up behind her and pokes her shoulder. She turns and gives him a big hug. She's a hugger, that Brooke. I'm glad she's sticking around.

"You're late," Kath tells him as he edges around her and stops behind me, his chest inches from my back.

"Hi," I say without turning to look at him. Simply knowing he's there is enough.

"Looks like I made it just in time," he replies.

Isaac is down to his last few bites. Everyone starts chanting his name, urging him on. He takes a drink of water, swipes a hand across his forehead, and takes the final bite. He did it. Challenge complete. The place goes wild. Isaac beams, then burps and slumps against the table.

I survey the happy crowd, all the residents of this little town that's beginning to feel like home. I may be only temporary, but even if I'd lived in Granesville all my life, the connections I've made here would have no guarantees. People move on and drift apart. Logistics and statistics aside, nothing in life is permanent.

Liam's hand grazes mine, and I take it and hold on. *Never again*, I'd promised myself. But never is a long time, and so is the time between now and summer. Long enough for lots of different adventures. *Or maybe*, I think as a plan starts to formulate in my mind, *even one big one*. Like my mother always tells me when we arrive somewhere new, we just have to make the best of things while we're here.

The familiar scent of onions greets me when I walk into Sadler's Subs the next day. Liam is behind the counter, wiping down the front of the fridge. I can hear Kath in the back office, talking to her mom. It's three o'clock and the place is dead, just like I'd hoped.

"Hey," Liam says, smiling. He flings the cloth over his shoulder and walks toward me. "Here for a sub?"

"No." I take out my phone and open my email app, then click on the latest one. "I'm here to show you this," I say, handing him my phone.

He stares at the screen, his expression going from curious to confused. When it finally sinks in, he looks back up at me, stunned.

"My parents said to count it as an early Christmas present," I explain, resting my elbows on the counter. "And birthday present, and graduation present. Basically, it's my retroactive gift for the next several years."

"But..." he says, looking down at the sign-up confirmation email again. "But the deadline was last Thursday."

"Well, you know what?"

"What?"

I take back my phone and grin at him. "Deadlines can be extended."

The shock fades from his face and he leans across the counter to kiss me, his mouth curved into a smile. I kiss him back as the shell cracks and the wall crumbles, leaving me wide open and ready for my biggest adventure yet.

The population of Dublin, Ireland is approximately 565,000. But for a couple of days in May, at least, it'll be 565,002.

About the Author

Rebecca Phillips is a copywriter by day and a TV-series-binger by night. Oh, and sometimes she writes novels. She lives in beautiful Atlantic Canada with her family and spoiled senior citizen cat. Find out more on her website: www.rebeccawritesya.com

Other books by Rebecca:

Out of Nowhere
Faking Perfect
Any Other Girl
These Things I've Done
The Girl You Thought I Was